Eric Meloy

Tru

FLAME
BOOKS

Flame Books Limited, England

www.flamebooks.com

First published in 2007 by Flame Books

Tru © Eric Melbye, 2007
All rights reserved

The moral rights of the author have been asserted

Printed in England by Cpod Ltd

Cover Photograph, 'Cold Foggy Morning' © Joseph Burge, 2007

Tru was edited by Sean Dagan Wood for Flame Books Ltd
www.seandaganwood.com

Layout & Typesetting by REPUBLIKA D&MPB, Italy
www.rdmpb.com

ISBN 0-9556725-0-3

About the Author

Eric Melbye is an associate professor of English and Creative Writing at Miami University-Middletown, and Editor of *Segue* online literary journal. His fiction and poetry have been published in a number of magazines and online journals. He co-edited, with Michelle Lawrence, *Under Our Skin: Literature of Breast Cancer* (The Illuminati Press, 2006). A Wisconsin native, Eric currently lives in Ohio with his wife and two children. *Tru* is his first novel.

For the tru believers:
Mom, who showed me my first library and the wonders of literature,
Dad, who encouraged me to write in spite of not really having a Plan B,
and Peg — supportive critic, careful editor, and patient saint.

November 27

In the afternoon, we prepared to leave our bodies.

The others had been edgy, they had been waiting a long time. Days previous I'd seen them cheating their medication and bartering it round in the hallways. Everyone wanted the green and the pink pills, which weren't abundant. Reds were OK, too. The white ones, which everyone had, were worthless for leave-takings, and caused constipation. The others didn't look like drug addicts or crazy people. They looked like ordinary folks doing ordinary things — they *were* ordinary. You could see the hungry wolf in their eyes, their teeth. Now they were dressed in their Sunday suits and dresses. Today was a special day of leave-taking — my birthday. Riding on cheated medication, they were already leaving for happier places, places memory alone might not take them. I hoped to go there, too. When you're dying, you want to make everything right. We get up to these hijinks every so often.

From the nurse's station Marilyn, the supervisor, rang a tiny silver bell, and its echo hung in the air through the rest of the afternoon. I took my extra greens with a quiver of excitement I hadn't felt in years, and sat in my rocker by the window, waiting. A fat young man we call Onionhead, or just Onion, appeared from behind the counter carrying the special occasion silver tray, with the little paper cups half full of water, and smaller cups of candy colored pills beside them, all lined up in elegant rows over white squares with our names on them. Onion has a round, shiny head — like an onion — and an odor. He is an orderly, all of them are orderlies, though they explain to us they are Eldercare Health Technicians, or some such.

I watched the plan unfold. Helen settled herself at the piano bench and played "That Old Time Feeling" and everyone made up their own words. The ones who could dance did so, bodies far behind their ballroom memories. Alice and Tom were there, dancing like a tree in a breeze — she trembling and fragile, he gnarled and immobile. Old Ed sat by the nurse's station sucking oxygen and staring at me through the dark thickets of his eyebrows. We call him Old Ed because he acts his age. He has the oxygen tubes in his nose and tanks at the back of his wheelchair. Looks like some sort of astronaut. He bought himself a wheelchair for Christmas to hold the tanks because he says hauling them around aggravates his bursitis. He should be a writer, the stories he tells. *Prevaricator.* Old Ed was the only one who could have ruined this afternoon, but I won't let him — I wave him away, and he goes.

Agnes appeared in a beautiful lavender evening dress with a bow at the waist and a ruffled overskirt with white trim. She says she wore it to church the day she met her husband, a famous jazz musician named Buddy Baker, who vanished many years ago. She is forever modeling such finery for me in an effort to change my plain wardrobe, but I don't need fancy dresses. No one believes Agnes' dress is as old as she claims, or that if it was she would still fit in it, or that if she still fit in it she would wear it to church, or that if she wore it to church any self-respecting Christian man would look on her with anything but moral indignation. I would call her a liar, too, except that Agnes certainly would wear an evening dress to church, and if the rest is a lie it's a fine one, and I don't care. She doesn't care either if it's true or not, if we believe it.

Agnes looked regal and acted like a clown. She took the two reds Onion gave her and spun in a slow circle, raised the water up, smiling. We cheered her on. Onion watched the water to see it didn't spill on his tray and she slipped a pink out of the pocket of her robe and into her mouth with the other pills. A casual grace. With her back to Onion she stuck her tongue out at me and I saw the pink capsule dangling between the two reds, and remembered better days, or made them up. It's all the same now.

The entire day shift came for the party, and even some of the night people. Slowly filling with noise and movement, the day room changed. *Metamorphosed.* The orderlies had moved some of the couches and chairs to the walls to make room for extra folding chairs and tables. White paper tablecloths hung over the tables, centered by little glasses full of chrysanthemums from the garden. Around their edges the orderlies had stapled red streamers that kept catching on the wheelchairs. For not caring, the orderlies had tried to make things nice. They had even set their radio on the main desk and played a station I couldn't hear well — a tinny voice, staticky old music. Much different than the deep angry stuff we normally heard from it, so loud and clear after Marilyn went home for the night. I wouldn't let them move my rocker. It's fine right where it is, by the window. If you sit a little too far on the left, one of the legs creaks at the joint. It's a familiar sound — at home, how long did I listen and wait outside Maddie's window, as her rocker creaked like that, like a metronome, how long did I watch for Morrow, to see if he was even alive in there?

But I don't want to remember that. Take me somewhere else.

A handsome elderly man from the city appeared at the piano where Helen was playing and whispered something in her ear. I don't know how he was able to get her from her seat — if there's entertaining to be done, she insists you look no further. The city man sang and told jokes about aging and the foibles of the young. That was his word. *Foibles.* We sat around the extra tables and chairs and gave the poor man a hard time. I sat next to Agnes. I always sit next to Agnes. She has an air about her that I like. Agnes is an exotic creature who spent part of her life in Europe and still carries Europe with her. Helen made little comments about the city man's technique under her breath that everyone could hear. She used to teach drama. Agnes threw in her own punch lines that stole his thunder.

City man: "Here's a song to help you remember what it was like to get out to a new, hip joint and dance all night."

Agnes: "Now I'd be happy with a new hip joint..." And in a whisper those just around her could hear: "I think Old Ed has one in his zipper bags." A titter rippled through us all, even Alice, who blushed, and Tom, who grunted with approval. It felt good, sharing the same laughter like that.

"What — " I whispered back, "a new hip, or a joint?"

Agnes raised her eyebrows at me. "Joint?"

"I heard it on the TV," I said, and watched a little smile quiver on her lips.

Before the laughter left us I noticed everyone pull their zipper bags a little closer to their bodies. *Fanny packs,* I've heard them called. They all carry their real valuables with them in little zipper bags. Cigarettes, money, letters, jewelry, photos, cheated medication. They're little bags of home, carefully guarded, and no one talks about them, though everyone pays attention to everyone else's. They buy them in bright colors and patterns, decorate them with pins and things, strap them to their waists, their walkers, their wheelchairs, in plain view. I've seen the kids in town carry flashy little music players with the plugs in their ears the same way. They say, I want you to look at me, at this interesting me, but you can't come inside. It's childish, but I think I understand. We're all children here, so needy, we all want someone to come inside, and we say so in our own ways. But we're weak too, and so we're suspicious, and guarded. If you forget your zipper bag somewhere, someone will snatch it up, claim your valuables for their own. Take pieces of you, claim your memories. I don't carry a bag, because I don't have anything to carry, except for this journal, which nobody touches, and a pencil, which I keep on a string around my neck. This is the safest way. They see zipper bag, they think "fair game." They see my journal, they think "hers," and stay away. They don't want to know what's inside me. Agnes doesn't have a zipper bag, either, because everything she has, she is.

The song the city man played was a good one, and he got us all clapping while he smiled at us, bobbing his head to help us keep time. Onion sat in the middle of us, working hard to clap right, taking it all a little too seriously. Marilyn stood at the back row, observing. She is a large, strong woman with a severe air — she has high-angled eyebrows and a long nose and is so tall she must always stare down it, as though aiming along the barrel of a rifle, to speak to you — but a soft heart. Sometimes she would walk to either side of our makeshift rows, pretending to watch and listen to the entertainer. But she was watching us. *Reconnoitering.* She knows we get up to hijinks, she sniffs us out. But I was watching her, too, we all were — Helen, Tom and Alice, Agnes. She has to move around my rocker with each pass. She didn't see anything, since the leave-taking had already begun. I could see it in Alice's face, a kind of soft glow, when she looked at Tom. And in Helen's face as it tilted up toward the past, and if you got close enough, you could almost hear her reciting great lines of the great dramas she called her own — My Shakespeare, she would say, or My Sophocles, and launch into grand monologues. I love to say the names of the Greek dramatists and their characters, light and dry and clean as marble. Aeschylus, Euripedes, Aristophanes. Perseus,

Oedipus, Clytemnestra. Homer, unfortunately, is now a cartoon on the TV.

Then people were talking and bending over me to take my hands in theirs and say, *Happy Birthday, Gertrude!*, their funhouse faces moving in and out of focus. Eight hands. For awhile I couldn't stop laughing, my sides hurt from it, how long had it been since I laughed like this, I didn't care, I was laughing now and couldn't stop. Then I realized I had stopped laughing some time ago. What I had thought was my laughter was really the ting of the nurse's silver bell in my ear, that light silver tone circling round and through us all. I looked for the bell across the room in the nurse's station, but there were too many people. Where had they all come from? The room was suddenly packed. No one could move, but everyone did. Some moved through one another. Translucent shadow-bodies flickered in between the people I knew, a profile here, a closed hand there, sometimes a red corner of down-turned mouth or a shoulder dipping away. I shouldn't have been surprised. The dead had arrived. I hadn't gotten anywhere, and tired of waiting, they had come to me.

I stared through the spinning forest of limbs for something familiar. I had seen the dead many times before, my dim memories, my familiar strangers, but never so many as now. The regulars had turned out for the celebration: Father, standing in a doorway, staring always from a distance, my mother, just a warm whiff of bread and blur of red, Brice, standing still amid the whirling bodies with his fists clenched at his sides and his jaw working from side to side, Madeleine, poor Madeleine, a shock of shadow trembling in and out of vision. As I watched them fade and flit, more and more of them rose out of my past, countless faces without names, all the people I have slighted, maligned, slandered, condescended to, hit and bloodied, screamed at, turned from. Sometimes I think that if I could forget them they would go their way, but memory persists. Whenever I'm sewing and my mind wanders I look up and there they are. I'm always surprised that they're still there, that they go on existing without my thinking about them. This is my pain, worse than the flaming swell of my joints, and no medication dulls it.

The dead used to fascinate me. That was when I was a girl, and innocent. When I had no past for the dead to remind me of. Now I am too near to them. They wander through a world they no longer belong in, befuddled, sad, lost, angry. They haven't grasped their situation. The dead pass through the halls of this home and my memory with no destination — they have forgotten where they came from and where they're going to. They move without getting anywhere, they have become their traveling. It's no way to live! And we are much like them, here, forever middling. At times I wonder if the dead have crossed over into our world, or if we've wandered into theirs. But we are not the same, we have an end in mind. That's what makes us different. And afraid as I am of endings, I would rather have them than not. I need to know it won't go on like this. I need to know that there is no leaving something without returning to something else.

"Welcome to the party," I called out to them. "Come one come all!" And they did, and they do.

I turn away.

Outside, across the way, the sinking sun mellowed the bare black trees and the flattened earth of a cornfield. There's a farmhouse further on. Highway 8 divides us, the road in and out of the city of Delamond. I have never met the farmer, though I have seen him on his tractor. I wonder at how many people have passed between the farmer and I on this road, exhilaration and terror driving lives to or away. I like to watch the way he works the land and the seasons, the slow cycles of labor, growth, harvest, and death. His field stretches to either side of the window frame and past his house, which his two young sons freshly painted an eggshell white this summer. Through the low mist of morning I hear him at the far corner of the field beyond the house driving the tractors and their machines that plow and rake and water and harvest. By late morning the fog has risen and I see him nearer, staring forward or leaning over one side of the machines to look at his land, engrossed in his work. The low grumble of the tractor comes to me disconnected from him.

His sons work on the other side of the field, caring for the animals. By late afternoon he has made his way nearer the roadside and I can see him clearly, a wiry, rough-edged man wearing a flannel shirt, dirty baseball cap, jiggling and bouncing in his seat. Most others would look silly jiggering around like that, but he doesn't. He accepts each tiny jolt into his spine. He is a man of perspective, I think. He knows his place between heaven and the earth. He will die in the winter, to give his sons time to adjust to running the farm on their own before the planting season. He has already made this decision in his bones. He will be buried on his property, and forgotten by all but the land he worked.

That could have been my father, that could have been our family.

*****

One afternoon when I was a child, I opened a window in our house. I stood there as a wind wandered through, and changed everything forever. The wind passed through each room, left something there, and in its wake, revealed a mystery in the world that I couldn't solve. Everything was a clue—the shape of air beneath a bird's wing, an empty chair against the wall, the paling of my mother's cheek as she swiftly took ill. Father pretended not to see the mystery, though it was everywhere, huge and fantastic, like a gigantic butterfly resting on his bald head, slowly fanning the air with its delicate painted wings as he sat in a corner reading yesterday's newspaper, looking for a job that would tolerate his club foot.

Odd jobs for odd folks, he would say. His little, pinched mouth.

Father's hands were rough and scored with paper cuts. The mill gave him a few hours a week, not enough, out of pity for his club foot and for his sons, who died in a boiler explosion there. Have I forgotten their names? — but they've been dead seventy years. The mill gave everyone in town a dead relative or two. The mill's charity had been enough when Father's sons were alive, more than enough. But then I had come along, a girl. Useless.

My mother started singing songs in her sleep that we didn't recognize, and they found their way into my dreams. In the morning there might be a spatter of blood on her pillow, like musical notation. In the night I would stand out on the back porch and listen to the long grass whisper. Sometimes I saw Father's lantern at the far end of the field next to my brothers. The wind caught the distant sound of his crying, or was it the wind itself? The lantern winked out, and the last light arrowed into the dark. And the silence — like a hand — how it closed the night.

A great-grandfather I never knew built our house when times were rich. After my brothers died, Father closed off the two upper stories of the house and much of the first. The second and third stories seemed to weigh down heavily on the first, the whole sinking into itself. A few acres of open land surrounded it, exposed it. The land had been used as a pasture, but now it was just an open field of long grass. From the kitchen, where I spent much of my time because my room was just room and not very much of it, I could see the field where I ran and played, and beyond the field the occasional copse of spruce, like an oasis. The house stared out impassively as a mountain, infused with my grandfather's and Father's stoic will. Father invested the family's money in a few head of cattle, which began dying off after the wind passed through my mother's window. They died quietly, one by one, each in a matter of days. You could tell they were sick when they stopped eating. They tended to stand and stare. Some wandered aimlessly to the pasture's edge. In the next few days they would sit down and refuse to get up, then lie down, then die. In the house, too, an invisible force seemed to pull our heels down when we tried to walk, so that standing or sitting in one place became easier than moving, trying to move. Watch the night descend. Wait. Then only two cows remained, stationed in the barn most of the time, for no one knew what the others had died of and it was thought the land itself might carry some disease. It became clear to Father, and finally to us all, that the family would never return to its past prosperity.

I believe I began seeing the dead around this time. Beyond my field, the river cut through the hills from the mill and down the west side of Delamond. I don't know where it goes after that. I used to bathe and play in the river, a lot of kids did. There was a spot a way north that no one went to because it was too close to the stink of the pulp mill and the sawmill loggers — loud, gruff, violent men. A calm pool in the middle of a run of sharp bends, where I could hear the river's roar without feeling its bite. Sun on the water, sun on my shoulders, voices all in the distance and the river just mine, mine, mine. Sometimes a few loggers would stray down in groups of three or four. I would backpedal, watch from the shadows on the bank. The loggers would stop and look around at this little paradise, sometimes sit on the opposite bank and smoke and laugh and curse the river for the lives it had taken. Many men died on that river. The loggers would name the dead, and stare up or down the river, to where their own bodies and souls might go someday. They met the river with an aggressive fear because they knew each day on it could be their last. After the wind passed through our house, I saw the dead congregating on the opposite bank, standing or sitting around, doing nothing. I stopped going to the river not because of the dead — they were less threatening dead than alive — but because there were suddenly so many men around, and I preferred to be alone. But I still heard the stories of the dead. On a quiet day I could listen to them as I sat in the long grass of my field — a tiny, constant yelling beneath the river noise, tumbling downstream to further country.

I saw the dead in school, too. Many had dead brothers, and once I overheard their stories, the empty shells of their spirits appeared to me and never left their living siblings. They hung from the body at odd angles or dragged behind it like something escaped from a circus, then so ordinary I forgot them again. These were not animated or outspoken. They did not speak at all, but gazed at whatever happened to be in front of them. They seemed content to simply be. Stop staring, classmates said to me, when a new one appeared, but I wasn't looking at my classmates. When they realized this they teased me and I bloodied their noses. How I fought, then! They all feared me. I loved it. I shouldn't have done this, felt this. After a beating, I apologized to the dead, who understood the nature of things. Then my classmates ignored me, kept me to myself. This was all I wanted in the first place. I searched my body for my own brothers; on my stomach, my head, behind me. But they had gone before me. I was their dead limb. *Vestigial.* That's what Father saw, that's why he wouldn't look at me, and felt guilty for trying to un-see me.

*****

From my rocker by the window, I watched across the way. The farmer had gone in and the day had begun to fade. A dusty figure — a man — followed his feet through the gravel along the edge of the road between us. He stopped in the middle of my window, set his bag down, and turned to the farmer's house away in the field. The lowering sun flashed bright off the molten roof, windows dark. The traveler's arms stretched up into a slow, trembling Y on a piece of blank sky, and fell. He gazed behind at the blue-shadowed trail of his footprints, touched his face, then moved on. I watched him go. Behind the traveler, a strange alphabet in the dirt, and the empty sky. I pressed my hand up to the window and pulled it away, watched my fingers' steamed imprint dissolve in the glass.

Inside, the music and the jokes had stopped and hands still surrounded me, still setting little gifts into my lap gingerly, as though my legs might crumble. I was opening each package slowly. I had never received gifts before, not from people. I held one in my hand and worked at the bow with the other thinking, *I have hurt many, many people*. Now they all gathered round me, wearing the little secret smiles of lovers and killers. I wish I could tell them: *I didn't know, I didn't know*. I wish they would listen. But it wouldn't matter. We know what we know. I am a *prevaricator* though, a teller of tales. I wouldn't believe me. I would give me what I have got in life. Agnes gave me a deck of playing cards with pictures of shiny, brooding men on them. I haven't had much luck with men. Drove Father insane, drove two lovers, Brice and Father Still, to unspeakable acts. Drove my twin sons out of my body before their time, drove my grandson Morrow out of town. I wonder where Morrow has gone, where he's going. He would be old, today. I cannot place him anywhere but here, now, at the edge of my life, passing through. A traveler, forced to foreignness.

"Chippendales!" Agnes cried, taking the cards up and waving them around for everyone to see. "Ain't I a lifesaver?"

Dear Traveler: What word do you bring me now? How do I read your footprints? Coming or going? But you've already gone. I have not forgotten what it's like to be like you. How the world looks back at you — the wonder, the loathing. I remember your face, your hands, your why. Would you remember me? Do you remember me, Morrow?

*****

They gathered around me—Agnes, Alice and Tom, Helen, Onion, and Marilyn. It was strange, they were ceremonious about it. Marilyn presented me with a package. She stared down at me and held it out, made me feel guilty for taking it, though I knew better. Inside was a carved wooden music box. I lifted the lid back, and a little ballerina turned on her toe while song chimes rose up beneath her, carried her along. It was a familiar tune, though I couldn't place it. The satiny white lining the ballerina twirled in looked like a cloud. It was supposed to be heaven, I thought. I watched her until the song began to slow. Her passive gaze, pale moon skin. She wore a floaty dress material I've never seen before, a gauzy, carnation-pink. It looked strange stitched onto this mysterious night creature. She seemed out of place in heaven. I imagined she would go on dancing after I closed the lid, even after the song stopped. She had black dots for eyes. As I lowered the lid, the ballerina folded down and the eyes swelled, bigger and bigger.

"It's from all of us," said Marilyn.

"Happy birthday, Hayes!" said Onion.

The dead pressed closer around me now, the air dimmed and left me, and I got the joke. The gift came from the dead. The ballerina wasn't in heaven, it was a coffin. The dead don't let me forget. My mother died without knowing Maddie or Morrow. She would have loved them, as I did. She had much love in her, and much to love.

Shortly after my mother took ill, a doctor came. He spoke with my mother, and I listened from the other room, trying to hear. He and my mother went on for a long time. The doctor came into the kitchen and shook his head, gave us medicine. Outside, he spoke with Father, and Father didn't come back inside until night. My mother had been well liked in Delamond. She didn't belong with us — Father must have been a different man when they married. I think Father expected that one day my mother would go downtown and never return, but she always did. The townspeople probably wondered why. She was the best seamstress and dressmaker in Delamond, though she had only a few regular customers — just enough to help us by. She would have done better on her own, without us. She could have married better, and I don't know why she didn't.

My mother taught me about stories, about the life and the truth in them. That's nearly all I remember of her. She kept a small stack of books in a back room we never used for anything else. She said she had found some of them in this house, left behind by our ancestors, but most she had collected herself. There were fairy tales, and stories and poems about wars, women, adventurers, children... There were strange books about mathematics and science and books in foreign languages we couldn't read. These I would look at with my fingers, tracing over the diagrams and unpronounceable words. Little maps of broken roads.

My mother was a different woman with a book in her hand. We would sit in the kitchen by the stove, where the pages would glow with firelight, and it seemed the glow came from the books themselves. She held each one in her strong, gentle hands like a baby, or a world. She had hazel eyes the fire turned amber, and a mouth like the ornamental hunting bow that hung on the wall in the General Store; all elegant curves. She had life. She would read — she had a voice like a soft bell, clear and subtle — then pass the book to me, and I would finish it for us. After, there was just us and the fire. Little sounds erupted from distant rooms. My mother stared out the darkening window, over the plate of dinner she had fixed for Father. I breathed on the glass and stared at the smudges and prints that formed there and disappeared. This had become a favorite game of mine, searching for messages the dead left behind. I listened for messages in the house-sounds, then on the breeze outside. A muted clatter of tools from the barn — Father was working late again. He never interrupted our story time, even when he needed help. Sometimes he would come in halfway through and sit down with his dinner and his newspaper, a harmless presence we paid no mind. The stories made him harmless. My mother described herself as avid about literature. That was her word, *avid*. I didn't know what it meant, but the way my mother's face changed when she said it made me want to be *avid* all the time, *avid* about everything.

When she grew ill she still took in sewing work from her bed, and we still read her books, though her mind wandered from them more and more to some other place only she could see. She might stare into the fire, as if to get a better view in the flames of what was going on in the story, or simply close her eyes and watch from there, her lips moving silently. I tried to bring her back.

My favorite is Walt Whitman, I confessed to her.

She replied, He was a great man. She opened her eyes, and stared across the bed to the doorway, out into the kitchen. I looked, too, half expecting to see the poet stroll in from over the horizon. My mother laughed. He's in there, she said, pointing at the book in my lap. Then she looked out the window again, and whispered — to herself, I think — But the whole world is a story, too.

If my mother hadn't belonged with us before, she did now. No one in Delamond would have received her fever-talk with anything but fear and scorn. But I believed her, and I believed in what she saw. When she spoke this way, I could see reflected in her face the invisible world beyond her fever. In these moments, I felt I was seeing all of her for the first time. Not reduced by fever and racking cough, but revealed: she was more than my mother, brighter somehow, fuller and more complete, and she spoke with the clarity and truth of dreams. Yet though I held her hand near me, she spoke from a great remove. I hoped to be with her again, the way we used to be. What world was she reading? And what made it so enticing that she would never return to us the way she was? I hoped to see it, too, and I kept searching, because I understood that the world I was in then was ending.

I'm still searching.

When my mother began looking too much like the dead, I snuck upstairs to the rooms Father had closed off, to see what I had missed, and if anything of the past could be salvaged. Most of the rooms were bare. In some, furniture wrapped in bed sheets, frozen, as though I had almost caught the chairs and tables moving and breathing. A feeling of lives that had gone on living without our knowing. From a third story bedroom, a curved bay window gave onto a view of the last pine trees marching slowly north over the horizon, away from the sawmill. *Exodus.* And to the south, the squat buildings of Delamond, settled in the bottom of a shallow misty kettle and clinging to its sides, like the stained bottom of a teacup ready to be divined. Further on, in Harrington, was the train station. Sometimes on a still day I could hear the engine whistles. I never saw the station, but every time I heard an engine whistle I knew exactly what the station looked like, I knew every traveler getting on and off.

On one wall hung a small wooden cross blanketed in warm forgetful dust. Delamond's church — the Church of the Assumption, I think it's called — sat toward the north of town, with a pointed white bell tower rising up above all the other buildings. I could see it from the window. Our ancestors must have been religious. We were not. I had never been to church, had only a vague idea of what went on there. Why hadn't anyone taken the cross down off the wall? It hung there like a secret. It made me curious about the church. People who talked about God seemed happy in a way that I wasn't. But those people were Delamondians, and their god was a Delamondian. My ancestors had been Delamondians, too, but something had happened. Now we were Hayeses.

I imagined the life in this house years earlier when the land was greener and the money more plentiful. The dead rose from the shrouded chairs. I greeted the faded presence of unknown family with the polite indifference of a child meeting dry old aunts and uncles at holidays. I watched them act out their mundane dramas over and over in these rooms, speaking words I couldn't hear and moving around with pointless urgency. Who were they, anyway? When I asked my mother about our ancestors, she said they were proud and prosperous people. Father only said they'd all gone away, and dropped the subject. Yet here they were, arranging invisible things on the tables, speaking mutely, walking through walls and returning on endless small errands. Their lives didn't seem so grand, after all. Sometimes they would pass through me and pause after, look at where I stood, and shiver. Sometimes I teased them, walking along inside them, making them jump to see what they had stepped in. These idle games bored me quickly. Though they often have their way with the living, there is only so much you can do with the dead.

Soon I did all the reading for my mother. I sat in the chair by the bed in her bedroom, and now it was my face lit with fire. I felt it working in me. There was a window above her head. She couldn't see out from where she lay, but I could. In between stories, I watched for the wind that had brought all this upon us. When I had read all the books I started making stories up myself. It came naturally. I was trying to entice her back with a world of my own, and I was trying to keep her from straying too far into her fever-world. I was trying to keep her alive. She had led me to believe the words had that power.

She laughed once at a story of mine, in damp hot dresses under sheets that clung and twisted, an alien landscape. Her breath was sour. As we laughed we shared a glance, and in that moment, we both knew. Sometimes sickness is the way to a cure, sometimes you just get sicker, and sometimes you die, though this too can be a cure. I played the story out as long as I could, added a second knight and then a third to fight for the princess. Father watched from behind his newspaper in the other corner of the room. I resurrected a dragon as my mother worked on the dress she swore she would wear when she could walk again, a strawberry red dress with little yellow flowers and bees. When she laid the dress over her body and tried to sleep through the fever, I corrupted another knight with lust. When she couldn't sleep I said, Mama, I don't know who's who anymore, we'll have to start all over. Her eyelids beat like moths against a pane. On the other side of the room Father turned a page. The brittle paper crackled. My mother spoke in half-sleep. Outside, a wind wished through the long grass. I looked out at the night. Something was happening — it looked at me — passed me by.

Now I remember the stories more than I remember my mother. They are as guilty of killing her as the wind.

*****

I looked back at the swarm of waiting faces. Alice stood at a distance, hands folded, smiling down at me, and Tom at her side, preoccupied with a hangnail. Agnes glanced away, leaned over the piano best as she could to flash the entertainer some cleavage. Old Ed was around here somewhere, Helen, Marilyn, somewhere through the limbs hanging before me, waiting. They were waiting for me to say something. There was a music box in my lap. What did it mean, where has it all gone? So much blind longing. Do we even know what we want?

"Are we there yet?" It was me talking.

"I think she means 'thank you,'" said Agnes, smiling sidelong at me, then turning to the crowd. She was so beautiful, so free. I wish I had known her in Europe.

The orderlies surprised us with cake and punch, then withdrew into the nurse's station. Onion served us up. The cake was white and decorated with little plastic dancers in red tutus. I don't why there were dancers, or why the music box. I don't like dancing. It must have been all the bakery had on the shelf. The orderlies had planned another generic afternoon, a waiting room event for anyone who happened to be waiting there. The longer I looked at the day room, the more I saw all the normal day room things — saw them more clearly than I usually did: The faded and bowed couches, the mismatched sitting chairs (and the one new one that everyone fought over), the yellowy reading lamps on every dark end table, all bought on clearance, I'm sure of it, from a hotel auction somewhere. Dust swirling in beams of hazy light hanging through the windows. And wherever an elbow might be placed, there sat a short stack of magazines. The magazines are all old, and the address labels list names and addresses you've never heard of. They pop up like weeds, growing underneath the things you set down for a minute — cups, newspapers, sewing. Pick it up again and there's a new old magazine. And there, right next to the new smell of mums and the sound of the radio, more normalcy: the same old odor of ointment, breath, lavender, and bleach. What I thought was someone blowing a party horn was just someone blowing a nose. The day room hadn't changed at all, only been moved aside for awhile. And having moved only after standing still for so long, it didn't stand out of the way, it just stood out.

The cake was too sweet, the frosting was worse. All around the day room, red plastic plates with little mountains of frosting rising up, little white forks fallen on their backs. Tom and Alice danced through the dead. Everyone else sat around, disappearing nicely. Watching the others warmed me. The pills kept me far between. The orderlies slouched in a little knot in front of the main desk, bored and arrogant. They had to watch for Marilyn, too, who would get them busy if they didn't look it, but Marilyn was behind the desk doing paperwork. Only Onion sat with us, eating the frosting we left behind. Old Ed was sitting away in the corner by the TV, behind the orderlies. He was frowning at his knees, his hands, the floor around him, agitated about something. Then he was whipping his head around and making little sounds. Nobody paid any attention to him. I was too far away to say anything, either. I didn't know if maybe he was having the big one, as we say. He was panicked, and afraid, and raging. Moments like these make you realize we're all the same, all fighting the same fight. All I could do was watch. He was going, but the rest of us were already gone. One of the orderlies eventually glanced back at him, who was by now thrashing around in his wheelchair. A larger man than he would have tipped the thing over. The other orderlies looked, too, and the city man looked, and stopped playing, and we all heard Old Ed yell, "My magazines are gone! My *magazines* are *gone!* Someone *stole* my magazines!"

He squirmed to the left and to the right in his wheelchair, trying to see into the pockets at the sides of the chair where he sometimes stashed a few of his magazines. Old Ed's pockets bulged out at the bottoms with shapes of things no one could identify. He needed the larger pockets because his magazines wouldn't fit in a zipper bag. He collected *Time,* of all things. If it weren't the truth I'd be called a liar. For a man who wanted to die, it was funny. He fingered through the photos and headlines until the pages were limp and faded, and he guarded them as if we cared.

His body was stiff and couldn't lean over far enough. He clutched at the arm rests, and his arms seemed to be barring him from further movement, as though there were invisible shackles at his wrists. Looking at him from this distance, sitting in his big chair and squirming and yelling out like that, he looked so ugly and weak, a roach on a pin in a dumb boy's bug collection. And it's funny on Old Ed, but I wonder, do we all look like that? Children in old useless bodies that can't turn to see what's in our pockets? When Marilyn rose up from behind the counter and shot a glance at the orderlies, one of them sauntered over and began poking around in the pockets of the wheelchair. Old Ed got even angrier, started shouting in his little nasally voice. We all watched without watching, tending to our cake and memories. This is the way we deal with theft and death.

Someone had given me a brooch — a silver leaf with silver berries at the stem. It sat on the arm of my rocker. Someone had put it there — maybe me. Someone had stood there, but I don't remember. Then Agnes appeared at my side, as though she'd been there all along, waiting for me to return to me. She leaned in close to my ear, whispered, "This is your real gift." In my hand there was a package wrapped in delicate silver paper with an ivory bow. I looked at her. "The playing cards?" she said, and waved away a piece of air. "I have a reputation to uphold. This is the one that counts." The gift, how it appeared in my lap, as otherworldly as Agnes herself. There was a pattern of swirls in the paper. I could lose myself there. "Some people open them," said Agnes. I was afraid to. The moment felt more important than I was ready for. *Momentous.* "For Christ's sake, Tru, it's not Pandora's box." I felt superstitious. I tugged at the paper, afraid to rip it. But I did rip it, again and again. Inside were three books, a dictionary, a thesaurus, and a journal.

I looked at my new journal. The cover was a wrinkled brown. Mummy-skin. A thin red ribbon dribbled out of the binding. Something rose in my stomach. The dead pressed around us. I turned back the cover and looked at the open plain of the first page and its gilt edge, like a sliver of sun sinking beneath the horizon. My fingertips tingled, the way they did when I was young. I had been young once. I looked at my palms, my parched fingers. Whose hands were these? Coming or going?

"Well?" said Agnes. "Say something. You're going to make me think you don't like it. Tru?"

"But what should I write? The pages are so...blank."

"Write anything." Agnes leaned back, rested her hand on my wrist. "'The journal is the destination,'" she said, "'isn't that the saying?".

"Funny, Agnes."

Then she leaned in again. I could feel their breath on my ear. "You still tell stories, yes?"

I wondered if the dead were speaking through Agnes. They seemed to grin at me through her, deadly tricksters. They wanted me to write it all down. A confession, maybe. But I do not want to write any more than I want to die. Stories always end. I am afraid of endings.

"Start with a word. Any word." Agnes was standing up now. She set the dictionary in my lap. "The dictionary's for finding words you don't know you know. The thesaurus is for finding the right words. You must use the right words, always. The great poets will tell you." She leaned over, plucked the dictionary out of my lap, handed it to me. Her eyes were glittering. This was exciting for her. I had told her about my mother, and the books, and I had told her all the stories. Agnes had listened silently, even after I had finished talking, staring at something invisible. I shouldn't have told her anything.

"Open it," she said. I opened the dictionary. "What word do you see?"

I looked at the columns of words, broken up with dots and accents like footprints. They were beautiful. I was in. "*Afternoon,*" I said. Agnes pressed her hands together in a silent clap, and smiled. I wish I had felt as happy. I did my best, for Agnes. "You're glowing," I told her.

"'Glowing'?" she said. "My dear writer! How plebian!" She thrust the thesaurus in my hand. "Try again."

I looked it up. "You're...*vivacious. Gleaming. Radiant. Joie de vivre.*" I didn't know such books existed. All these words at my fingertips. They tingled again — the words and my fingers.

"Will you use it?" asked Agnes.

"The thesaurus? *Avidly.*"

Agnes' smile waned a bit, and she leaned down again. She dug the journal out from where it had fallen beside my leg and pressed it into my lap. "Will you use this?" she whispered. She was so close she was only a voice in my ear. "For us?"

I stared at the thing in my lap. "I don't know what to say." I wanted to ask her something, or tell her something, but it wasn't on my tongue. "I don't know what you want me to say." The mummy-skinned cover warmed under my hand. When I looked up, Agnes was long gone.

Across the room, the orderly tried to calm Old Ed in a half-hearted way, knowing it wouldn't work. Old Ed started accusing the orderly of the theft. The orderly was just a young boy from town who didn't care about anything. He stopped trying to talk to Old Ed and focused on the many pockets around the wheelchair. Some were built into the wheelchair, others Old Ed had attached himself. The orderly disappeared behind the chair. Old Ed tried to turn and see what he was doing. He was going to hurt himself doing that. Then the orderly popped up with the magazines in one hand, plopped them down over Old Ed's head and into his lap, and returned to the others at the main desk without a word.

Now it was OK to laugh, and we did. How we laughed! Not just at Old Ed, but at all of us, all of it. Maybe it was the pills. Maybe it was relief. We were all so busy dying, here, some elegantly, most badly. Even the air seemed thin, fading. Even us, losing our breath in little panicked hiccups. And suddenly I wanted to tell the dead something. Not just an apology, but something about leaving. Suddenly I wanted to enjoy this moment, this afternoon, here in this room. I thought they might understand if I didn't want to leave anymore. So many moments had already been lost. So many tiny deaths. I remember, when the sun was high on the field of long grass, when Father set my mother in the chair on the back porch to watch me run. In the far corner of the field my brothers' stones, two gray humps still in the waving flower like a displaced sea serpent. Happy to keep you company, I laughed, stroking its coarse swayback. Returning, I stopped to peel a flower from my heel. Flattened against my foot it looked like a hieroglyph. My mother, wrapped in a cocoon of blankets, arms raised up at right angles to her body, ready to clap at my next joke, Father turned to profile, watching the cattle graze and the storm clouds flex. The light dimmed a little, color faded into the past. I had missed it, whatever it was. We all had. So many words unspoken, stories we never told. My brothers were dead before I knew them. I held up the crushed flower and laughed against my will. We are all strangers, bound by our longing. It's not the moment that we want to leave, it's the longing for the moment. Of all that slips by us, we hold only to its passing.

There was more singing and dancing as the afternoon descended. The entertainer vanished somewhere and Helen reappeared at the piano. People began to leave slowly, so slowly I didn't notice them until they were gone. Alice and Tom had gone — where? They had given me a gift, a shawl, that Alice knitted in a pattern I taught her, that my mother had taught me. Alice had blushed, Tom had grunted something. He hates respecting me, but does it for Alice. He used to be a preacher. I have a record with preachers. Had? The dead, too, faded back into the past, though this was no relief. The empty spaces where they had stood stared at me. I clambered after something solid, with seams and edges that could be seen and felt and traced from start to finish.

"Agnes?" I called. But she wasn't there.

The stragglers departed for the blissful ignorance they never knew as youths. Some of them found it. They raised their cups to toast the day, and to laugh and forget the fading hour. I laughed with them, and watched my laughter circle around the room with the dying echo of the nurse's bell and away. In spite of the dead, it had been a good day. There are things to love in this world — aren't there? If you can hang on to it. If you can beat back the dead. Friends and dresses and dancing, zipper bags and laughter. Long after the partyers had gone to their separate worlds, my laughter came back to me. I drew it to me and held it tightly to my breast, where it trembled in the dark of my fist. I fell asleep then. While I slept I ran on boundless legs through a field toward the horizon. When I got there I stopped, peering through the invisible pane at the rest of the sky. An old woman's face stared at me translucently from the other side. The dead will never leave you. I was awake, staring through my reflection out the window. Outside, behind my old eyes, it was the violet hour. Sunless, nightless. Pale stars shone out of my forehead, quiet and far away. As I watched, the night spread and revealed a map of deep lines across my face, connecting luminous points of light. Beginnings, and endings. I'd rather have them than not. Then the night deepened, the stars disappeared, and there was only me staring back at me. And there was the journal, suddenly in my lap, nested in gauzy paper.

I'm afraid, I'm afraid, I'm afraid.

Before she came to the nursing home, Helen was a teacher in the small southern town of Colby, Mississippi. Tom was born fifteen miles away in Harrington and spent most of his life in a seminary there before finding his way to our home. I spent time there too, and I suspect Tom remembers me. We've never spoken about it, but it's in the cold edge of his voice whenever I'm around. We still don't know where Agnes came from originally, or how she wound up here. The others came to Delamond because they had family here who said they'd take care of them. When they took up residence in the home their families died off. A lot of times it works out like that. Alice and I are the only ones who spent our lives in Delamond. She's the only one of our gang that knows me the way Delamond knows me. In her previous life she was a god-fearing housewife — a widow after the war — who naturally took to Tom when he arrived here. All of us are displaced people, come to the nursing home to nurse what was lost, and what remains.

When you arrive here, you are encouraged to decorate your new room with your own belongings, but it's a ruse. The things that reminded you of who you were — smell of stew simmering in a pot, wind through the long grass outside the window, sight of grandchildren romping in a field — those things are displaced. It's unsettling to see your familiar things, the things you took for granted and stopped seeing for so many years, filling a strange room. Like a museum set, with a note outside the door: *Replica, c. 1915-85, of how Resident 2A once lived. Notice the afghan, folded and unused at the end of her bed, just as it remained when she was not so far gone.*

The reds, the pinks, the whites, the coveted greens that see us through — anyone reading this would think we are drug addicts. We are. Some need the medication to cope with the pain of rheumatism, arthritis, old war wounds, surgeries. Sometimes medication brings you here, when you need so much of it you can't remember what to take when, or the side effects make you sicker than you were before, and you need more drugs, more drugs, more drugs. And the medication keeps you here — the cure of one pain and the cause of another — and the orderlies who deliver it, the nurses who monitor it. Establishing a routine binding as a contract. They take over your life, the caregivers and the medications and the schedules, and you lose yourself. It seems safer than dying, but take away your drugs and your routines and what do you have left? Look at us. There are many ways to die that don't require dying. We are scholars of the art.

Some need the drugs to maintain the pain. These are the Old Eds of the nursing home. Agnes says if their medication isn't on the tip of their tongue, the word is. They ask for their pills by their long names hours before each dose. They take them in their hands to count and name them before pushing them through their lips, one by one. Agnes teases them, especially Old Ed, but once, by the stone bench in the garden, she confessed there was something sadly beautiful in the ritual of his suffering, the religious devotion he gave to it. Those were her words. She said his pain made him happy. She doesn't know, but Old Ed has asked me more than once to give him a week's worth of greens, so he can disappear and never come back. I won't do it. He tells me I'm a coward, and he's right. The dead are my private hurt, and I won't add him to it. We all want to die, here, though not all of us know it. And those of us who do are afraid of it, including Old Ed. For all of our leave-taking, we never stray very far from here. I tell Old Ed he would never off himself, and every time, he wheels himself away from me.

I asked Agnes if she ever asked Old Ed if he was happy, because he doesn't look it. She said, Why would he act as he does if it didn't make him happy? I said, I think he's more misguided than happy. Agnes laughed and said, Don't be silly, Tru. We're not guided at all.

November 30

Before there was Delamond, when the white folks and the Indians shared the land here, the Indians would sneak into the homes of white folks and swap their own babies with the white babies. This is true. In a few nights the Indians would return and swap again, leaving the white baby in its crib, dressed in beads and leathers. No one knows why they did this. There's a story people here tell that once, when the Indians brought one of their own babies back home, it carried a white man's disease with it, and it died. The white family didn't know. The Indians placed the body in a wooden box and got the box up in the branches of a tree, as was their custom. It stayed there, concealed by the springtime leaves. In the fall it presented a curious sight to passersby, this treasure chest wedged in the naked branches. Later, when snow and wind forced a part of it open again, a tiny hand could be seen inside. There must have been other boxes in other trees, too, a grove of winter's strange fruit.

Why does Delamond remember this story?

Dear Traveler:

I am haunted by what you remember.

I can't keep the wind in a zipper bag, would that I could — trap it all inside and throw it away is what I'd do. Put it up in a tree, or bury it, or scatter it on the wind. Give the disease back.

December 5

As a girl I would sit in Bulb Park on Main Street, where I could watch the comings and goings of things. The park was a small grassy lot with maples and benches and a winding path. Mothers and their children picnicked there, and businessmen read the paper and smoked cigars. They always kept their distance from me, even moving away when I sat near them. It used to bother me, but after the wind passed through our home something else filled me. A peace — it felt peaceful. I was right in the middle of town, yet separate from it all. But it was an eye-of-the-storm peace. Just across the street beat the heart of Delamond — the Manor House, where travelers stayed, the dry goods store and the tailor's, where I bought sewing supplies for my mother and me, the Fuller Opera House, the bank, the general store where I got our food. All the people up and down the street, wearing my mother's handiwork.

The tailor's name was Inchbald. Most of the things my mother needed to sew she bought at the dry goods store, but Inchbald had connections and could order the more exotic fabrics and buttons she used for evening gowns and such. I don't think Inchbald sold supplies to anyone but my mother. They never spoke much, when I went in the store with my mother, but Inchbald was a strange, quiet man. I can't picture my mother standing in Inchbald's, isn't that odd? Only remember the store, and Inchbald. I imagined he had a crush on my mother. In my heart of hearts I know my mother would never have cheated on Father, but she was also too kind to be unkind — that's probably why she married Father! So I imagined she knew and sympathized with Inchbald's broken heart, and let him perform these little acts of kindness for her, but kept him at a safe distance. While we stood at the counter watching him unroll the fabrics or count out buttons or spools of thread, I would watch his hands. He had extraordinarily long, spidery fingers, and when he was working they came alive, moving softly and surely, each with its own mind. I loved his hands. I would watch those hands and wonder what life might have been like if my mother had chosen Inchbald instead of Father. This was before I found out, years later, how Inchbald despised me.

I never saw a show at the opera house, and now it was starting to crumble, as traveling entertainers had stopped traveling here. I always wanted to see a show. Instead I watched the Manor House, and the travelers coming through there from the train station, and imagined where they were coming from and going to, and the shows they had seen. The lives they were living. They were all sorts of people, black and white, old and young, alone or with family. Soldiers, sometimes. And I imagined myself among the travelers, too, watched the men tip their hats and smile at me, watched myself passing through to places I could only imagine: Chicago, Paris, Troy, Camelot.

Delamond had a bookstore on Main Street, too, called Bishop's, after the owner, Henry Bishop. It used to be run out of Filbert's, the grocer, before he sold it. Bishop was as cheap and sleazy as the books he sold, but he did a good business. He sold mostly magazines and dime novels — stuff travelers and men would read. There were almost always a few men hanging around inside, smoking and talking over the books and newspapers. Some of the men were travelers passing through from the train, wandering men looking for work. I would study their clothes and their hair and their manners and their smell, trying to see the places they had been and were going to. If the store was empty, Bishop might let me inside. In order not to appear too sleazy to Delamond, he had a shelf of hardback books by respectable authors, and a catalog you could order from. I think no one touched them but me. Those books were too expensive for me, but I liked to go through the catalog, ticking off the ones I was going to buy, as though I had a plan to. Beneath the smell of smoke and cologne, I could smell the stories — the exotic spice scent of lives in faraway places.

I didn't question why Bishop let me in the store in the first place — never look a gift horse in the mouth. He never took his eyes off me. I thought he watched me so closely simply because he didn't trust me. I didn't care, so long as I got to look at the books. Sometimes I would wander behind the shelf of dime novels, which was almost as tall as me, pretending to be curious, just to see if he would say anything. He didn't, just kept watching me. Now I think Bishop wasn't watching me, he was imagining me. Some of the books had pictures on the cover of whorish women, or shadowy men with guns. Because they knew they were cheap, these books had a false pride. I imagined they came from the forest north of our home. They were stories of crime and war and romance, fodder of lurid dreams and impossible hopes, Delamond's children returned home. *Prodigals.* They weren't the real thing, not the walking talking living breathing stories the wind carries into your house from the forest. What would Delamond do with such a tale? I never bought any of Bishop's books.

One afternoon after school I was inside, running my fingers across the hardback spines, looking for something I could tell my mother. Through the window, across the street, I saw Brice staring at me. Brice was the quiet boy in our class. He looked years older than he was, or maybe he really was older. The other children watched him watching them. They were not afraid of him, there was safety in numbers, but when they were alone they crossed the street to avoid him. He had a face that didn't move, but inside you sensed a storm brewing. A wave of black hair shot up off the narrow rock of his head. He ground his teeth and there were rumors about what the teeth looked like.

When the war came, the Conscription Act sent Delamond's boys overseas, where most of them died. There were military men at the post office signing boys in. The train station was a beehive of weeping mothers and stern-faced fathers. Brice tried to get himself drafted. He tried to keep it secret, but the whole town found out. The government rejected him, and the town decided it was not because of his age, but for psychological reasons. Brice was a closed fist of a boy. On the surface, Brice didn't change at the news, but what we were seeing was the calm eye of the storm. Inside him there was a hardness. He clung to that hardness as a storm raged around his brain.

In school earlier that day he had quietly appeared before me with an invitation or a flower or whatever it was. No one ever spoke to me unless they wanted to tease me, so I didn't listen to what Brice said. I should have listened. But why would he speak to me at all? Maybe he felt the storm in his brain coming the way birds sense a drop in air pressure and grow silent. Maybe he wanted an anchor, someone to hold him in one place. I could have done that for him. We were alike in many ways — both outcasts. Brice had a crooked smile and wet lips. He spoke in a low, quiet, halting voice — that I remember. A boy's voice, I thought, not a soldier's, yet Brice was more a soldier than any of the other boys. Before the other boys went to war they tried to make themselves into men, swinging their shoulders when they walked, barking declarations. They were still terrified boys, as much at war with themselves as with the enemy overseas, and they wore their new manhood uncomfortably. It was too big for them. Kids staying at home looked at these boys differently, in awe, but also in fear, for they knew these boys may not return, and dying for love of country wasn't everyone's dream.

Brice, I think, knew exactly what was at stake. He was braver than the rest for facing his fear with honesty, he stood naked before his fear and let it consume him. He was the only one the other kids teased about going to war. They wouldn't even give him that much respect, but used him like a trash bin for all their fear of war and death and adulthood. They called him "little soldier boy," or just "boy." He never responded, and I thought this was another sign of his bravery. His bravery earned him nothing from me that day in the school hallway, though. As he stood before me, glancing up and down from his shoes to my neck, I waited for him to finish talking the way I waited for buggies to pass before crossing the street. I looked past his shoulder as he spoke because that was where I was headed next. I hadn't meant to be heartless. If I had known what I was facing I would have done more — smiled, touched his hand. I didn't. I don't remember what I said, or if I said anything at all. When he walked away I heard him crushing his teeth to gravel.

I didn't know anything about love or boys or sex. I never thought about it, because it never occurred to me then to think about the world as something outside myself. Growing up in that tiny corner of Father's house, surrounded by the dead and diseased, I had to create my own world or succumb to that one. It would be easy to say that I trapped myself in the boundless world I created, that it held me prisoner from the joys of this one, but that wouldn't be entirely true. The two worlds bled into one another so that I never knew exactly where I ended and the world began. So when Brice approached me with an odd shine in his eye, he didn't seem real, in a human way. I ignored him, like one of my classmates' dead brothers.

None of this excuses me.

In the schoolyard later there were cruel jokes. I watched from high up a maple tree I sometimes climbed to read books and see what I could see. I enjoyed feeling breezes the others couldn't. On this day I just wanted to get away, and climbed the tree to wait for everyone else to leave before making my own way home. Sometimes a group of boys would get up a game of baseball or other made up games that gave them an excuse to tackle and beat each other. Brice normally found his way into these rough games because the other boys always needed more bodies. The games usually ended in fights with Brice. I sometimes wondered if the games weren't just setups to trap Brice into fights he couldn't win. Now I wonder why he always agreed to play with them, knowing they would beat him. Was this the price of acceptance he was willing to pay? Why didn't he find a tree, like me? Yet on some level I understood why he would willingly go to slaughter. Because he was ready for it, because he had prepared for death early on. Inside Brice there was a twisted black thorn where his heart used to be which came from god knows where, dropped there by a malignant wind, perhaps, like my mother's illness. And though he feared death he would not run from it, even as the boys circled him and began teasing him for talking to me.

Brice and Trudy, wouldn't it be nice! But when he kissed her he gave her lice!

Little soldier-boy!

They called him worse things than I'd ever been called. And there was no way out of the circle. Brice stood there looking at them. One of them pushed him into the other side of the circle, and someone else pushed him back. They shoved him around, and he let them. They were only waiting for him to fight back so they could really begin on him. Some of the girls had come over to watch too, and one of them spat on him. Everyone laughed. I looked toward the schoolhouse for the teacher, but she wasn't coming. I felt around for a branch to hurl down on them but knew it wouldn't do any good, would only make things worse for Brice. This was about me, not him. I had started this fight when I walked away from Brice. If I had only talked to him. They wouldn't have fought with me, I had beaten them all in the past. The boys began to close ranks on him, and as they did, Brice looked up at me. His face had turned to stone. I couldn't win.

Brice stocked groceries at Filbert's after school. He must have been going there now, and stopped when he saw me in the bookstore. When I walked outside the bookstore I looked back at him. He warned me, in his way. His nails digging into his palms warned me, his clenched jaw. From across the street I thought I could hear his teeth. I told myself there was nothing to be afraid of. I walked down the street, bookless, but with ideas. I used to imagine the walk home as a celebration parade — my parade, celebrating me. The sidewalk rolled open before me. The telephone wires, which were new enough to still surprise me each time I looked up, became festive ribbons lining my path. The lampposts ushered me on my way through the crowds of stores standing at attention. A curious cloud peeked over the top of a store to see who was passing. No sound except footsteps behind me. It was Brice. He tried a smile, looked behind him, scurried up to my side.

"Where you off to?" he said.

This simple question — I didn't know how to respond. I was on parade, couldn't he see? Up close I saw just how much he had changed. He had lost the war. His eyes had turned to glass. The air around him shivered. I didn't say anything. He didn't say anything. He tried a different smile. It didn't work. He took my elbow and pulled me into the alley behind the bookstore.

There was nothing to be afraid of, I thought. With his iron

hands pinning my arms down to my sides and my cheek scraping the brick wall. I surrendered to him. Brice needed something from me. No one who wasn't dying needed me. He pushed my dress up. He took it out and stabbed me over and over. I felt myself bleeding inside. The whole time he gnashed his teeth and pushed my face across the brick. Above, a narrow strip of blue sky between two walls leaning together. A cloud retreated over the edge of the building, the sky fell away. The earth quaked as though a giant hand were pounding at it with a hammer. Even after Brice ran away the world kept shaking. Only then was I afraid, because it wouldn't stop shaking, and it wouldn't go away. I was thirteen years old. Suddenly, the world was everywhere I looked. I had been forced into this place, and I couldn't get away. I vomited and cried. No one came. Of course no one came, there was no one. I was alone. The emptiness ached. I held my stomach and felt for anything. There was pain, and nothing. I held on to that. I took it home.

December 6

I'm sorry, Brice. I'm so sorry I hurt you. I loved you.

December 7

The dead will never leave you. They may fade in and out of vision, but they are always *there,* in the silence. They hover around my shoulders all day long now, pressing down. They needle at my hands until I start to write. They are never satisfied. Memory is a needy beast. Once it gets a hold of you it has a way of clinging, and you don't realize that you've passed into a sort of waking coma that's difficult to rouse yourself from because you aren't always aware anything's wrong. Worst are the ghosts of guilt, the restless spirits of past misdeeds. Memories come and go, but conscience is stubborn, tenacious. This is how you know you're facing them, because they remain even after you blink, after you start sewing a scarf, fall asleep, and wake again. Otherwise they are not very different from the other dead, they are silent shufflers with quiet stares like the ghosts of memory. There is an air about them, though, they seem to vibrate faster or understand more clearly that something is not right. Their reach is longer.

I have hurt many, many people.

There are, I suppose, the dead who are a comfort to know, but I don't see them. Sometimes I see a place instead, like the green field of long grass between Father's house and the river. At the other end, near the sagging fence line, stand two round, worn grave stones, the brothers I never knew. My brothers never appear to me as other dead do. Never talk to me. I sit by their gravestones and talk to them. There isn't even the faint tingle of a departed presence about those stones. Only the trees, the wind, birds. I am always aware of wind, now. I climb the trees my brothers must have climbed, range around the field searching for lost things, but they have left me completely. Maybe their absence is meant as a sort of comfort, a reassurance that there is real silence somewhere. That there is rest. Maybe they grew tired of my prattle and retreated still further into the other side — proof that I have hurt even the dead. Eventually I stop talking to my brothers. Instead I run. The field is huge and I run all of it, back and forth from brothers to home to trees to brothers to fence and home and lost in circles, then collapse, breathless, on the ground, and stare up at the sky bending over me, soft grass sighing, safe, free, connected, earth hugging my back and nothing but sky to step into.

The last time I saw Morrow he was walking down a hallway at the courthouse. A normal hallway, white paint, wood floors, a lingering smell from the last mopping, and from the mill. And Morrow, in brown pants and a white shirt, blending right into the walls and the floor as he walked away, a few geometry books tucked under his arm. Just before they led him away, his face was so near mine I can still feel his breath. His face was still, but he was crying on the inside.

He said, Whatever I did, I won't do it again. Please.

Little warm breath, little warm heart, waiting for me to say the words that would stop the men from taking him away. The words didn't come, and the men took him away. Does he ever feel me now — the tickle of my pencil as I write these lines, could he follow them back to me from wherever he is? He was a part of the old story — could he be part of a new story? I would like to know him again, and I would like him to understand some things. I would like him to know me. I would like him to forgive me, maybe. But most of all, I would like him to bury me. If nothing else, let him bury me. I could die with just that.

December 10

Dear Traveler:

When you paused at the side of the road between here and there, you turned away from here. Did something in the farmer's field catch your eye — the sun on the roof of his house, the thought of a warm meal and conversation around a dinner table there? You could have turned the other way — to here, to me. There's warmth, here. You would have been fed. *Nourished.* You could have told the story of where you've been these many years, and though we would ask you where you're going, we would hope that you would stay with us, instead. There's plenty of room, here, and time. All we have is time, and I would give it all to you if you would stay.

A fat, bald man takes your bags to your room while Marilyn tours you around. This is the day room, she says, spreading her hands out at the room you're standing in, and the kitchen is over there. On the far side of the room, through the window of the kitchen door, you see the pots and pans hanging, hear the orderlies shouting over the dishwasher and the radio. Meals are served at seven, noon, and five, says Marilyn. We eat there — she points across the day room at four long tables. Marilyn follows your eye around the room as you look at the pictures on the wall, the knick knacks littered across the tables and shelves. She says, There are plenty of magazines to read, and a television, board games, arts and crafts to enjoy. You will find your hobby. Some of our residents put their work on display.

Marilyn keeps watching as your eye falls on the residents themselves. They are looking at whatever's in their laps — sewing, magazines, photographs — or they are clustered in groups of two or three, smoking or playing cards. One old woman is sitting in a rocking chair by the window. She is short, and swimming in a strawberry red dress much too long for her. Her hands are gnarled roots. She stares at a painting on the wall above her, then starts scribbling in a journal and muttering to herself. The painting — you recognize Impressionism — shows a rain-slicked Paris café at night, three women in puffy dresses and a man in a tuxedo, little vials of green liqueur, hazy yellow globs of streetlight. The old woman glances up at the air as you pass. She has the bright eyes of a little girl, and the sad eyes of a mother.

Marilyn leads you by the main desk — there will be some paperwork to fill out later, she explains — and leads you through a corridor. You trace your finger along the wooden railing against the wall. The varnish has worn through in places, and the wood is smooth and mottled. The carpeting is thinner and grayer beside the railing. In the middle, a deeper shade of blue still looks new. Marilyn stops at the end of the corridor and points to the left and to the right — there are ten rooms there, and another ten around that corner, she says. Residents share rooms in pairs, and each room has a private bath. There's no cooking in the rooms. We are adamant about this, though the residents sometimes complain. There are fire codes to follow, so no cooking in the rooms.

Marilyn doesn't show you your room. Instead she leads you around the corner to the right and to the end of the hall, through a door that leads into the back yard. Our residents get exercise here, she says, and enjoy the garden. You look at the garden, which isn't much to behold in this gray winter light. Through all the dead limbs you can make out a fountain in the garden's center, and a small granite satyr, mouth puckered open. The satyr looks like he's whistling. There's a sort of glee in his face that could be kind or wicked.

That's it, says Marilyn. She smiles like the satyr. She opens the door for you and leads you back to the day room, where she stands behind the desk and gathers up paperwork. As you wait, you look around the day room again. No one has moved, nothing has changed, except for the strange old lady in the rocker. She has closed her journal and is staring out the window at the road you came in on. The rocker makes a little noise each time it leans back. You've been hearing it in your mind since you walked in. It's quiet in here — that suddenly hits you. This is a place were you could be comfortable with your thoughts, or they could drive you crazy.

Marilyn is watching you again. She slides a short stack of papers across the desk and looks out at the residents. It's a peaceful life, she says.

But you aren't so sure. What about her? you ask, pointing to the old woman in the rocker. She looks fragile to you, like a broken and mended teacup you would have to hold in the palm of your hand. But would you hold such a thing, would you even keep it around? Maybe better to just throw it out.

You notice Marilyn's smile deaden a little as she watches the old woman. Never mind her, says Marilyn. That's just old Gertrude. She's a little…

Touched. Affected.

The old woman is still staring out the window. Walk over and look outside with her. Rest your hand on her shoulder a moment. Her bones are hard, she is stronger than you thought. She's looking at where you were standing. You remember the road beneath your feet, you can still feel it. From somewhere beneath her bones, you feel her trembling. She is afraid, afraid, afraid. She lifts your hand from her shoulder — her own hand is dry and warm, the skin like paper. She closes your fingers around the journal she was writing in.

You can't stay here, she says. But take me with you.

Outside, you stand at the edge of the road and look in either direction. The journal rests snugly in the breast pocket of your coat. You remember you were going somewhere. Start going. The gravel crunches in time beneath your feet. You remember the creak of the old woman's rocker. Remember the satyr's grin.

Continue down the road, arm turned to wood from the long weight of the pack in your hand. You listen to the rasp of your breath and the scrape of your shoes through the roadside gravel for a time before it becomes a part of the sound your blood makes on its course through your veins. In the ditch to your right, dead stalks of grass stand at angles in a frozen brown puddle. The cold hardens the road, hardens everything. Your feet are hard and numb in your shoes. You walk with your head down and watch your dusty shoes push along. In time they detach themselves from your body. All you see are the top halves of two brown shoes bobbing up on either side of your field of vision and falling below it again, over and over, until they begin to lose their definition, and then they aren't shoes at all, but two raggedy brown animals popping in and out of their holes, trying to find each other.

As the final bit of orangey sun melts over the horizon, your stomach begins to growl. At the top of a steep hill you stop — Delamond is below, settling into the night. You drop your bag, and a host of pains shoot through your body up to your head, where your brain hammers against your skull. Delamond pools at the bottom of a large, shallow kettle. The kettle's uneven rim appears like a giant mouth opening wordlessly to the sky. Main Street glows palely through the city's heart, and to either side, sparse lights from the darkening houses spread and thin in all directions, to the hills you have just come from and to the forest to the north. You continue down the hill. A few cars move silently up and down the distant streets, more house lights come on, traffic lights wink red, yellow, green, red. As you descend you hear a dog bark, and you smell Delamond: the rotten cabbage reek of an unseen paper mill, the cold pine forest, gasoline, pavement. With your left hand you take up your luggage, and a new pain nettles along one side of your spine. Walk.

Down Main Street, search for food and shelter. People notice you, their eyes flicker. Some seem to recognize something in your face, and it makes you uncomfortable. You want to be alone. There's the Manor House on the left, where you can take a room, and a little further on, there's Filbert's supermarket. You'll take some groceries back to the Manor House and get a room. Filbert's throws off a bright white light through its wide front windows into the purpling winter outside. A few people move around inside, insulated from the quiet rushing of the breeze through the pines. Inside, it's another world. Music plays from somewhere as you walk the aisles, picking non-perishables off the shelves. You can hear your footsteps again, and begin to feel your feet. In the produce section, you look at fruit.

You could sneak something into your coat pocket if you wanted. This suddenly occurs to you, and your heart flutters at the idea. You haven't thought like this in years, but in Delamond, the past is carried on the air, attached to the pollen and paper mill odor. You can almost see it as a fine grit that makes the air look like television static. You remember a time when pilfering a few apples seemed more thrilling, when you were a child and supermarkets were just little shops and there were no hidden electronic cameras. Filbert's used to be one of those. It was just you against the shopkeeper, then. Now it's you against something bigger, vaguer, and more threatening. Filbert's is nearly empty — you've only seen a cashier at the front and a young man in a white shirt and tie who shuffled by you in the snack aisle. He would be the one to prosecute you. He would do it, too, he had a surly look. Then, as quickly as the idea entered your brain, you pluck two apples from the pile and slip them into your coat. You do it without deciding to do it, and you're surprised at how well your hands remember how do it right. And it does feel thrilling, after all, so you do it again, put another apple in another pocket, and you're dizzy and your heart's about to explode. When this madness finally leaves you, you feel like a stranger watching yourself. Afraid, curious, a little sad.

Hands in your pockets, you stroll away, search for canned goods. In one aisle, there's a boy kneeling on the floor, stocking a shelf with cans of soup. He glances at you through a dark curtain of hair, face pimpled and stoic. You try to imagine a life for him outside this store. Is he happy? Is he a fighter? Does he have a girlfriend? What kind of man could he become, if given a chance? You ask him for tomato soup, and he hands you a few cans without a word. His eyes catch on your coat pockets — one of them is gaping open, and you can see the top of an apple peeking out. When he looks at you his face doesn't change. He has an ugly scar on his temple, and a scarred look about his eyes. An old soul in a boy's body. You push the apple down into your pocket and wonder if you should say something, but the boy has already begun working again. He works quickly, graceless but efficient. He will always be this way. He will grow into a man worn down by life, and he will die too soon in some stupid accident, but unafraid, and with few regrets to linger on after he's dead. In Delamond, not only pasts but whole futures quietly open and close before you, too, like slow blinking eyes. Your eyes.

At the checkout, the cashier chomps at a little green wad of gum while she slides your food across the scanner. Her fingernails are painted green, like the gum. The only people you've seen in here are children. Do you remember, dear traveler, being a child?

You'll need to lie to yourself. You'll need to believe in your innocence. Push those apples deep into your pockets. Remember the long grass outside your house, remember the books I brought to your room, the math books that absorbed you...how I tried to read them with you...I still have them, dear traveler...remember the little noise your mother's rocking chair made against the loose floorboard in the kitchen...keeping time for the whole house...remember the court house, the men taking you away. It wasn't your fault. Believe the world owes you something, that Delamond can give you back the life you should have led here. Believe that you'll get it.

— What else can I do for you? the cashier asks in a deadpan voice. You misread her tone and it sounds like she's saying, I've already done everything I can for you, what more could you want, here? It sounds like Delamond is speaking through her.

You don't have an answer, so you take up your bags. Outside Filbert's the air is a solid thing that pinches your lungs, and the breeze brushes against your face and curls your hands into fists. You stop to let your lungs adjust. The streetlights and store lights only cast shadows over this city — dark figures walk up and down the sidewalk, a few dark cars cruise by. The people are hustling between their cars and the stores, running errands through the cold. You try to imagine your unlived life in Delamond — the real life you should have led, that I let them take away from you. A house, a job, a car, running to the store for a gallon of milk or a new toaster. A life of school, then work, then war, of bills, vacations, television, errands — a family? But it was never there. All you're seeing is the other life you lived, the sham life you left behind when you came back to Delamond. A life as near as fiction and far away as memory. I remember, long ago, you invented a geometrical definition of time and space. It made true that time and space are bound together. That an image takes time to reach your eye and your brain, and that the further away an image is from you, the longer it takes to reach you. This means that everything we see is always in the past already, and the present is a story we tell ourselves is real.

Everything is removed from you now. You have been traveling so long it has become difficult to tell what is moving and what is not. Waking from dreaming. People, traffic, noise, are unreachable. The white light from Filbert's throws half of you in shadow. In the distance there is the black of the forest against the black of the sky. Just through the window behind you, the checkout girl is standing still at her register, staring at nothing, bathed in that otherworldly light. You dig your hands into your pockets beside the stolen apples. It was foolish to take the apples. You're not a child. It's not the lying that ages you, it's hanging on to the lie knowing it's a lie. We are old, dear traveler. I don't have the words to hold you here forever any more than I did when you were a boy.

Just down the street, the Manor House is yet another world. You lean through the heavy glass door and stand in the lobby a moment, unwilling to drop your bags because you know the blood will return to your arms hot and angry. The room smells like air freshener and dust. A crooked and delicately cobwebbed chandelier and a small lamp by the manager's counter spread a yellowy glow over the room. Behind the counter an open door leads into another room, more brightly lit. You hear the sound of silverware tapping plates and smell something warm. Your stomach growls. At the counter you tap the bell, and a short, bald man appears in the doorway wiping his mouth with a napkin and frowning.

— Who is it, he says.

— I need a room, you say.

The man in the doorway stares at you as though you just reminded him of something important. He holds his napkin to the corner of his mouth. You stand there like that for a moment, the two of you, regarding one another. Let him look. You have all the time in the world. The manager limps up to the counter, massaging his hip, and lifts a large musty ledger up onto it. In the dimmer light of the lobby, he looks older. A woman calls out from the other room about a bank payment, wants to know what 2,375 times four point nine is, then divided by four. Automatically your fingers begin twitching at your sides, touching each other in a pattern only you understand. The manager squints and makes a low sound in his throat, glances at you.

— Sign here, he says, pointing to the ledger. — Fifteen dollars a night. How long will you be staying?

— I don't know.

— Pay in advance. He takes the book down and lays your money in a cash register. From somewhere down below he finds a key and sets it on the counter.

— Room Two is through that doorway on the right, he says

— Restroom's down the hall, on the left.

— There's no cooking in the rooms! shouts the woman from the other room.

— Tell them there's no cooking in the rooms!

— Quiet! yells the manager.

— 2, 909.38, you say. — Your bank payment, per quarter.

The manager stares at you, hopeful, vaguely suspicious.

— You're some kind of accountant?

— A mathematician, you say. The manager's face grows more hopeful and more suspicious. He turns his head slightly to one side and his face screws up tighter. — Have you been here before? he asks. — In Delamond? You look familiar.

— Who do I look like?

— I don't know. Someone.

— Could be.

— Where you headed?

— Up to my room.

The manager stares, waiting for you to say something more, but you've told him everything you know. You lift your bags, sighing with the pain in your arm, and make your way up the stairs to your room. The other rooms along the hall are silent, and there are no lights beneath the doors. You have the floor to yourself. Inside your room you turn on the light — the same yellowy light as the lobby. The room is clean and spare. There is a bed, a nightstand, a small table and chair, and a dresser with a flimsy, warped mirror. From below, you can hear the manager and his wife yelling at each other. Between the bed and the table is a thinly curtained window looking out over Main Street. You set your bags on the floor and unpack your things. You only have a few clothes in your bags, a little food, three stolen apples, and the journal in the breast pocket of your coat. You set the apples in a row on the window sill and crack the window up with your good arm, let the cold air seep in. Outside, a cone of light falls on the sidewalk directly below. Occasionally a man or woman appears in the light, a splash of dark color, then disappears through the other side.

A wind is picking up, knocking on the wall. In another room, a floorboard pops. If you close your eyes you can see through the walls into the other rooms, all the same as yours, and feel the echoes of the voices of travelers passing through. Between your unlived life in Delamond and the unreal life you left behind, all you have now is the road, and this journal. This journal is my living memory. Memory is a needy beast. Even now I see every paper cut on Father's hands, I hear the wind in the long grass, I feel the warm fire as I read to my mother. Small things, maybe, things to forget. But these are the forces that shaped me, the things I can't unremember. What I have forgotten haunts me, too. My mother must have yelled at me once, she must have made me cry. Father must have laughed. I must have done something right. What kind of grass stood in my field — meadowgrass, sorghum, clover, ryegrass? And those poor dying cows! Didn't I visit them, even once? My brothers had names — why can't I remember them? They had lives, they are a part of my family and me. What I have forgotten fills the empty space around these words, and the emptiness forms me sure as memory hardens the bones inside me.

Memory can be fooled, too. Agnes doesn't want to remember that Buddy left her, so she lives a memory of waiting for his return. We all remember what we want. I write a birthday party with friends and gifts, and in time, that's what happened. If I write you in Delamond, you will harden into memory here. Why don't I give my brothers names, then, or invent a whole new life for myself, as I do for you now, dear traveler? I'm trying to tell you a story, a story of what I am. I could write a happier story this time around, but certain things I can't forget, and certain things I don't need to remember. And there are certain things I need. Memory is more than truth and fiction. Memory is what you need.

I need you, dear traveler. This journal is everything I remember, everything I've forgotten, and everything I need. I've been working on these words with care, and now I'm giving them to you. That's all there ever is. You'll see, when it comes time to get your own story up a tree, how things fall apart, and what to make of it. You don't have to believe this story, you only have to trust it. I will take you other places, show you new things. We will search for a new beginning somewhere. I need you for this.

December 13

The dead haunt Agnes, too.

Afternoons you can often find her in the day room, sitting alone at a little round table near the window, sipping tea and staring through all the residents. If you sit down with her you'll see she is not in the day room at all.

"Smashing day," she will say.

She is in Paris, in a café on the street, sipping something stronger than tea, maybe even absinthe. The locket around her neck gives her away, and her smile. The locket hangs on a silver chain, delicate as her mysterious little smile. There's an image of Artemis on the locket, and inside there's an empty space where Agnes sees a picture of Buddy Baker. She is fingering the locket and taking in the city. She is watching the poets and the beggars and the military men and the expatriates, and suddenly, so are you. The day melts away and you play Paris, you and all the seekers and the makers, with luxuriant decadence, thrum Paris like a sad old guitar. Up from the street and through the click of a thousand heels, the hum of voices, the tink of silverware and glass across tables crowding the sidewalks, the song of Paris rises. Someone is always laughing or crying or drinking or dancing, there is always a war on this or that horizon. There is never enough food or money, but always enough to write.

I took a chair beside Agnes and raised my tea cup to hers. "To Paris life," I said.

Agnes raised her cup to mine. "'Life is the farce which everyone has to perform,'" she said with a flourish. "'True life is elsewhere. We are not in the world.'" She drank deeply from the cup and smiled. "Rimbaud." Our afternoons in this Paris café were always full of this back-and-forthing. *Repartee.* But it was more than that, too, it was conversation, and it was a kind of confession. Our favorite writers gave voice to our hearts' truths. It was easier to be intimate that way, because they weren't our words. It was more intimate, too. With our writers in front of us we weren't afraid to say everything. Agnes quoted her favorite poets, I quoted Whitman. She respected Whitman in spite of his being American.

"'We convince by our presence,'" I said.

"'I is another.'"

"'I celebrate myself, and sing myself.'"

"'And as the Damned soul rises, so does the fire.'"

"'Nothing can happen more beautiful than death.'"

Agnes chuckled lightly — more music from Paris. "You Americans," she said. "You're so plucky."

"'And your very flesh shall be a great poem.'"

"Not a poem, a burial site — 'The beautiful uncut hair of graves.' Now there's your Whitman."

Agnes always got the last word this way, using my Whitman to one-up me. I didn't mind — she wore Whitman well. Hearing us from the piano where she was playing, Helen strolled over and joined us. She was sipping absinthe, too. "How I love a little Mozart," she said to Agnes. She never looks at me. "Paris was made for Mozart." For Helen, this was all acting, and she was out of her element. She should have been playing jazz.

Tom and Agnes joined us, too. Tom was eating leftover

whipped potatoes from lunch, scooping them out of a Styrofoam cup. He paid more attention to the potatoes than to us. Tom knows it's best to play along with Agnes, but he thinks we enjoy it too much. He tempers Alice and makes her nervous, but she could be plucky, too.

"You sure you don't want some potatoes?" he asked Alice, raising a spoonful up to her.

Alice wrinkled her nose at the potatoes. "They do serve the most dreadful pâté here," she said, looking at us. "I dare say it tastes like whipped potatoes." We always used this odd lingo. We didn't speak French, and American didn't seem appropriate for this Paris. British, or something like it, seemed the next best thing. *Pidgin*. It felt right for this otherworld.

"I rather enjoy the pâté," said Helen, eyeing Alice's spoon. "They refused to give me enough at lunch. The servants here are atrocious."

Tom stuck the spoon in his mouth and spoke around the pâté. "That's hard cheese for you," he said.

Helen frowned. The three of us laughed at Helen's reddening face and Tom, who had slipped into Agnes' world against his will. Hard cheese, indeed.

A silence crept over Helen, Tom, and Alice. Alice squeezed Tom's hand in apology as he looked away toward the kitchen. He had an appetite for potatoes. Helen drummed her nails on the table and stuck her chin out in the air, acting as if she'd forgotten about Tom's remark. Around Agnes and I, Paris buzzed. As we sipped at our absinthe she gave me a conspirator's wink and grin, and touched my knee. Old hands are rarely beautiful like Agnes'. My hands are like a deformed ginseng plant, hers are the white wings of some rare, exotic bird. Her fingers were like warm feathers on my knee. Even after she left in search of a restroom I could feel the feathers all around me, and the city, a close embrace. I wanted that feeling to stay awhile, to stay forever.

Agnes, mother of my dreams.

Agnes is the woman I would like to have been. Her name means "pure." She has never picked up a musical instrument in her life, as far as I know, but all her life a kind of music has played itself through her. When she is happy, you'll notice in her walk an occasional eighth-note skip, or she'll sing in a bold falsetto just this side of laughter. There are dirge-moments, too, when she mopes about the garden in her bathrobe, picking the petals off flowers and letting them fall behind her, or settling into chilly gray stillness on the stone bench by the garden. But even in her quietest moments she is a struck tuning fork whose note settles gently in your blood. She is not sorry for misdeeds of the past.

Agnes and I were friends, I believe, before we met. She was the form of my childhood days. My past is a string of events in response to the pluck of Agnes' music. I heard her in the wind brushing through the long grass as I stood, a girl, in the field outside my house, wondering past the horizon. She was a voice my mother and I heard outside her bedroom window one afternoon, singing a song we'd never heard, as my mother lay dying. I polish my words like brass as she would — my thesaurus and dictionary sit like eager dogs at my elbow. *Fervent.* I try to see as Agnes sees, and think the things I think she thinks. I have never told her this, and I will never show her this journal. It would go to her head.

But nothing stays forever. These weren't Parisian days of war and poetry, these were the evaporating hours between medication and faraway dinner, and after a time, the others were still silent. Without Agnes, our Paris had vanished. I was jealous of the others. They had their own places to go. Where was my Paris? Even my journal was a travelogue of the all too familiar. If I sat here too long in this silence I would start to write again, and I didn't want to write. I don't. I could feel the sudden weight of the pencil on its twine around my neck. The dead began to arrive from their own distant places. Their feathered breath at my ear. I'm afraid, I'm afraid, I'm afraid. I finished Agnes' tea, searching for a taste of mint, but the tea had gone cold and bitter. Agnes hadn't come back from the restroom. I wanted her back. I had an appetite for Paris, any Paris.

"Where's Agnes got to?" I asked.

The others snapped back to here. Agnes could get herself into danger when she wandering through time. We tried to watch out for her.

Alice put her hand to her cheek. "Maybe she went to her room," she said.

"Or outside?" said Helen. "Though it's so cold out there…"

Tom snorted. "You southerners," he said. "It's practically Indian summer out there. Maybe Agnes went back to Paris." And he snorted again. Tom doesn't believe Agnes has ever seen Europe. He says that if she lived in Paris at all, it was probably Paris, Illinois.

"You're an ass," I explained to him. I can't stand when a man snorts like that. *Dismissive.*

There was no real alarm. Agnes was probably in her room. The orderlies were supposed to keep track of us, but they didn't always, and we liked it that way, so we didn't tell them about Agnes now. Marilyn would know, and Onion, but Marilyn wasn't here yet, and Onion was busy in the kitchen. Across the room by the TV, Old Ed was watching us. He had a wounded puppy look on his face. He always had a wounded puppy look. As an outsider among outsiders, he's a member of our little gang, though we never invite him in. We don't like the way he wears his wounds. He saw the question on my face and shook his head, no, he hadn't seen Agnes.

I went looking. I poked my head into Agnes' room, but she wasn't there. I couldn't help but stand there in the doorway a moment. Agnes' room is something to behold, a museum of weird artifacts from her time in Europe. A quiet chaos of photographs, paintings, musical instruments, journals, letters, books, books, more books, on the bed, the dresser, the nightstand, the chair, the floor. Strange folk I'd never heard of before. I had read most of them — Agnes loaned them to me and only to me. We didn't talk about them much, we didn't need to. We just knew each other through them. A perfume hangs in the air, something that smells to me like India. A rich bronze odor, and you catch yourself sniffing after it long after it's left you behind. Agnes is a place, a place I know well, which I have never been to.

I looked in the back yard. I usually find Agnes on the stone bench by the garden, but she wasn't there. The sun was up and melting the snow — you could see the black earth around the trunks of the trees, and almost smell it. I stood on the patio and called out. The yard is penned in on all sides by a wall of pine trees. *Sentries.* This is where the orderlies parade us about like tired old circus animals when the weather is fine, goading us to lift our knees and swing our arms. A stone walkway follows a flowerbed to the right, turns behind a stone bench on the far side, then leads through a garden before finding the patio once again. The garden is the most beautiful thing here. In the spring, red-berried shrubs and patches of wildflowers bloom along the path as it winds around low sculpted hills of shade trees. Now the flowers were dead. Wet black stalks poked up through the snow. I kept calling out as I followed the walkway around the yard and into the garden, stopping at the fountain. The granite satyr grinned down at me. Agnes sits here sometimes. She likes the satyr, the note of jazz in all this chamber music.

She wasn't here, but I could see her past the garden, on the other side of the pines. I might not have seen her but for the bright green cape she was wearing. When she wore the hood up like that I called her the Green Reaper. The way she was standing, though — so still, with her hands resting on top of a chain link fence —

something wasn't right. I walked up slowly and stood next to her. You can't just sneak up on someone when they're staring off. First, you have to just be there, let your existence remind them of the world they've left behind. She was looking out past the grounds. A fragile little smile trembled on her mouth, and a tear had fallen down her cheek and splashed on the back of her hand. She was staring off. You see this in the Alzheimer's patients, the slack jaw, the glassy stare. Beyond the fence was an open field, probably filled with pine at one time. Everything seemed so far away. If I turned around, I wouldn't be able to see the home through these trees. The home would be gone. Beyond the fence, the field spread out and out, with patches of brown earth showing through. In the distance, a wavery black strip of road where little cars moved back and forth.

"I didn't know there was a fence here," I said. I didn't. I spun in a slow circle and followed the fence with my eyes all the way around the back yard and back to Agnes. I stuck my fingers through the wires of the fence and pushed, and they clanked lightly against the poles to either side. I realized I had heard that sound every time the wind blew strong enough. One part of me knew of the cage, the other didn't want to know. Had Agnes just found this out as well, and found an escape? There are many ways to live that don't require living.

"Buddy drives a Ford," said Agnes. "He'll give the signal when he comes so I'll know it's him."

"I don't see him, Agnes," I said.

She threw me a quick smile. "You know he's always late, Martha," she said. "Up all night, playing with the band, then he can't get out of bed in the morning. He was nothing when he left Delamond. Now he's a star."

"You're probably right," I said. Martha was Agnes' dead sister. I hated Martha, though I'd never met her.

"We'll have a house in Paris and one back here, so you and I won't lose touch. And you'll visit us in Paris. It's worlds apart from Delamond, Martha, worlds apart. We'll go shopping, and I'll buy you a dress — you really do need a proper dress, you know, instead of these old things. Buddy will introduce you to all his friends. He's got a lot of connections, you know. Last time we went to a party at Gertrude Stein's and I met so many lovely people — Surrealists, Martha! Imagine!" Agnes pulled me close and grinned. "Buddy doesn't know yet," she whispered, "but I think I might be pregnant."

"That's wonderful, Agnes," I said, and we hugged. She never hugged Agnes like that. I was jealous of Martha, stealing this intimacy from me. I wanted to be cruel, so Agnes would never return to Martha's memory, and stay here with me instead.

Behind us I heard a crash — I imagined the satyr had finally had enough and was barreling straight through the brush, granite arms and legs kicking aside everything in his path on his way to a better place. "Agnes?" a voice bellowed. It was Onion. "Gertrude?" He and the rest of our gang appeared through the trees, smashing through the bushes and flowerbeds. Onion was all circles and bright colors — he wore a puffy, berry red coat that made him look even bigger and rounder, and a yellow woolen cap shoved back on his head. His eyes were wide and round, and his mouth, as he cried out again and again, "Agnes! Getrude! Agnes! Gertrude!" Arms waving around stiffly as he tried for balance, he looked like a cartoon, a very dangerous cartoon. The others, too, as they bungled along, alarmed. I could have laughed, or killed them. I waved them off.

"Maybe you should sit down, Agnes," I said. "Are you tired?"

She turned back to the road and her face fell. Without moving her lips she said, quietly, "Yes. But we'll be better off in Paris, away from these people." She nodded toward the home.

"Who do you mean, Agnes? What people?"

"These locals, this place. Everything is so dried up here, it's miserable. I'd leave it in a heartbeat. No regrets. We could make it in Paris, Martha. Let's leave them all behind. Let's tell Buddy we're leaving it all behind."

"Agnes. Buddy's not coming, Agnes."

Agnes looked at me, suspicious, staring at me as though I'd just lifted a mask off my face. "You aren't Martha," she said.

"I'm Tru," I said. "I'm your friend. Your best friend."

"Tru?" She touched my cheek, considered me. "That's a lovely name. Tru. Very American, somehow. My husband Buddy is a musician. We're going to Paris. Have you ever been to Paris, Tru?"

"I haven't been anywhere."

"You should go."

Later

I wonder if Agnes haunts Buddy. Living or dead, if he feels her watching for him on the horizon, if she fills the notes coming from his trumpet on some dark stage in a cramped Paris nightclub. If we are all somebody else's dead, haunting somebody's past. There's a strange comfort in that, and a fear that it might not be so. That's why we lie.

Dear Traveler, let me haunt you now.

December 14

This afternoon the orderlies set up the folding chairs again and made us listen to a city man talk about the history of Christmas. "How we do attract the city men!" Agnes said. The orderlies had decorated the day room for the holiday. There was plastic garland around the window frames and frost on the pane that Onion had sprayed from a can. I couldn't see outside from my rocker, so I rubbed some of it away. Christmas carols played endlessly from somewhere. Little santas and elves and angels and things sat on top of the magazines, and some of them lit up or said things or played music. If you put down your sewing you might accidentally set one off. In the corner by the front door stood a Christmas tree that everyone was welcome to decorate with personal things. The tree was real, and smelled wonderful. There were so many different things on it that it didn't look personal at all, though. At first I thought it was like the day room, brimming with impersonal personality, but then I thought it looked nicer, more like Frankenstein's monster — you only saw the whole wondrous thing, and never stopped to think, That was somebody's arm once, that was somebody's head. Even the monster never asked Victor the story behind each cut and stitched piece. But when it was all thrown together, the separate limbs didn't matter. The whole is greater than the sum of the parts, isn't that the saying? In its ugly confusion of pieces, the monster had become something beautiful. Victor — Father, Creator — should have seen that.

The city man told us the history of St. Nicholas and whatnot, but he was very dull. He was still speaking when our little gang started our own little debate on the matter. I didn't know there was so much history to Christmas. Helen told us the tradition of the Christmas tree traced back to the Romans, who decorated trees during a festival called Saturnalia, honoring Saturnus. Agnes told us no, everything we currently understand about Christmas was invented by Charles Dickens and greeting cards. Tom reminded us that Christmas is about Christ, not pagan orgies or children's stories, and he looked for a nod from Alice, who gave it. He even interrupted the city man in order to give us a sermon on the true story of Christmas. The city man was polite enough to let Tom talk about the wise men, Joseph and Mary, and the rest of it. Agnes, who hates religion, wondered out loud why it's no longer fashionable to have illegitimate children in the barns of slumlords. The stories were all lovely and frightening, as stories always are. I believed them all.

Tom and Agnes went at it until supper, and the city man never did get to finish. He left rather sullenly. After supper, we sat by the window. We always sit by the window, in the same chairs. I get the rocker. Winter nights, when the sun sets early, we talk. I listen. The others were telling stories about their own past Christmases, the same stories every year. At this age the only new thing to look forward to is death, so we look backward. Tom, who only has stories from his seminary, doesn't have stories to tell that Agnes won't poke fun at, so he keeps mum. Helen's stories of Christmas pageants that her students put on at school, Alice's little stories of singing around the tree with her family at home. Agnes' stories of

Paris, where she danced once with Winston Churchill, and stayed up nights drinking absinthe with the surrealists.

I remember cold, and the flat field of white snow stretching away to the gray sky. I remember the wind rattling at the windows or sneaking under the kitchen door. I remember the fire being never quite warm enough. Some years Father dragged home a tree we'd set up in the corner of the kitchen. I don't remember decorating it, but I remember it decorated — wax candles when we had them, red ribbon, apples. Smell of pine and apple warming by the candlelight. I don't remember presents. I always think of winter as death, and spring as life, even though Father and my mother both died in the spring. I didn't bury my parents, I planted them.

December 16

Everything was changing for us. Father sold the last cow for a pittance. He withdrew deeper into silence and distance, coming in the house only to eat a little and sleep a little, then rise before the sun and leave — I don't know where. Sometimes I saw him limping through the long grass, head down, looking for something. All he found was an Indian arrowhead. It was the only arrowhead ever found on our lands, far as I know. Someone must have dropped it there. I thought maybe it had fallen out of the ribcage of a skeleton sitting in a wood box up in a tree. Someone had looked up at the tree, looked down at the arrowhead, and walked with it for awhile before it dropped, forgotten, from his hand. For awhile Father kept the arrowhead on the kitchen table. I tried to read the arrowhead for a sign, something to point me in one direction or another. I discovered it some mornings in different positions, pointing at the door, out the window, toward my mother's room, but I couldn't read what it meant. *Void.* The meaning of things had gone. Father's prospects had dried up completely, my mother was dying. The dead had returned to their netherworlds. Brice had disappeared from Delamond, no one knew where. And deep in my gut, I felt a tingling. I believed I was pregnant. One morning the arrowhead was gone from the table, and I didn't see it again for a long time.

I stopped going to school in order to help with my mother. I sat by her bed and coaxed her to restless sleep with the news of the day from yesterday's newspaper. I had ceased telling stories — they had stopped making sense. I wanted to tell her about Brice, I wanted her to help me. I didn't know how to raise a child. But I couldn't tell her. She would have been disappointed in me, as I was in myself. It would have killed her. As she slept I stared at the rise and fall of her chest for so long it didn't seem to move anymore. At times I wanted her to die, so her suffering would end, and so she would never learn of what I had done. I thought of whispering my secret into her ear as she slept, hoping that when she awoke she would know as if she had always known, but I couldn't say it out loud, even to no one.

When I couldn't bear to be with her, I revisited my place in the back alley behind the bookstore. I called it my "spot." In the beginning I would just walk by my spot, glance at it from the sidewalk, and remember. Later I would stand in the exact place, at first for little snatches of time, then sometimes for the luxury of an hour. Eventually, I couldn't stay away. I searched through the dirt for Brice's footprints. I laid my cheek against the wall and relived it. I pressed my lips to the faint stain of my blood in the brick. I deserved it, all of it, the things I did and the things that were done to me.

No one deserves this.

No one but you, Tru. Nothing was done to you. You did it all.

It's true. There are things I could have done to avoid all this, and there are things I shouldn't have done. Why am I evil? I searched for signs in the bricks, the thin strip of sky, the dirt at my feet. They must have known more than me, but they couldn't help. The fact remained. I have hurt many, many people.

Before he ran away, Brice dropped out of school and quit

Filbert's. I would see his mother in Filbert's from time to time, a short, thin, dark woman with a sharp face, clutching her purse to her stomach. Her name was Thora. Thora was always the kind of woman who expected the worst, and got it. After the rumors flew that Brice was too crazy to go to war, she grew worse. She had a hard voice, hard little eyes that could only accuse. Maybe because she loved her son and wanted to protect him, or avenge him, or maybe because she feared and hated him like everyone else. It was hard to tell. I'm sure Brice never told anyone about us. Brice must have felt he was unfit for anything. This must have been worse than going to war. The people kept their distance from Thora, and rumors started about her, too.

I only saw Brice once more, downtown. I was coming out of my spot. It was noontime, and there were many people on the street. Brice stood across the street from the bookstore, just where he had stood the last time we met. Still as a post, but for the grinding of his teeth. I slowed to a stop in the middle of the sidewalk. He wouldn't look at me, or maybe he didn't see me, but then he started backing away into the alley behind him. I stood there watching him, letting him go. I was feeling something, but I didn't know what it was until I looked down at my hands. They had closed into fists. I realized suddenly that I was furious, and that I had been furious for a long time. I looked around at the people and at Delamond. I could see every hard corner of every red, pocked brick, the grit of the sidewalk rubbing off on my shoes. The sun shone down on it all like a harsh yellow lamp. It was all too real. The birdsong, when I followed it, came from a simple robin. When I touched my face it felt cold and thick and heavy as clay. The rest of my world had been bled of its magic, and it seemed to me that this world — this world of downtown Delamond — should have received an overflow of the fantastic. But it hadn't. Nothing had changed. Since Brice, I had harbored secret hope that the magic I had known for a brief time had disappeared, but not gone. Now, suddenly, I knew it was gone, and I was stuck in this world. It had all happened, and it had not gone away, and it would not be erased by a trick of my imagination. There would be no more signs or messages in the world, no more stories to tell.

And as soon as I saw how angry I was, the anger faded away, and there was nothing. Nothing to be afraid of. The world was just the world. Without thinking I pointed across the street and shouted, matter of factly, That boy raped me. People stopped. By then Brice had already disappeared. The people looked at me, I looked at them. Some shook their heads at me, I shook my head at them. For them, the problem was me. For me, there was no longer a problem. This world was easy, such a small, ordinary thing. And I laughed.

It was a long walk home — past the last house, over the corduroy bridge, up the long hill. The easy laugh that had barked out of my throat downtown had gone away and I felt every footstep, every rock beneath my heel. Felt myself growing heavy and tired and hot. The hillside rose up and up to the sky. We hadn't had much rain, and the grass was brown, and the sky was pale. Everything looked so plain. *Wanting.* I pressed my hand against the ache low in my belly and thought about the future, but nothing came to mind. There was only the uneasy weight of me. But as I walked and grew heavier, the weight demanded more of my attention, and I was able to go inside of it. I felt my bones pistoning, my muscles working, my blood pumping, my heart straining. The thing in my gut heaving around. I didn't understand it yet, but I was feeling myself growing stronger, growing into a woman.

At home, I caught Father in my mother's bedroom. He didn't hear me. He was kneeling on the floor by her side, his face pressed into her hand. I could see his mouth moving, but there was no sound. There was no sound in the whole house. I could feel the empty weight of it pressing in on us in that room, I could feel the whole world pulling toward this eternal moment. My mother's eyes were closed and her face turned slightly away. Her lips were open a little — was she breathing the silence in, or was it coming from inside her, filling the house and us? Father's shoe scraped against the floor as he rose, the noise like thunder, and I hid behind the door. Later, it didn't seem like any of it had happened — seeing Brice, laughing, seeing Father — but when I returned to her room, my mother's hand still lie at the edge of the bed where Father had been holding it. When she was awake, she always held her hands together. I told myself she was fighting to hold on. I moved her hand over to her other hand. Father never understood a thing.

Over time, I put it all out of my mind as best I could by sewing. My mother had unfinished orders from before the sickness overcame her, orders her customers were too afraid to ask about, and I took them up and completed them myself. I did it automatically, without thinking, while I watched over her. Sometimes she watched me, too — my hands as I worked the needle and thread. There was no expression on her face. Then she would whisper the name of whoever's order I was working on, and look at me, sometimes smile, usually not. The doctor came in — a glance at my mother, a frown, sometimes a packet of medicine for me to give her — and out. If Father and the doctor spoke, I never knew it. My mother never improved. In time I stopped watching her and took greater care in the sewing. There was nothing I could do for her but wait.

Father was waiting, too. He had seen my belly growing, and he had stormed through the house, pounding the walls and breaking dishes and yelling, Who? Who? Who? I didn't tell him anything. He would have killed Brice. He wanted to kill me, too, but then the rage passed into a quiet, seething wait. He kept out of the house most days, and stayed up late at night in the kitchen. I could hear his boots pacing the floor, and when they stopped, I knew he was looking out the window toward the graves of his sons, wondering what might have been, and what would come.

As my body swelled I took to wrapping cloth around my belly, to hold things in, and wearing loose dresses. I spent more and more time sewing for my mother. I had only made clothes in the past to help my mother during the busy season, but now I sewed like I depended on it. My mother's customers paid for their dresses and new orders came in, and a few new customers. I called them "my women." Father noticed the people coming to the house but never said anything. The customers would stand on the back stoop uncomfortably, because we could feel Father's stare from the far side of the field, where he stood like a black mark on the golden grass. My women and I exchanged orders for money quickly, with little ceremony or eye contact. I didn't know what Father was thinking then, though I felt resentful and afraid of him. I believe now that he didn't know what sense to make of his life and had stepped out of the center of it, to the edge, to watch it pass from a safer distance. I believe he was already grieving for my mother's death, and I wonder if he saw in my distant figure, standing on the stoop welcoming customers into the kitchen, the future ghost of his wife.

When the weight of his stare grew too heavy, I cleaned out the front parlor entrance and took orders there. In time, some of my women stayed for tea. They were not interested in me or conversation, though. They were all gossips, and they used me, the thirteen-year-old spinster, to vent opinions that would offend polite company. I assured them in their views and took care to conceal my belly. They didn't notice because they never looked past themselves. We were not friends. In town I was still just That Hayes Girl. They would not wave or say hello. They looked at me the way they looked at Father.

When my women left I returned to my mother's room for more

sewing. I wanted to tell her about the women and how they behaved downtown — I didn't think they were the same with my mother as they were with me. I wanted to complain, and to poke fun at them with my mother, but she was always tossing and turning through fever-sleep. I continued sewing and let her talk, her voice like a rusty door hinge. One day I realized she had awakened, and was talking to me, and I had missed her words. I set the sewing down on my belly. She looked at me. In her watery red eyes I saw one future — I had come to realize that there were many futures perched upon my shoulders. I realized I had been crying. I may have been crying for months without knowing. The tears had pooled and dried over my dress so many times that a trail of salt stains ran from my chest to my stomach, where it collected in a pale white circle. I felt weak, suddenly. Bone-tired. I hadn't slept in how long. Then her white hand on my cheek like a cold fire, lending strength. Outside, a voice was singing. Are you sad, she said. *Breathe.* And I did. I took in the song, I took in the whole sky in one breath. I took in my pasts, for there were many pasts as well, one for each day I had lived. I took in my futures. I took in this story though it hadn't been written yet. My mother laughed. We laughed together and were cured. For a moment, everything was possible again. Everything else was in my mind.

Then she fell asleep again, a deep, silent sleep. I rearranged her blankets, straightened her bedclothes, propped up her pillows. There was something underneath one of the pillows — Father's arrowhead. It was light in my palm, and still sharp. I held it close to my mother's bow-shaped lips, tried to imagine it was a word shot from her mouth and turned solid. Father never knew what it meant. I put in my pocket.

In the weeks that followed, I began thinking about the future more. It was there in front of me, I was aware of it looking at me, but I didn't know what to think or do. Necessity became the new presence in the house, replacing possibility. I took its heavy weight on my shoulder. I set the little extra money aside for the baby — it had become, finally, a baby, a reality, and not a thing, though it was still just a baby, and not yet my baby.

*****

My mother's hum turned to a rattling wheeze. She seemed to breathe blood, and so pale I could hardly tell her from the bed sheets. The doctor had stopped coming, though Father always seemed to have a supply of useless medicine on hand. I sewed beside her, piling material over the globe of my belly. Father had been busy doing something outside in the field. I had stopped using the back door altogether — couldn't remember the last time I walked through the long grass or heard the river. The day I did look out the back window, I saw Father had been building a new house, a cottage at the far end of the field, near to where the diseased cattle used to stand and stare. He had burned the grass away and tilled a patch to one side of the house, ready now for my own food. He had used some of the wood from the old red barn for my new front door. The red paint made it look like a warning.

The day he finished the house he walked into my mother's room, where I was sewing. After I had sewed a wardrobe for the baby I had begun work on the dress my mother had started sewing so long ago, the strawberry red dress. I had found it crushed at her feet beneath the sheets. I had finished it and washed it and while she slept I had put her in it. She lay now as though she had just fallen asleep after an exhausting day. Father stood in the doorway, breathing. He breathed in short, shallow breaths. He smelled like mud and sweat. I looked up at him. He was shaking. He was seeing his wife from long ago, before all this, the woman who, in his mind, he had already buried.

Get out, he said.

I did. I picked up my things that night and moved into my new home. It was solid and clean, with a kitchen and a bedroom. Father had piled wood by the fire and stocked a little food in the pantry. And he had built a crib for the baby. My first night there I lay on my side in bed. I tried humming like my mother, to fill the house with something, but the tune was wrong. I breathed on the windows to see what shapes and signs might appear, but that was so long ago. If I craned my neck I could just see Father's house through my bedroom window, a gray shape against the night. The empty field stretched like a desert between my parents and me. My brothers in their home at the other end of the field completed a triangle, like an arrowhead. We were all strangers connected by this shape. I watched for other signs in the flight of birds, the patterns of new grass growing at my doorstep. I listened but the wind brought me nothing. I chastised myself. The wind was just the wind. The world was mute.

One night I had the baby myself. I was peeling potatoes when a flood of water spilled out of me and terrible pains shot through my gut. I cried out, fell to the floor, crawled to my bed. The pains stabbed me so quickly they merged together into one enormous and prolonged shock. I pushed it out of me, and both of us screamed with the effort. I may have blacked out for a moment, though the crying sound stayed with me, a small but shrill voice. So angry, I thought. When I looked up Father stood in the doorway, then disappeared, then reappeared beside me, doing something between my legs. I felt a tugging, a slippery mess, then nothing. Father held the screaming thing in a bloody towel, stared at it for a moment. The moment stretched into another, slower time. His face went soft. I wanted to hold them both, my baby and my father, and reached my arms out to them. Father's arms slowly straightened out, the baby suspended in the air between us, its cries coming from somewhere else, another world, and falling, like tears, finally, into my arms, a red, raw, powerful, fragile little girl. She exhausted herself in time, fell asleep.

Father stood near the door and watched me holding her. Her name is Madeleine, I said. Isn't she beautiful? But he couldn't see through the tears in his eyes. He wouldn't move one way or the other. The doctor came, nudged him aside like a piece of furniture. The doctor glanced between my legs, pulled Madeleine from my arms and looked her over. He said she looked healthy and that I would be alright. For a moment he loomed above me, his eyes flicking from me to my girl, his mouth pressed into itself, a barely perceptible turning of his head from side to side. Soon everyone would know what I had done. They too would show me this face, but I had seen it plenty before this, I was accustomed. I looked away, at Madeleine. She had opened her eyes and was watching me, too. Eyes black as a pit. The doctor finished with me and left. When I looked up again Father had disappeared, too.

I stayed in bed for two days with Maddie. Father brought food and left again. On the third day, my mother died. From the kitchen window in my cottage I watched Father bury her next to my brothers. Maddie lay in my arms, staring up at me. Father died just a few days after that. I suspect he poisoned himself. He had strayed to the border of his life, then quietly slipped over the edge. Father was selfish, and weak, and a coward. I found him when I got up the courage to stop at the house and ask for food. He was lying in my mother's bed, on his back, dressed in a new shirt, with a look of relief on his face. His brow was still, swept clean of care. No remorse. I slapped him, hard. I slapped him because I had loved him. He barely moved, it was like hitting a wall.

Then I cried, all day, with Maddie. I stayed in the old house the entire day, partly because there was nothing Father could do about it. Sometime during that day — I hardly remember — I went to my cottage, came back to the house, pried Father's mouth open and fingered his arrowhead deep into the back of his mouth, where he could chew on it, or choke. His teeth scraped my knuckle on the way out. Then I explored the rest of the house again, to take my leave of the family, but also to plunder. I rediscovered my mother's books, arranged in silent columns around the back room like ruins of an ancient civilization. I took them all. Beneath her bed I found a pile of the pictures I had drawn for her so long ago. Father had been keeping them there all along. I set them aside. Upstairs I found a few paintings and pieces of furniture that might fetch money. There was no resistance. Any ghosts I had greeted as a child had either faded with my parents' deaths or were content to let me steal their property as long as I never returned. I didn't intend to.

I buried Father next to my mother. Between the digging and looking after Maddie, it took all afternoon and long into night. I used an ordinary shovel, the first one I found in the barn. Dried cow dung crusted over the rusted blade. Before I shoveled the dirt back over I dropped the pictures I had drawn over his body. I told myself I wanted to surround him with what he could no longer have, but a part of me also wanted him to remember me, and hold me, and protect me. Maddie cried next to me, but not out of sorrow. She was never sad. Her cry was outrage at the things that had been taken from her before she had them — a father, a family, a future. As she cried and I slammed the shovel over Father's mound I wanted to tell her about the special soil on our land, how it would help my mother to grow into the light of that other world she was reaching for when she was alive, and how its disease would attract and trap Father in it, and only let him seep and spread down into the cold clay. Maybe Maddie already understood. I picked her up and rocked her but she would not stop crying. Above, the stars shone down. I had read that the stars comforted some people, as though the stars were watching over them. To me it seemed the stars were turned the other way, part of a vast audience and me at the back of the room, straining to see. I wanted to see things again, the way I had as a child. But the things I had seen then had been no different from these stars, strange signs I could no longer read or understand, and didn't care to.

After I finished with the graves, there was a moment. The stand of trees off to my left, black against the night's indigo, stood like an exit, a dark portal into another place. If I dug another hole, I thought. A small, deep hole. And stood at the edge with Maddie in my arms, and leaned forward, loosened my hold of her, just a little, a little bit more. If I covered the hole, covered the crying, buried my past and walked through that portal to nowhere. The thought made me dizzy. It isn't the fear of falling, or the fear of your child falling, that terrifies. It's the fear that one day you will not check your desire to let go. As if she knew, Maddie stopped crying and looked at me. Her black eyes shone. The rest of her body lay still, too still for a baby, but she was not a normal baby. In her mind, she was already digging a hole for me.

December 19

Dear Traveler:

As you take the steps down into the Manor House lobby, the manager's wife stands behind the counter, watching you. She is a short, old woman, sunk into herself. Her head sits low on her shoulders, and her shoulders slope to the ground. She has small fleshy eyes and pursed lips, a tired woman who wanted something more from life than cleaning up after travelers. She tries not to stare but she can't stop, she even goes a little pale, seeing your grandfather so alive in your face. The older ones here will see you as a vengeful ghost. They have not buried their dead. They will fear and hate you, and they will try to hurt you, because the only thing they can't do to you is the one thing they want: make you go away.

Try kindness. Tuck the journal away and unfold a few bills from your pocket, smile and give them to the woman. Tell her, — For today and tomorrow. Her lips tighten and her eyes harden. She takes the bills and draws a line on each one with a marker, then slides them into the cash register. She looks at you. She doesn't trust you. Try flattery. Tell her it's a lovely room.

— I know who you are, she says. — You're that Hayes boy.

Spitting image of your grandfather. Though he didn't live as long.

— I never knew my grandfather.

— He was crazy, she says. — You look just like him. He was murdered, you know. Only murder we've ever had in Delamond.

Her eyes are sparking flint. She's enjoying this.

— Who killed him? you ask, and with a conspirator's wink, whisper: — Was it you?

She gasps and scowls. Don't be angry, dear traveler. You can't hate them back. We all have our dead. Just leave it behind.

You push the hotel door open with the sore arm, the one that carried your bag, in order to make it exercise. It has loosened up, but still complains when raised too high or asked to lift or push too much. At night those feet at the end of your bed complain, too, though they've hardened to wood. You don't care for this body's complaints. It's gotten cranky and uncomfortable in its old age. Outside, a mess of clouds scatters across the sky. The sun flashes and dims. Follow your feet, as you always have. Make your way first through the downtown streets. There is traffic up and down the road, and a few people in and out of the post office, in and out of restaurants, men and women wearing ties and high heels and a few older folks sitting at bus stops. The noise and smell of traffic echoes back from the surrounding hills and swirls around the kettle, boiling up into a soupy racket. But above the city noise you can still hear the wind moving through forest and the hills, a patient, persistent rush. If you hold your hands over your ears, your blood makes the same sound, as if you're carrying the wind inside you. The people seem of a piece with the city noise. Of a peace. That's why they notice you, because they feel in their own blood the wind you've brought back into Delamond. They are all aware of you, watching you, afraid and suspicious.

If you walk away from downtown into the quieter streets, you'll see this more clearly. Where the two-story houses, all the same structure, huddle close together, and the lawns are trimmed but a little shabby around the edges, and the curtains are opened just a crack. A police car cruises silently by. Briefly, you consider not leaving. You can't imagine the life that you should have led here, so you try to imagine the life you could lead here now, but you can't do that either. There are too many questions, too many possibilities. All of it is beyond you, anyway. Try to understand this. You're a traveler, not a homesteader. I can't keep you here. You'll die, the story will end. You must keep walking, uncomfortable as it is. The houses all look the same, and it seems that every time you arrive somewhere new you hear the same dog barking nearby. The daylight shifts from bright to dim with surprising speed as the clouds scuttle across the sky. The neighborhood seems to change with the queer light, real to unreal, and you cannot tell which is which. You are lost. You listen for the sound of downtown traffic but all you hear are birds chirping, and occasionally, the barking dog.

Keep walking east and you'll eventually pass by Delamond Elementary school. Children play on the playground, which is surrounded by a high wire fence. There is a teacher among the children, a young woman in a dress directing the children in a game. They run around her laughing, and she blows a whistle, and there is a red ball bouncing around among them. Other children are playing on a swing set and running through an obstacle course made of wooden planks and old tires. Off in a corner, behind the teacher, two boys are grabbing after a football. They shove at each other and a fight breaks out. There is always war. Another child scurries over to watch, joined by others. The teacher, lost in her own game, never sees.

Across the street there is a vacant building and a parking lot. The old elementary school used to be here, and later a recreation center, which closed. At one side of the parking lot stands a giant willow tree, many, many years old. There's a branch about halfway up where you could sit and watch the world pass by.

Higher up you can catch breezes that the people below don't get. In the tree, you're close to the goings on below but far away, too, and it's more peaceful than lonely. You're too old to climb up there now, but you can lean your back against the trunk and watch the children fight their endless battles from a comfortable distance. But the longer you stay at a distance, the greater the distance seems to grow, and the less comfortable you are. One of the fighters is lying on the ground getting pummeled. Children didn't fight like that when you were young. So much angrier now, so much more pain. Finally the teacher notices and runs over, starts loosening the knot of limbs. There is blood on her dress. You could have stopped that fight. You should have done something. But you didn't, you couldn't from this distance. What are their wars to you, anyway? Dear traveler, they will bring their wars to you, and remind you that all life is a violent drama, and you are a part of life. There is no safe distance. If you don't create your role in the drama, one will be assigned to you.

That Hayes Boy
Little Soldier-boy!

A police car swings into the parking lot and stops beside you. An officer steps out.

— Afternoon, stranger, he says to you. — Live around here?

— I don't know, you say. You know you're asking for trouble with such an answer, but the question is too difficult to think about right now. Across the street, the teacher has pulled the boys apart and holds each one at a strong arm's length. Now it's her turn. You can almost see the veins popping out in her neck as she yells at them. You can almost feel her nails digging into collarbones. You wonder if some part of her is remembering being abused long ago on some other playground.

— Have you ever been to war? you ask the officer.

— Sir?

— War. You nod across the street at the playground. The officer looks with you, then back at you. He's wondering if he's got a nut job on his hands.

— Why don't you tell me why you're standing here, he says, more firm than polite. Look at him. He has a clean-shaven face and blue eyes. He looks like a boy playing at Halloween dress-up. He's a young man, proud in his uniform, with a bit of swagger. He taps his fingers against the butt of his billy club. You wonder how he fared on the playground, if he was a bully who is still a bully, or if he was beaten, and is now taking his revenge on the world. The afternoon sun gleams off the metal on his uniform, then dims suddenly when a cloud passes over. The boy's face turns gray, his badge dull. In an instant, he is old, and then the sun returns. And it occurs to you what a passing thing life is, a whim of light and shadow. *Ephemeral,* like a ghost. You have to be a ghost to hold to such a thing. You have to be alive to leave it behind. Because the dead will never leave you, you must leave them. Those other lives — unlived, unreal, imagined lives — you can't have any of it. You're a traveler. That's your role. You're only here to say goodbye.

— I'm just passing through, you say. I don't want any trouble.

— Then I suggest you move along.

— I will.

Let me go now, Traveler. Find a new beginning; better to have them than not. The dead can only continue, but the living can begin again. If you start over, you'll know you are living. Not many can start over. There's a certain power in it. Feel it. As the officer turns back to his car, tear pages from the journal and let the wind do its work. Walk away. The officer will stay behind for a moment, entranced by the apparition of agitated pieces of paper fluttering and dancing around the lot.

December 22

When I was just a girl, they called me Trudy. When I became a woman I was Tru, and I still am, though now they call me Gertrude. I'm no longer a woman in their eyes, I suppose, just old. Only Agnes calls me Tru now.

I didn't know I had become a woman until I was Tru. This was long, long ago. The logging camps had followed the treeline north, and then were deserted. They left behind stubbled hills that families gradually turned into dairy farms. The pulp and paper mill still did a business, though, and stayed open all the time after it began making writing paper in addition to wrapping paper. Its stink had long since become a part of the town. Delamond had grown southward into rich farmland, and Main Street had been paved. The influenza and the great war had come and mostly gone, and the town bustled each day to distract itself. I loved the city, but hated the people, because they hated us. I walked into town only when we needed food, or sewing supplies. I think they hated Father first, and then everything that reminded them of him. I suspect they even grew to hate my mother, though I don't remember. They definitely hated me. Going into town filled me with one part dread, one part anger. Sometimes one or the other would win out.

After Maddie was born and the war had ended, I didn't have much time for sitting in Bulb Park the way I had as a girl. My women kept me busy, and Maddie, too — she was already growing into the quiet madness that had consumed her father. The same stone-faced, black-eyed expression conveyed every emotion in her. After Maddie, the people in the park — the women, in particular — got nastier. *Whore,* some whispered, casting sidelong glances from Maddie to me. I deserved it, but Maddie didn't need to hear it. She was three, just old enough to ask me what that word meant, and why I was one.

We picked up and walked across the street to Inchbald's for fabric. I ordered fabric through Inchbald just as my mother had. I imagined I reminded him of my mother, though I didn't look a thing like her. After my mother died, Inchbald became a colorless man who spoke in quiet murmurs — a purely functional man, nearly invisible, unless he was working on a piece of clothing. He was avid about his work. With a piece of fabric in his hands, the real Inchbald would emerge from his shadow, a redness would flush his cheeks and lips, and those hands — those strange and lovely hands. Inchbald wasn't as good a clothesmaker as my mother or I, and he knew it. He and I had an unspoken arrangement that developed shortly after my mother died. I didn't always have money to pay for fabric, but he gave it to me on credit. In return, I made most of the clothes on his back free of charge, and I kept my time in his store as brief and quiet as possible. Whether he saw me as business competition or as the ghost of my mother or as the local whore who would ruin the reputation of his business, I don't know, but our arrangement suited him. I didn't think much about it, and didn't care to. I didn't get credit anywhere else.

When Maddie and I walked through the door Inchbald was bent over the counter, examining the seam on a torn shirt. His fingers worked along the tear, feeling it out, and he was breathing through his mouth in little breaths you could hear. I saw him like this a lot. His eyes flinched toward us as the bell over the door rang out. When Inchbald saw it was us, he stood up straight and dropped his hands at his sides. As his cheeks paled back to their normal shade of paper, he kept his eyes on the shirt, and his fingers kept twitching. I looked around the store to see if anyone else was there. I did this automatically. Our arrangement had grown into a ritual. If anyone had been in the store, I would have quietly slipped out again. Like the rest of them — the Delamondians — Inchbald didn't welcome us in, but long ago he used to speak a few words to me once in awhile, asking after my mother. Today the store was empty, and Maddie and I walked over to the counter. The quiet tap of Maddie's footsteps. I always heard Maddie's footsteps on wooden floors like this one. I remember this because they were the opposite of how I had expected a child's footsteps should sound. In my mother's books, children were always described as "tripping happily along." Maddie's footsteps were always measured and deliberate.

At the counter I placed my order. Inchbald wouldn't look at me, just stared at the torn shirt on the counter. When I finished speaking he walked round front to the rolls of fabric and began measuring and cutting my order. This was part of the ritual, too. Inchbald would fill my order, place it on the counter, pull my money toward him, and slide my goods toward me, eyes trained on the exchange. Then I would leave. We practiced this for four years after my mother first took ill. In that time, I'd gotten pregnant and given birth, my parents had died, and my lover had disappeared, leaving me with Maddie. I lived in a cottage in the field I used to play in, in the shadow of Father's house, making clothes for my women. More an outcast from Delamond than ever, but freer than ever, too, for certain things had been left behind. I had stopped telling myself the stories of travelers and faraway places, and I no longer saw or heard the dead the way I had as a girl.

As Inchbald began measuring and cutting my fabric, I watched his hands, and for the first time in many years, a whole imagined history opened to me. As a girl, I had imagined an entire tale of unrequited love between Inchbald and my mother, and how my life might have been if my mother had chosen Inchbald instead of Father. I had imagined what it would have felt like for those hands to hold me, walk me to Bulb Park, to school, to the lake. Warm, strong hands. Protective. After my mother died and I had Maddie, I stopped imagining. My life with Inchbald would have been exactly the same as it really was. Delamondians don't bother to understand a thing, only judge it. But I understood Inchbald, or thought I did. After my mother and Maddie, I thought I saw Inchbald's shoulders develop a permanent stoop beneath an invisible weight, and he stopped speaking to me at all. And now, just as quickly as it opened, that history closed itself off again, and I saw only this long procession of lifeless exchanges between Inchbald and I, extending onward for countless years, further and further away from the warmth of those strange hands. It occurred to me suddenly that Inchbald had never said a word to Maddie, who stood now staring up at him with her black eyes. He had never expressed condolences. He had never expressed regret. He had never gone after my mother. He hadn't spoken to me in three years, except to tell me what I owed him: silence, and this dead ritual of money and cloth.

I watched his hands now as they set my cloth on the counter, and I placed my money down. As his hands reached over the money, I swiped it up and held it to my face. He had to look in my eyes now. I stared at him and said, I don't owe you anything.

Surprise, very brief, lit his face, then a moment of disgust, then that soft, blankness I had seen for so long. *Impenetrable.* Seventy-two cents, he said.

I don't owe you anything, I said.

I keep you in business, he said.

I keep you in clothes!

Seventy-two cents. His hands still hovered over the space where my money had been.

I don't owe you anything! I said. I would make him understand this. That now, suddenly, everything was different. That our history was gone, and our stupid rituals, that a door had been closed long ago. I wasn't a girl anymore. I repeated myself again, hissing, I don't owe you anything.

Then why do you keep coming back?

His face settled into the expression Delamond had saved just for me since I can remember, the weary contempt in the downturned mouth, the resigned sigh. He looked at Maddie beside me. He wanted to say something else, maybe to her, but she stared back at him, and he looked at me again. And in that quiet little voice, as though he had repeated it a million times before, he said, Who do you think you are, anyway?

He had thought about this. Over these many years, he had been thinking about me, too. Imagining me. His silence had been full of it. I saw it all now in his face. But in his version of me, there were no parks or schools or lakes. He simply imagined me gone. My wind left me. I would have conjured the dead then, if only to hold me up, to feel some support. I would have conjured my family, but my family was gone. Inchbald never would have said such things to my mother. Father would have been more prepared for it. I had nothing. For Inchbald, I was nothing. The empty space around me expanded outward. Inchbald was a mile away. The floor spun, and little Maddie gazed up at me from another world. She was holding my hand. Her little hand, cool hand, holding me up. I had Maddie, and she had me. She was staring at me and giving me strength. Those black eyes, portals of night. Something was coming through them, filling me up. It was me.

I held a hand to my breast, steadied myself with myself, and opened my mouth for air. I said, I'm Tru.

This was the first time I had spoken this name. I hadn't planned it, or thought about it. It had been there for some time without my knowing, waiting to make itself known. I liked the way it sounded. At the heart of me, I was real. *Actual, accurate, constant, undeviating, sure, sincere, genuine, legitimate, rightful.* Maddie slid inside my arm and wrapped it around her, kept holding my hand. With the other I set my money back down on Inchbald's counter. I stared him right back. I was whole. I commanded the distances. I said it again, louder:

I'm Tru.

A corner of his bloodless mouth curled up, and Inchbald *snorted.* The man who never made a move or a sound unless it involved a shirt, the man who was wearing my shirt on his back.

Hayes, he hissed. That's all you'll ever be.

Beneath our stare, his hand took my money and slid my material at me. I still hear this sound now, coin and cloth over worn wood. Sound of bondage. Before the hand pulling my money away reached the edge of the counter, I put my own hand over it — my father, what might have been — and shoved it at Inchbald. The coins scattered on the floor behind him — the bounce and roll of the loose change through the dust and dirt and landing in forgotten crevices he would never reach. For a second he stared at his upturned palm, then kneeled down for the money, trying to scoop it up while it was still moving. He looked so clumsy, his fingers panicked. I knew I had done the right thing, then, the only thing. When he saw me watching him, he stood up again.

Get out, he said.

I gathered up my fabric. Outside, it was a bright day. There wasn't a cloud anywhere in the sky, which was unusual. Although I had become a woman and was Tru, nothing had changed, and nothing would. The next time I visited Inchbald's we would fall into our old ritual again, as though today never happened. The people parted around us without looking at us, without touching. *Whore*... Some of them were wearing clothes I had made. Some of them were travelers going to foreign cities. I could take up with a man and leave this place. *Whore. Whore.* No, I couldn't. The world had hardened, and I had hardened with it. The mystery of things had dissolved long ago — back there, in the alley. What happened in the alley was everywhere. I had become bitter, but my bitterness had made me strong, and my strength had made me Tru. I had become a woman. Maddie tugged at my sleeve and I looked down at her. She said, Let's go home, Mommy. That face! She was frowning into the sun, a beautiful alien. Let the travelers have their faraway cities. I lived in those dark eyes.

December 23

"'The purpose of life is to be defeated by greater and greater things.' So says Rilke."

"'Oh while I live, to be the ruler of life, not a slave, to meet life as a powerful conqueror, and nothing exterior to me will ever take command of me.' So says Whitman. So say I."

Christmas

Agnes is right, Christmases are all Dickens. In the day room, greeting cards are wallpaper and knick knack — they line the mantle over the fake fireplace, crowd the message board, attach themselves to door frames and window frames. They stand upright and announce themselves from end tables, dinner tables, game tables. The big pretty ones relax on chairs and couches where their owners have carefully forgotten them.

And Christmases are times of special hauntings, though not by the dead. Here, Christmases are haunted by the living. Parents appear all day in the front door, smiling awkwardly, children clinging to their coats. The families find a resident and hover over them for an hour or two. One parent dotes, the other pretends to be distracted by the children, who scatter across the room and regather at the shelf of games and the dishes of cookies and candy. They're musical, these children — all squeals and laughter in spite of their dour parents. And then they're gone, and then there's the emptiness again.

None of our gang has family that visits, unless you count Old Ed. His family came today in the afternoon — his son, the wife, two grandchildren. They all look like Old Ed, even the wife, with her dark hair and sallow sagging skin, her flat eyes and lifeless mouth. The two boys did not run and play and snitch candies like the other children. They stood next to Old Ed's chair, where their father had placed them, and looked across the room out the window. For a few minutes one of them played with the lever that steered Old Ed's chair. The mother pulled his hand down. They watched a documentary about World War II tanks. Onion offered to take a picture for them — his family snapshots filled a message board by the front desk. Onion huddled them together into a wall, parents on top, kids to either side of Old Ed. Onion said "Say cheese!" and the boys did, but their mouths didn't move. No one smiled, or you couldn't tell if they did. Looking at them all in the photograph is like looking at the cold, rocky face of a cliff. They watched more television, and the father spoke into Old Ed's ear while the mother fidgeted with the boys. As the father spoke Old Ed stopped watching the television and stared into his lap. Then he lifted his hand, and the father stopped talking, and they all left.

Old Ed doesn't know what he's got. Or maybe it's me who doesn't know. Maybe family is better than memory, even Old Ed's family. The dead have kept silent since I began writing again. They only sit at my elbow now, press at my pencil. Are they satisfied with my stories? Lovers or killers — they're just waiting to be one or the other. Would a real family weigh on me this way? I'll never know. But the dead are just as real for me as a relative breezing through the door on Christmas. Only difference is the dead don't leave — for better or for worse, I don't know. I wonder what I would do without them. I wonder what I would be.

The residents without families to haunt them are led in card-making and letter-writing activities, and the cards and letters are collected in a sack that Onion, strange Santa, lifts over his shoulder and carries off to the post office. "Nothing to send again this year, Hayes?" he asks me every year. He means well. He doesn't understand that word, *Hayes,* how others use it as a cuss word. How it stings me. I shake my head at him and take out my book of Whitman. Out the window, the farmer's frozen field gone to deathly slumber, the hard white road stretching away. I write my letters here and there.

Dear Maddie:
"What is it then between us?
What is the count of the scores or hundreds of years
between us? Whatever it is, it avails not — distance
avails not, and place avails not."

You didn't wait for me. I miss you terribly, my strange angel. May you drift forever through godless fields of purple butterfly violets.

Dear Mother:
"What chemistry!
That the winds are really not infectious,
That this is no cheat...
That it will not endanger me with the fevers that have
deposited themselves in it,
That all is clean forever and forever"

Dear Father:
Hope the arrowhead fits OK. It's authentic!

Dear Twins:
"But the mother needs to be better,
She with thin form presently drest in black,
By day her meals untouch'd, then at night fitfully
sleeping, often waking,
In the midnight waking, weeping, longing with one deep
longing,

O that she might withdraw unnoticed, silent from life
escape and withdraw,
To follow, to seek, to be with her dear dead son."

They buried you in the seminary grounds, my babies, far away from your family. I will seek you there in memory. I will hold you there and rock you to sleep.

Dear Brice:
　　"Whoever you are, now I place my hand upon you,
that you be my poem;
I whisper with my lips close to your ear,
I have loved many women and men, but I love none
better than you."

I called it rape, that day in the street before you ran away. Were you running from that word? I'm sorry I hurt you. It wasn't rape, I know that now. Wait for me. I will see you in that better place.

Dear Morrow:
　　"You will hardly know who I am or what I mean,
But I shall be good health to you nevertheless,
And filter and fibre your blood.
Failing to fetch me at first keep encouraged,
Missing me one place search another,
I stop somewhere waiting for you."

Find a better place than this, dear traveler.

*****

Now gather round me, you dead. Now comfort me.

December 31

A few weeks ago we convinced Onion to drive us downtown in the jade chariot. Our little gang gets up to these hijinks every few months, to pick on Onion and to get downtown, where we don't know what to do with ourselves. In order to convince Onion, we harass him. We complain about the things we lack — tobacco, medicines, magazines, thread, dye. Drugs and routines. We want out of the routine. We want the chariot and the city, we want a day that ends when we say. This is a game with a purpose, and we play like old wolves. *Savvy.* I march out piles of clothing and show Onion holes, tears, rips, things we'd be afraid to die in. Tom begins drumming the table with his pipe and reaching after an invisible pouch of tobacco. Alice silently paces around the day room, worrying her hands and knitting her brow over Tom. Onion starts to pant and his skin shines. Agnes and I discuss our progress in coded conversation about onions. The others never catch on, it's only our secret.

Agnes says, "Onions are shiny this time of year, but not ripe yet, not ready for travel. We should press them harder."

I say, "One must be gentle, Onions' skins are thin."

Helen's developed a repertoire for the piano designed

specifically to annoy. It involves show tunes sung out of key, and we all join in. *Cacophony.* The other orderlies play their own game, busying themselves with nonexistent paperwork and cleaning, seeing who can work the longest without working. They are as merciless with Onion in their way as we are in ours — even more so, because sometimes they tease him to his face, and mean it. In the end, Onion wants to go as badly as us.

Before we left, as I was dragging my dresses back to my room and Helen and the rest were still singing on in the day room, I had a moment. When I turned down the hallway, the noise from the day room suddenly ceased. Time slowed, time paused. I caught up to my body. The watery light, the cool metal of the guard rail, these things were suddenly more real. More now. The worn path in the carpet, stretching forward and back, blurring into less real. Voices, echoes from a distance, a different time. My body had continued on without me, but now here I was. Everything was quietly revealed. I was old. The air thickened. I saw my breath escape through my mouth on one wing. I watched my feet move forward, my new feet, newly old. The end of each bone complained against its neighbor, a walking civil war. When had this begun, the confusion, the slow pain? I could not remember, I had always been this way. I called forth proof against me, a girl running forever through a field of long summer grass, but it was the story of someone else's life. So is this one. Where had I been? What was there left to do? I was going to my room for something. The dress. Leaving. Onion was close to cracking, and I wanted to get ready to leave. Going downtown still makes me nervous, though I'm drawn to it. I need time to prepare, to catch my breath for a moment, alone. I hadn't been downtown in some time.

I watched my feet moving forward, and knocked into Old Ed. A copy of *Time* with a black and white photograph of FDR on the cover limp in his lap. Old Ed wanted to be dead, I believe that. But he did not want to die. When he looked up at me I could see it there, a longing. *Petulant.* I always told him he deserved to suffer with the rest of us. I told him he was already dead. Nothing I said kept him away. Others had little patience with Old Ed. Maybe they saw too much of themselves in him, longing after death in their quiet moments. Perhaps for the same reason, I bothered to listen to him.

He thrust his voice up out of the phlegmy swamp of his lungs — "Going downtown, I hear," — then it dropped back down and disappeared.

"Come along," I said. "We'll stop for the latest *Time.*"

"I can't go out there with all this." He petted the tubes running out of his nose. "Pick me up some cigarettes." I could count the demands people have made of me in on one hand: *Check on your mother. Make me a dress. Seventy-two cents. Get out.*

"What are you trying to do, kill yourself?"

Old Ed scowled. His whole face wrinkled and folded inward. "I know you cheated your medication," he said. "Give it to me. You don't need it."

"I need it more than you. I just want it less."

He traced over FDR's face and opened the magazine, flipped the pages past his thumb. They were so worn they didn't make a sound as they fell. Agnes was right, there was something beautiful in the ritual of his suffering, but it was also dull. I was suddenly bored. Suddenly tired. So tired. When had these legs, these wooden legs, ever run, except to run away?

"We both want the same thing, don't we, Gertrude?"

"Don't you presume to know me."

He gave me a look. "We all know each other at this age," he said. "I would help you if I could."

Meaning he'd be happy to kill me. "I can't help you, Ed."

"You won't."

"No, I won't."

A clatter behind me made us both jump. Agnes strode up, an

airy yellow shawl billowing about her shoulders. She stopped alongside me and looked down at Old Ed. "What's this?" she said. "Not dead yet?"

Old Ed's face went big and soft as pie, and calloused over again only when he remembered himself. Agnes loved him too, I could tell. They were as unlikely a pair as you could imagine, that's what made them storybook. The look in Old Ed's eye when Agnes was near told everything: he did not long for death, he longed for her. Agnes was more subtle. Anyone could see that the hardness in her eyes when she spoke to him was too hard, and her words too sharp. If she knew of her own feelings she denied them, and I never asked. Love in old age is a peculiar thing, heady at first like pure, childhood love, then wary, as you begin to wonder if you're only in love to make the Final Wait — the Final Weight — bearable, and whether or not panic can induce true love. This between them was true love, I think, because neither of them wanted it. Love is violent.

Agnes touched the fabric of my dress at the back of my elbow. She was physical that way, always touching to talk. It always surprised me. "Onions are in season," she said, "and your chariot awaits."

"Maybe I will come along," said Old Ed.

Agnes barked out a laugh. "You think you can keep up with a Cadillac in that contraption?" Agnes took my hand up and patted it. My withered hand, yet I felt so gawky. *Maladroit.* No, *girlish.* Agnes glanced at me like a woman, like grace, as though it was normal to touch me. "Onions won't keep long, so unless you're staying — " she nodded toward Old Ed and rolled her eyes, but he was already steering his chair away. I called after him. "Let him go," said Agnes. "Old sot."

The plush seats of the jade chariot were wide and long and made us giddy. We complained about the temperature and bickered with great delight over where to go next, our feet banging uncontrollably against the seat backs while Onion craned his neck to scold us from the rearview mirror. Helen took up the front passenger seat by herself, humming a bit of opera. She waved an imaginary wand out the window, conducting the road as it dipped from farmland into Delamond. The rest of us fit in the back. The back of Onion's head looked like the stub of a fat, amputated limb. Agnes silently pushed the button that raised and lowered her window. When the air rushed in it revealed us. It passed right through Agnes, as though she and it recognized each other as the same. When it hit Tom's face next to her he looked young again, and I could see what Alice saw in him, the passions he still remembered. Alice pulled her skirt down against it and fidgeted next to me — she was nervous about keeping my company, That Hayes Girl. She leaned into Tom. I watched Agnes, that little smile on her face. It wasn't the wind. It was really all coming from her.

Nearer downtown we quieted, and gazed out separate windows. The present and our private pasts separated from each other and fought for attention. There was Bulb Park, new benches, new playground beneath the shade of the same aging maples. The tulips were up and wilting already. There was the Manor House, and what used to be the dry goods store, the general store, the opera house... The dead were here, too, reminding me I hadn't finished what they wanted me to do. How they push and pull, drive me away and call me back! Bishop's bookstore, Filbert's, all the buildings that shook after Brice had finished with me. The stores are different but the place is still there. What passed between Brice and me is still there. In the cracks and holes of the pavement and bricks, there are tiny gasps of air that never escaped. And there are molecules that did. A molecule is a tiny, tiny thing. There are millions, maybe billions, that have made their way on the wave of a butterfly's wing across the globe. By now, half the world has breathed my breath from that moment. Specks of dirt from under my feet, droplets of blood have traveled from hand to hand. And something in us all remembers, now, just for a moment — I'm afraid, I'm afraid, I'm afraid — and then we forget. The people walk right over it, we drive right past, as though nothing changed. But everything has changed.

*****

Dear Traveler:

I see you in the city, too, searching for a new beginning. I see you in Bulb Park, dressed in shades of rumpled brown, like hardened furrows of earth, unfeeling of the cold. I see you on Main Street, reflected palely in shop windows. Your body is restless and has a mind of its own. You need to walk, much as it hurts and tired as you are. Even your dreams are restless visions of open landscapes where you shove through air thick as mud toward an unseen spot on the horizon that never approaches. Or you dream you are walking up a busy downtown sidewalk against the crowd, and everyone who bumps into you knocks something off — finger, hand, toe, foot, arm. At first it doesn't concern you, you even laugh it off and continue walking, then hop-lurching along. You wonder where your pieces are going, and then you notice that the passersby are munching on the pieces of you, a hurried lunch on the way to the office, and you think, "At this rate, I'll never make it home!"

But that's just a dream.

You *are* home.

*****

Agnes started in on her oral history of Delamond, which she had been making up since our first chariot tour of Delamond way back when.

"In the winter of 1886, a storm buried Delamond and trapped

the outlying homesteads under four feet of heavy snow. Stoic, and possessed of great fortitude, Delamondians did not panic. A few industrious thinkers dug out a path to the Church of the Assumption and Loggers Tavern. Consequently, not one Delamondian in the city died. Not as fortunate were the homesteaders in the forestland to the north, however, where a man named Barnabas Small and his family of four were frozen and starved dead.

"Here is Delamond: When curious parties finally cleared a path to the Smalls' home, Barnabas Small was found hunched at the dinner table over a bowl of vegetable soup. Mrs. Small sat stiff in her rocker knitting a summer dress for little Elsie, who kneeled on the floor by the burned out fireplace with her brother, Barnabas Jr., a game of checkers in progress between them and Barnabas facing a triple jump."

As we cruised along, Delamond changed its face yet again, or maybe it's only we who change the world. The people up and down the street — so rounded and heavy with clothes and concerns and bags of serious things! Helen reached over and honked the horn at them. Some looked our way but didn't seem to see. Timeless for a time, now we were the ghosts.

"Let's go to the school," said Helen.

Helen liked to watch the children and remember her teaching days. The others didn't mind — the point of our excursions wasn't to go anywhere particular, just to go. I wasn't so crazy about the idea, but I kept mum. What could I tell them — that the sight of the school broke my heart, because that's where my lover grew to hate me? No one wanted to know such things about me, and I didn't want to confess. We were a gang because we were all outsiders after a fashion, but we weren't all close friends. Alice, I'm sure, had told Tom all about That Hayes Girl, and Helen seemed to sense the outcast in me. She was gracious from a distance. I could confess to Agnes, but she may or may not be listening. I only have this journal.

Delamond Elementary School sits right across the street from the old school, where I learned about war and boys. The new school is a low brown brick building with a parking lot on one side and a playground on the other. Onion swung the car through the parking lot and by the playground. Kids laughing and screaming. I didn't look, but I heard it. It's the same sound the kids made all those years ago, across the street, me in my tree above them all, looking down. The tree is still there, shading an empty parking lot, and I'm still in the tree, watching Brice look up at me while the others close in on him.

Little soldier-boy!

"Recess was always my favorite thing," said Alice. "If we behaved, Teacher might let us draw with crayons. She had eight crayons. We drew pictures of dresses in the most outlandish colors!"

"I organized plays for the other kids," said Helen. "We made them up as we went along — what fun it was! What did you do at recess, Tom?"

"Read the Bible."

"Of course you did," said Helen. I could hear her smile spread across her teeth. "And you, Agnes?"

"I taught the other kids how to smoke cigarettes."

Gasps all around. "Precocious youth!" said Helen.

"Shameful," said Tom.

"I didn't inhale," said Agnes.

Out of the corner of my eye, I saw Helen's head tilt toward me, and she froze like that for a moment. Social grace demanded that she ask me about recess, too, but she didn't really want to know. I didn't mind. What would I tell her? What could I say to any of them? They didn't want the truth any more than I did, but that didn't mean I needed to burden them with it. I could lie, if I could unremember. If I could climb out of that tree.

Brice and Trudy, wouldn't it be nice!
I should have done something.
What could I have done?
Something, anything. I should have.
You didn't.

"Let's buy tobacco," I said. "Agnes can teach us how to smoke." There was another silence as they considered this. No one wanted to say yes first. "Tom needs tobacco for his pipe," I added. So it was OK now, and we went.

Tom knew the owner of the tobacco shop, and Agnes convinced him to give us free cigar samples. Helen refused to try, wouldn't pollute her golden lungs, but she took one anyway, and waved it around like a wand. Agnes snuck one into Alice's hand when Alice wasn't looking. Alice blushed and looked for Tom, who was talking to the owner and didn't notice. Onion stood at the door, rocking on his heels and glancing from his watch to us to his watch. Alice held the cigar like it was a giant insect, disgusted and fascinated at the same time. I had never held a cigar before. It felt silly, such a giant thing, but I imagined the men I'd seen smoking them, how they looked so powerful, and I felt that way, too. Agnes lit up like a pro, and showed Alice and I how to smoke them. We stood in a cloud of smoke getting punchy and acting like fools. We wandered around the store fingering cigars and pipes and soft pouches of tobacco with thoughtful frowns and sucking and smacking at our cigars. Alice, tiny Alice, trying to smoke this smelly tree limb of a thing by kissing the end of it! I smiled at her and patted her back. She wasn't a bad old egg. She sort of smiled back, then started coughing. Agnes patted her back until she stopped. Alice smiled again, a victor's smile. She giggled and waved her cigar in the air. Tom finally noticed what we were doing and stomped over, stared down at Alice. Alice blushed and bowed her head, let him take the cigar. He threw it to the floor and crushed it out. Alice folded her hands in front of her and stared at them, mortified. Agnes watched Tom and puffed at her cigar. I wished I could be that brazen. Tom was a fool and deserved some sharp words I couldn't conjure. I felt too bad for Alice. Tom was looking at me.

"Haven't you corrupted enough good souls?" he said. I couldn't say anything. He was right. He stared into me. He would have been a fearful father.

"Haven't you?" said Agnes to Tom. She rested her hand on Alice's shoulder. "Alice is a big girl now."

"But you aren't," said Tom. He was still looking at me. "That's the difference. Alice knows better. You... God pity you." Tom gripped Alice's hand and led her away.

"If that's the state of God's men on earth," said Agnes, "I pity God, poor sot."

Dear sweet Agnes. Always with a kind word.

We bought more cigars for later and by the time we were back in Onion's car we were all in our cups. Onion asked us to put the cigars out but we were too old and deaf. Agnes reached over the front seat and jammed an unlit cigar in Onion's mouth. When we went on our excursions we always tried to shower Onion with gifts, partly because we knew it was against the rules to buy things for the orderlies. He's such an easy target, and fun to annoy. I have hurt many, many people. I don't want to hurt people anymore. Onion let the cigar hang out of the corner of his mouth. The car quickly filled with smoke. We rolled down the windows and rested our elbows out as we cruised Main Street. Helen leaned out the window, conducting the symphony of people that parted the way for the jade chariot. We were on our way to the Thread Shed.

Agnes continued: "1920 claimed three lives by suicide, another five by starvation or hypothermia. Because farming production had decreased, the hunting season became more necessity than sport. Hunters unable to bring down sufficient game were marked for doom. During the leanest years of the depression, church attendance increased dramatically and then fell sharply as Delamondians gave up hope, and a heaviness fell across their shoulders. The mayor at the time, Theodore Wrigley, saw his people dying, and formed a plan. Shrewd and compassionate as well as extremely rich, he raised public morale by the institution of The Children's Festival, a celebration of Delamond's future leaders, complete with contests, sporting events, and games. All prizes were food items provided by Wrigley. This enabled him to give away food without injuring the people's pride. The Children's Festival was such a success that Wrigley created nine others throughout the year. In time, however, even Wrigley's enormous financial resources dropped off, the festivals grew smaller and the prizes less plentiful, the celebrations rote activities for the grimfaced Delamondians.

"Here is Delamond: in a photograph of The Children's Festival Spelling Bee on page one of *The Delamond Post* in 1922, two young boys, dressed in torn and sewed and torn again pants and wool shirts and caps and grinning wildly, hold up a prize potato. A couple, presumably one of the boy's parents, stand to one side, mother with her arm wrapped in her husband's, smiling vaguely at the ground, father with his arms crossed, frowning at the potato. According to the article, the boys tied when both spelled 'tithe' correctly, but missed on 'salvation.'"

The others laughed, more or less. Delamond remembered enough rough winters, famines, and near-deaths for such jokes to hit too close to the bone. Delamondians in general are stoics, tough and proud, but usually too simpleminded to laugh at themselves. Lovely in their flawed way, brave and tightmouthed. *Dunderheads.* After the others soured on the joke I couldn't stop laughing, and revealed myself as not one of them. Never have been. The others remembered again, too, who I once was, the oddwoman living on the edge of Delamond with the legacy of her deranged and murderous family. That made me laugh more. What else do you do? The air thickened between us, my friends stiff and distorted. Intimate distance. They were the townsfolk who would never come for me. I was the ghost they tried to ignore. I stopped laughing. It wasn't the things I had done in my life that separated us, it was the things we shared. Who hasn't felt like an outsider? Who hasn't done bad things? Now we *all* live on the edge of town.

Here is Delamond:

Soldiers returned from the great war, triumphant and haunted by the dead and their former lives. Some took back their jobs at the mill, which had been suffering, and others tried opening businesses downtown. Most stood on street corners surveying the city, fists crammed uselessly in their trousers. The city hadn't changed, but they had. They were men now who hadn't been boys long enough. There was one soldier who walked up and down Main Street for hours at a time, day after day. He was Billy Tanner before the war, going to be a millwright like his father. Billy's father died while Private Tanner was digging a trench in Germany, and Private Tanner had lost a hand to shrapnel. Now he walked Main Street — strolled, even. There was no hurry in his step, or panic, confusion, madness. He was studious. Down the street, his hand would trace the brick and glass of the storefronts, as though marveling that something so petty and fragile could feel so solid. The ghost hand at the end of his stubbed limb felt the walls, too. I used to watch the ghost hand. It was searching for the tripwire that would bring the whole city down. Not just the street's shallow front, but the whole easy permanence of cigars, candy, newspapers, groceries, hot meals, haircuts, suits and dresses, gossip, laughter, business, day, night.

A stranger to Delamond wouldn't have noticed him. Billy Tanner was a good-looking man. He wasn't unkempt, and he didn't lurch, zombie-like, like some of the others, or rant at the invisibles in his mind. If he had, the townspeople might have known what to do with him. The others were sent to special hospitals, or kept away in their homes by their families. But Billy was almost normal, so instead, Delamondians watched him for awhile, then quietly closed their doors on him. They saw their former lives, too, their dirty buildings, the close walls, the jewelry in the windows and the toys and the fancy clothing. What they had sacrificed their men for. The world as it was, lives and cities for nothing. So arbitrary. Billy's family put him on a train to who knows where. The town council planned a parade to mark a new beginning. There would be music and speeches and banners and food. There would be rejoicing. The people were proud of their fortitude.

Bodies and cities, what we leave and where we arrive: the comings and goings of imaginary lives. These are the things I thought about as we drove through Delamond on our nonsense errands. The dead entice us out of this world and pull us back into it. It ages and fatigues us. I lack Delamondian fortitude, and that makes me an outsider. But I don't want to be like them. I just want to be liked. I want to do something right. I had not a friend among my friends. Even Agnes, who was not of the world, but merely in it. This is what I thought about each time we came downtown, and forgot when we returned to the home. Downtown was Delamond, where I was always That Hayes Girl. Back at the home I could try to be Just Old Gertrude. But it would never work. There was always Delamond, and always Delamondians. Even our gang, who except for Alice and me were not Delamondians by birth, were Delamondians by nature. There was a quality that united them, so that wherever they went, they were never alone. There would always be more Delamondians around, always someone to talk to, someone to save you. What was the quality that bound them together? The ability to mark me, wherever I might go and whatever form I might take, That Hayes Girl. *Uncanny.* They are an impressive breed, these Delamondians. My cigar had given me a headache. I held my arm out the window like a wing and watched the tip of the cigar glow and cinder, break away. What kept the memories pressing in on me — is memory so relentless, or is it just that I need to call back the dead for judgment on me? But I haven't done anything. I haven't done anything wrong.

Oh my dear, you've done plenty.

Agnes kept up a lively banter on the subject of whatever caught her eye. The others joined in, even Onion after awhile, and the car filled with voice. When Onion parked they stepped out as a group, never breaking the conversation's stride even as they separated inside store after store, calling out to each other from across a sales floor to comment on a bolt of fabric, a picture, a shock-eyed fish on ice.

In the afternoon, Helen talked Onion into Blue Moon, a diner on Main Street. Helen told us they made their own ice cream. I had never been to Blue Moon. Long ago, it used to be Inchbald's place, the tailor. Nothing looked the same inside, but it felt the same to me, and I could still see Inchbald where the server now stood behind her display of ice cream, bright buckets of it submerged in crushed ice. The server was a funny old woman whose nametag read "Patricia." She looked out of place here. She stood behind the counter with a tightlipped and blank stare, and I could imagine her as a customer of Inchbald's waiting for him to cut her cloth, standing for years just like that in that same spot as Inchbald's shut down and new stores opened in this space, waiting in the vacant dark of night as those stores shut down too and in the bright lights and hustle and bustle of new stores, all the time growing old, waiting for fabric. I see Maddie here, too, or feel her, the weight of her silence as we watch Inchbald cut bolts of fabric. Inchbald was a son of a bitch. The way he treated Maddie and me. He wouldn't have treated my mother that way. I don't see my mother here, she's always churning in her death bed. Maybe I just don't want to see her here, to uglify her beauty. I don't want to picture myself here in Inchbald's, either, it reminds me of who I am now, how I'm just as evil as him in the way I've treated the men in my life. I wanted to tell Patricia that there was still time to get out, but in truth, there wasn't.

Standing with her back to the rows of ice cream, Agnes spoke at length on how flavor reflects upon the eater, so that we might choose wisely when considering exuberant raspberry versus reserved maple nut. Even Tom joined in a debate over the maturity of mocha fudge. Onion refused to let us buy him anything, as usual. He licked his lips and said he was on a diet. We all crowded around him on a little round table. He couldn't see anything but our ice cream. It wasn't kind, and I felt bad for him. Then the others — to keep Onion from temptation, they said — invented new and horrible ice cream flavors: onion, aspirin, meat neopolitan. Onion cringed. At least he didn't want ice cream anymore. Neither did I, really. I let the blue moon melt onto my napkin as Agnes watched me.

"What's wrong?" she asked. I asked her what she meant, and she pointed her eyes at my ice cream. "A sagacious flavor, sometimes nostalgic, but with a melancholy aftertaste." Agnes had chosen chocolate chip. She didn't say what it meant. To me the white, dark-spotted globe looked like a universe in reverse, viewed from far away.

"It's cruel, the way we treat Onions," I said. "It makes me want to cry."

"Onions will do that no matter what," said Agnes. "Anyway, I think they enjoy the attention. Have you seen the way the other vegetables treat Onions at home? They don't like him — Onions — at all. Onions are too strong. Have you noticed? Too singular and extraordinary. The other vegetables are so bland. I suspect they're jealous of the gifts of Onions."

"What gifts?"

"Why, kindness, my dear, to a fault. To the point of tears."

"All the worse for us, considering how we treat them."

"Onions aren't so unique," said Alice, blotting vanilla — not even French vanilla, or vanilla bean, but just plain old vanilla — off her mouth. She looked at Tom, who was busy with his lemon sherbet. She dabbed a spot off his nose. "I mean as far as vegetables go. There's rutabagas." She didn't know what Agnes and I were talking about. She didn't know what she was talking about, either, poor soul.

"Rutabaga's a tuber," grunted Tom. Helen nodded in agreement from behind a double scoop of shameful double chocolate fudge brownie with nuts.

"Turnips, then."

"Tuber again."

"Garlic?" asked Helen.

Onion sat there quietly staring into his hands while the others debated, looking very serious. His shift ended at three o'clock, and it was already past that. What was three o'clock to us? Coming or going? Such arrogant fools.

I reached over to Onion and stuffed a wad of bills into his hands. "Onion," I said, "please, go buy yourself some ice cream. Whatever you want. It's on me."

Onion looked over at me. "What did you call me?"

I looked at the others. The conversation had stopped and they were looking at me. I had broken the secret code. It would be all over for me now. "Gilbert?" I said. "I said, Gilbert, please get yourself something to eat."

"You called me onion," he said. I couldn't look away from his face. His eyes jiggled back and forth between mine, saying, Guilty. Guilty. Guilty. Then he smiled. "You called me onion!" He started laughing. "It must be getting close to medication time if you're confusing me with a tuber!"

The others laughed, too. Even I laughed, with relief. I shooed Onion up to the counter and he went. He returned with a Double Deluxe Banana Boat which he began pushing through his grinning black mouth. The others kept talking about vegetables.

"What's really bothering you?" Agnes asked me.

"I don't know," I said. I looked at Agnes. I wanted her to read me, understand all the things I couldn't say, but Agnes doesn't enter you that way. You drift into Agnes. "Here," I said. I handed her a *Time* magazine I had bought earlier. "I thought you could give this to Old Ed."

"Whatever for?"

"As an apology, Agnes. For the way you treated him earlier."

"You're certainly in a mood," she said, and set the magazine between us. "Old Ed doesn't need more *Time,* he needs more life."

Something in Agnes' eyes deepened, and she was gone. I wanted to leave with her. I wanted to forget who I was and be someone else. No, that wasn't true. I like being me. I just wanted the others to see Tru, not That Hayes Girl, or Just Old Gertrude. It would never happen. Memory was too strong for us, and the stories we've told ourselves. I could laugh myself blue, I could change my name, but I couldn't get away from here. Everywhere was Delamond, and everywhen. I have been strong through this, but I don't want to *have to* be strong. It isn't fair.

How childish you are!

But the others had other places to go — and Agnes was a world unto herself. Maybe she isn't a place, but just space, and time.

"Agnes," I said, "if I was in danger, and you were far away, would you come for me?"

Agnes clucked her tongue and touched my arm. "Of course I would. I've always told you I will never leave you behind, Martha."

I wanted to cry bitter tears without stopping. Onion held his spoon in his thick fist like a child, and with each bite of dessert let out a little laugh that showed me the mess on his tongue. Everything around me looked hard-edged, weighty. Permanent. I can't blink it away or laugh it away or eat or buy or smoke it away.

It stares at me with eyes of stone: God-damned Delamond.

January 4

Dear Traveler:

You keep walking through the streets, and along the way, torn pages fall from your hand and flutter away from you...

As you walk, you feel yourself come into yourself. Now that you have a purpose your body is yours again, no longer the strange moving cage it has been for — how long? Your rusty cables of muscle stretch and flex, your lungs draw and push the air, your skin flushes with hot blood and your bones swing and sing. You feel present. *Undivided.* Raise and lower your leg, bend your arm to your nose. You still ache, but then you are still old, my dear. You could almost laugh. When is the last time your stomach tingled without indigestion? You are hungry. It means you are living! Starting over.

Downtown, you sit at the counter of the Blue Moon diner. The waitress is a young thing who gives you a little plastic smile. You order eggs sunny-side up and toast and coffee, though it is nearly time for supper. The waitress pours you coffee and calls your order over a metal shelf into the kitchen. She chats with someone you can't see on the other side. It looks like she's talking to a hissing, sizzling mist hovering around the kitchen ceiling. There is no one else at the counter. In a booth over your left shoulder an old man is drinking coffee. He is unkempt — wrinkled clothes that hang off his bony shoulders, gray stubble in the hollows of his cheeks. You watch him slip a shaky flask out of his pocket and pour liquor into his mug. He has long fingers and massive knotty knuckles that used to move gracefully. He's settled into his life, all his decisions made — you envy him that. He stares at you over the upturned rim. In the far corner booth, a group of boys and girls sprawl around their dish-piled table. Laughter and sweat and cigarette smoke. The pale memory of your own youth makes these children vivid, their bodies open and glowing. Sated young gods they seem, beyond the cares of the world. Or devils, playful and murderous, bored enough to kill. You must have sat just like that, too, beautiful and terrifying, long ago in some faraway diner. It feels so distant, like someone else's life. Just a moment ago you were whole and present — where did that feeling go? You were never undivided. You had only welcomed your fracture into your bones for a moment, surrendered to it.

The waitress wipes a few things off, works a crossword from the newspaper. She is a confident woman in a vulnerable girl's body. You can see her whole life in her half-slouch, eyes sharp on the page and shoulders ready to turn to work, her quick, methodical hands searching and finding the words she wants, her clownish, sneakered feet, heels together, toes at angles outward, tapping. The children believe they will always be young, and their belief is powerful. Even the old man shares a connection to them, you can see it now in the way he watches his hands, still believing in the things they used to hold — money, clothes that fit right, women.

The old man calls the waitress over and she settles his bill, collects his dishes. The man is grumbling as she walks away, then calls out, — You still owe me seventy-two cents! Hey, missy!

The waitress ignores him. She sets his dishes on a tray near the kitchen as a hand slides a plate through the order window. The waitress brings it to you. As she sets up silverware and a napkin beside your plate, you notice her nametag says "Patricia." She doesn't look like a Patricia, though. She's grittier and more alive than a Patricia, a girl unconcerned with the dirt under her nails.

— Haven't seen you here before, she says.

— I'm new.

She nods and slides a bottle of ketchup over. — Welcome to Delamond. What else do you need?

That tone again, which you first heard in the grocery store, that question. Tired exasperation. It is Delamond asking again, *What more could you want, here?*

— Hey missy! You didn't get the check right over here!

— Patricia rolls her eyes. Never mind him, she says to you, then louder: He's just an old drunk.

— Is that your real name? Patricia? you ask.

She glances down at her nametag and blows a fistful of air through her lips.

— Only the manager calls me that. He's an idiot. I'm Tess.

— Do you live here? you ask, and she gives you a look that a Tess would give you, a deadpan *You seem nice, but you only get one dumb question before I end this conversation.* — I mean, have you lived here your whole life?

— Yeah, she says. She pushes her hands into the big front pocket of her uniform and jingles her tips and stares out the window. She's tired. She looks too young to be so old.

— What's it like here? What you really want to know is what it's like to belong in one place your whole life, and to have the place belong to you, but that would be dumb question number two.

Tess shrugs her shoulders. She's still staring out the window, like she's waiting for a bolt of something. — It sucks, she says. — But I'm going to leave or something, as soon as I save some money.

— What do you want to be when you're older?

— Rich. What are you?

— Poor. And I don't know where I'm going.

— Yeah, Tess sighs.

She looks at you and smiles a little, then walks to other end of the counter and begins wiping out the mouths of ketchup bottles. You watch her at this mundane task that she isn't even thinking about, the nervous tendons in her reddened hands jumping out, the long graceful cords of muscle in her neck. She is so alive. *Imperative.* She is tough and beautiful. She could go far, she could grow rich. There's a godlike spark inside her, and like all young folks, the goddess in her thinks her home is too small. She wants to be as wide and deep as she feels inside. She wants to travel. But you know all about the road, dear traveler, and being a stranger, and you want to warn her. You want to tell her she can start over right here at home, she can be great even in Delamond, and her greatness will spread beyond this town.

— Hey missy! I want to speak to the manager!

The shiny toast and rubbery eggs on your plate look slippery and fake. You reach for a local newspaper and spread it open, searching for something real you can hold on to. Bake sales, cold snap, layoffs, vandalism — you know the definitions of these things but their meanings escape you. You feel like an alien anthropologist, living among people but apart from them. You can touch without being touched. There is a certain power in this, but a great loneliness, too. This is what you want to warn Tess about. When you're a stranger seeking home, home is always a memory away. Can you find comfort in this distance? Remember you were one of them once, dear traveler. Remember time and space are the same. You may be far away, but you are never unconnected.

— Eggs OK? asks Tess. She's standing over you.

— Fine, thanks.

— Are you OK? You look a little sick.

— Yes, you say, staring at the eggs staring at you. — Where will you go when you leave Delamond?

Tess shrugs her shoulders, looks out the front window. — Maybe I'll go to college. Or maybe just travel around for awhile. Find myself and all that.

— It's hard, traveling. Being a stranger. You don't know anyone.

Tess is still staring out the window, unconvinced. What you meant to say is that no one knows you. Cannot. You have no roots, nothing for others to hold onto. They see what they believe in you, but they don't see you. You tell yourself you don't want this for Tess, though you're kidding yourself — it's you you're concerned with, not Tess. Starting over is one thing, but all you really want is to stay in one place, live a life less fictional.

— Where will you go to college? you ask.

— Far away.

— It's expensive.

— I told you, I'm saving money.

— As a waitress? How long will that take?

Things a dumb parent would say, and Tess gives you a betrayed look and changes, suddenly more girl than goddess. She is afraid to go, but she is also afraid she will wait too long and she will not leave or grow rich, only grow old, and become Patricia, vacant and stern and still waiting. She was trying to forget all this before you reminded her.

— I have to get back to work now.

That's what Delamond will do to you, dear traveler, trap you in a story you can't escape. It's fine until you're about to die. Those children in the corner — they are not the future of Delamond. Their roles will be chosen for them. Delamond is their future. The old man behind you is their future. That's why I won't let you stay. I've already waited too long.

A ball of paper bounces off your shoulder and lands in your eggs. You look to your left. The old man is gazing out the window. In the corner, the boys and girls are playing with the food left on their plates. Tess is standing at the far end of the counter, her back to the tables, wiping the mouths of ketchup bottles with a rag. The children couldn't have thrown the paper this far, and Tess wouldn't have. The old man, then. You pull the ball of paper from the egg yolk and open it. On one side is written, in shaky capital letters, GO HOME LITTLE SOLDIER-BOY!

The old man stares back at you, his face immobile as carved wood. Scalding hatred floods your chest. One of the old man's hands trembles uncontrollably. His lips are moving a little, like he's chewing on something small and hard. He's chewing on his soured life. Inchbald may be long gone from this place, but there are always Inchbalds, these detestable men who tailor prickled misery for themselves, and blame you for the uncomfortable fit. They will bring their wars to you, they will push you away. You could fight with the old man, you could talk to him. You wonder what he was before, if he was somebody's husband or father, if you might even have been friends in that other life. There are too many possibilities in this place. You want to feel whole again. Your hatred is useless. Hatred won't get you home. The burning in your chest trickles away, leaving you cold. He's just an old drunk.

Tess is standing in front of her ketchup bottle project, staring at the long row of crusty-mouthed bottles still to clean. Watch her instead. She is thinking about who she wants to be, Tess or Patricia. She balls her towel up into her hand. She gives a hard look to the children in the corner and the mess they're making of the booth, then at the mumbling old man, then at you. She is still just a girl, afraid of the goddess smoldering inside her. She wipes her hands on a towel and walks over to you.

— Something wrong with the eggs? There are dark fleshy gobbets of ketchup beneath her nails.

You ball up the paper the old man threw at you and set it aside.
— Lost my appetite, you say. You push the plate away.

— Anything else you don't want?

You shake your head. Tess slides the check beside your plate and walks away.

Another missile hits you in the back of the shoulder. It lies on the floor behind you. At first you think of a body part, something blown off in war, but it's just a ball of napkins soaked in ketchup. You can just see a few tiny droplets splashed against your shirt, and feel a wetness sticking to you. The old wooden man is sipping his coffee, the children sitting back and smoking cigarettes and flicking their ashes onto their empty plates. They've already planted a stubby forest of butts in a shiny red hill of ketchup. There's something grotesque about the misuse of ketchup in this place — there is blood everywhere, piles of it dripping and drying, and now you are covered in it, too. You notice little spots of it on your fingers and on your pants, and the wetness on your back seems to be spreading. When you were a child they wanted you to leave, and to take the memory — *their* memory — of Hayeses with you. You want to laugh, you desperately want to laugh.

— Why'd you come back here, anyway, little soldier-boy? calls the old man.

— That crazy woman a-yours is dead. That Hayes girl.

You tell yourself your resemblance to your grandfather can't be that strong. There must be a smell in your blood. Smell of Brice or smell of Hayes. This is the world you are entitled to. In the corner, the children are all laughing like hyenas, tongues bobbing from their mouths. One of them looks across at you. The old man looks at you, too. *What more could you want here?*

You swivel around on the stool, say to the room: Maybe I never left. Maybe I've been here all along.

*****

Everything stops. A universe quietly opens up and disappears.

*****

The children in the corner are making a sculpture with their dishes. The old man is staring out the window. Nothing stopped. They didn't hear you, it didn't happen. You stand to leave. Tess walks over.

— You owe me a buck for the coffee, she says.

She drums her fingers on the counter. Her knuckles are red and cracked. You imagine her hands reaching after things — dirty dishes, diplomas, paychecks, lovers, enemies. A smart girl, kind, tired, hopeful, afraid. In another life she could have been your daughter, reaching for your hand. Now she just wants you to go, as the others do. The sooner you go the sooner she can forget you. There's nothing you can say. She will be what she will be. You pull a twenty dollar bill from your wallet and rest it on top of the check. Let her at least forget Patricia for awhile.

— For the college fund, you say.

— Hey missy, just kiss him and get it over with! I want my seventy two cents!

— I'll go, Tess says to you. Frightening and fragile, the goddess in her is daring you to challenge her, and the girl in her is begging you not to.

— I know you will.

The old man watches you as you turn toward the door. Stop at his table, stand over him. His mouth hangs open a little. Up close he seems sadder and more fragile, less like wood, more like a cinder. In another life, you would not have been friends. All lives are the same for him. He would have hated you and pushed you away.

We will not be pushed away. We will leave on our own terms.

These Inchbalds don't deserve to forget. Tear pages from the journal and slide them under the ketchup bottle sitting between his crooked hands.

— There is no change for you, you say.

The old man will snort at you. He won't understand, and he'll pretend not to be interested in these pages. He will wait until you leave, and try not to look at them. Then, unable to get it out of his mind, he will read these words, and afterwards, he will sit quietly with unquiet thoughts. He will invent stupid jokes about us. He will keep telling the jokes long after he's stopped laughing. He will spend his remaining years trying to drink us away. He will try to remember the jokes. He will not be able. His memory will be our home. Too prickly a thing to forget, we will live in his restless head, the last thing he remembers before he dies.

Now Inchbald is dead.

Now walk away.

January 12

Malediction. In the ten years that passed since Maddie was born, Father had rotted and seeped through the crevices in the barren soil and soaked into the walls of his house and now hovered in the air over the land as a slight shadow that deadened the light. I kept the shovel I had used to bury him in my kitchen, leaning against the wall behind the stove. I hadn't used it since the burial. I kept it close by because it was a good shovel, and a sort of heirloom. Early on I used to touch the handle each time I walked into the cottage as a sort of ritual. I think it helped keep Father out. Sometimes when I was outside I spoke to him. As in life, he answered with silence. This is how I knew he hadn't left. The time had long passed for truce or reconciliation. Now there would only be reckoning, though I didn't know which of us would bring it, or in what form it would come.

By Father's presence I came to understand that the magic I had thought bled from the world had not gone, after all, it had only shown me its other, uglier face. It was a two-headed beast that breathed change into the world. When the wind blew through our home, my mother had died and the land had died, but I had seen more of my mother and my world than I might have without the wind. I wondered now what else was in store for Maddie and me. I tried to read for signs, but Maddie was difficult to understand and the world was dangerous. I guarded my hope carefully, and watched, and waited.

Maddie grew wiry and tough, like a dirty root. I expected every day to be her last. Whatever demons had tortured Brice had found passage into her, as well. Her beauty was terrible for it. At night I heard her grinding her teeth. I carved a piece of hardwood that I slipped between her lips every night after she fell asleep. In the morning I sent her out to play and found the hardwood in her bed. As I watched her play through the window I felt the grooves and dents in the wood and tried to read them like Braille. Maddie was a sign herself, and like all the other signs I hadn't learned how to read her yet. She was a curious girl. She never asked about the wood.

Maddie didn't go to school. She would have gotten on badly there, but the truth was that I couldn't bear to be without her. I taught her as best I could at home. I showed her the books I had taken from Father's house, but she was never interested. When I read to her she only stared at the words spilling from my mouth and scattering into the air. Sometimes she found the books on her own, and would examine them as though they were objects left behind by a forgotten people. Sometimes Maddie and I spent long days in the garden or in the kitchen sewing. I sang her songs and she hummed them back. My women gave me just enough business to buy fabric, seeds, little things for Maddie. She liked to draw and play with dolls. Most times I let her out to play in the long grass. I taught her about soil and seeds and growing things. I planted some butterfly violets to the side of the house for Maddie to care for. In high summer they opened their faces to her and she picked them out of the ground and held them like children, stroking their petals. *Velveteen.*

I wondered if she saw the dead the way I had as a child. She never explored the old house, and she never asked about it. It had weathered, but still stood defiantly at the other end of field, looking down on us. I explained to Maddie that I used to live there once, but that now I lived here with her, and that others who used to live there had died and were buried under the headstones. In the kitchen, I showed her the shovel I had used to bury Father. There was still a little dirt on it. I rolled a piece between Maddie's fingers. What we all become, I said. She looked at the crumbs scattered on the floor.

I saw her from the kitchen window standing by her grandparents and uncles at the far end of the field, one hand resting on a gray curve of a headstone, her body fading downward into the long thin blades of brown grass. The wind shushed through the field and bent the grass as it passed by her. She watched it go. She returned to her garden of violets and mouthed silent words to them. Then she plucked the wing-shaped petals off one by one and tossed them into the air and watched them flutter to the ground. She buried the stems and then came inside the cottage and watched me in the kitchen the rest of the day with a solemn stare. I wondered if she had been speaking to Father about me.

I never worried for her safety. She wasn't a part of this world, so it couldn't hurt her. Times she would disappear in the morning and return in the afternoon, standing in the open doorway, clotted with soil I didn't recognize. Eventually she ground her teeth through the day, too, and I made her keep the hardwood in her mouth all the time. I had to replace them several times a month. I loved her, but I feared her too.

Maddie was my fault. I reminded myself every day. I had been proud and stupid with Brice in school, though he forgave me later, in the alley. Maddie was Brice's madness barely contained inside the body of an innocent girl and turned loose in the world. She couldn't control it, she didn't know what it was inside her. I felt for her, for her future. I gave her what I could. It wasn't enough.

*****

I love you, Maddie. Some things don't belong in this world. We call them miracles, or abominations. You were both. I love you for that. I love you.

*****

I hadn't seen Brice since that day long ago downtown. He had backed into the shadows of the alley and no one had seen him since, except maybe his mother. Thora was a secretive woman, hard and dark and thorny, and no one asked her what had happened. Instead, the Delamondians invented rumors and stories. Brice had run away, Thora had sent him away, Thora had killed him and buried him in the forest. When news came of murders and mysteries from other cities, Delamondians would search for clues that Brice was at the center of them. Things like Brice didn't happen in normal Delamond, and when they did, the Delamondians turned them into legends and myths, strange and frightening things outside of their world. The Delamondians didn't see how strange they were, themselves.

After he disappeared, Thora grew further into herself. Her own sharpness cut her, and I could see her bleeding inside. Her dark hair was wild around her face, her dresses were threadbare. Whatever she had left she held onto tightly. I would see her sometimes in Filbert's, clutching her purse in one hand and snatching after food with the other as though she were stalking it, as though she thought it would try to escape if it saw her. We never spoke to each other, not once. Why would she speak to me? I was something of a legend too, another strange thing for the Delamondians to scare their children with. I was That Hayes Girl, and I was Tru. Thora must have sensed what she had become to the Delamondians, she could see it in their eyes. And she must have felt it was unfair. It was unfair, but she had to find a way to survive. Outsiders who don't want to be outsiders can't go speaking with other outsiders. She wouldn't want to know me.

Often I saw her walking up and down Main Street, glancing into the alleys. All the streets and sidewalks were paved by this time. There were cars, and the telephone wires had spread like webbing over the buildings and houses. Delamond chugged and hummed louder than ever, but I always thought I could hear Thora's heels clicking on the pavement as she paced Main Street. They had a hollow sound the rest of Delamond did not. Some said Thora was looking for Brice, others said she was looking for evidence of his murder she might have left behind. My women told me all these things. They told me everything they didn't want to tell anyone else. They revealed the secret heart of Delamond to me, a dark thing pulsing with a fear that it might not be what it told itself it was. If I saw my women downtown, they looked right through me.

It doesn't have to be this way.

I believed Brice ran away. I believed he felt Delamond pushing him out. I believed he was still alive somewhere, lurking on streetcorners in some faraway city, maybe even Paris, free now to invent a new life for himself. I pictured him at various jobs — farmhand, assembly line, watchmaker. Demanding jobs where he could work alone. I pictured him writing letters to me that he never sent. I wished him well. I wished Thora well. Whether she blamed his vanishing on him or herself or Delamond, it didn't matter. Whether she told herself she hated him or loved him. When the cold rains came each fall the streets emptied for Thora. She walked under an umbrella, or sometimes not, always glancing into the alleys. She saw Brice everywhere, or tried to. I knew she missed him. Now Thora was alone with Delamond.

What was Father searching for out in the long grass while my mother lay dying, while Maddie grew madder inside me? What signs did he see as he grew soft into the clay, listening to Maddie's footsteps pound across the field?

When the rains came my cottage dripped inside, a little more each year. Plates and then cups and then buckets filling with water in the kitchen. The cottage had begun to fold in on itself. I didn't know how to fix it right. Such things should have been left to the men in the family. Winters were cold, cold, cold, and there was never enough firewood. I made blankets when I could, and nights Maddie and I huddled together beneath them. In the bedroom there was a chink in the wall where it met the ceiling, and if there was a moon out, a round piece of the sky glowed through like a purple eye. It was Father's eye. I listened to the wood pulping in Maddie's mouth and stared at the eye all night, waiting to see who would blink first.

In the morning Maddie had a cough, and I resolved to fix the leaking roof. I would use wood torn from the old house, and Father's tools. That cold, dark, empty house. For days I sat with Maddie in my cottage waiting out her illness and staring across the field at Father's house, wondering if he would let me return. Had his feelings changed? Was he watching Maddie sleep at night, missing us? Maddie spoke in her sleep, words I couldn't understand. I thought of my mother. My feelings for Father hadn't changed. I wanted the arrowhead I had stuffed down his throat to freeze. He could watch us all he wanted and choke trying to speak. He couldn't say anything I'd want to hear. The sky scudded over with clouds and a wind blew in from the north. I heard the forest trembling before the wind snaked in through the walls. It was a threat. Father could hurt us this way if he wanted, riding on the back of the wind through the walls, dragging in some ancient dark thing from the forest. Awake, Maddie looked at books and drew pictures of purple flowers. I put the pictures up over the holes in the walls. *Talismans.* In time Maddie's fever passed, and I knew I had to get to work.

I went into Father's house the next morning when I thought he might still be asleep. I told Maddie to stay in bed but I saw her slip out and away before I even crossed the field. I let her go. I entered the old house through the kitchen door though I knew Father's tools were in the storm cellar. I stood in the kitchen. I told myself I was looking for useful things, but all I saw was the past. I looked at the old stove and the table where I ate and drew pictures for my mother, in the corner where we read our books together. Father was wide awake. I could hear his footstep in every heavy dust mote that fell to the floor. With each breath he settled into my lungs. I stood by my mother's bed. I had taken the mattress away the last time I was here, but now the empty frame seemed fuller than ever. I wanted to say a prayer for my mother but I didn't believe in God. My mother wasn't here, anyway, she had gone away to a better place and forgotten me, as she should have. The window above her bed shook in the wind and the air shivered beside me. Get out, it whispered. But I would leave on my own terms. I sat in the chair beside the bed where I had made up stories for my mother, where I had sewn so many dresses and thought about my future while my belly swelled with Maddie. This was a useful thing, this chair, but I wouldn't take it with me. Why did I long for this past which had been so painful? Maddie and I were happy enough now. Why was the pain all I could remember?

From the chair I rested my hand on the bedpost until the wood grew warm, and I said, Once upon a time there was a beautiful dressmaker who was the best dressmaker in whole kingdom, and she could have married any prince in the land, but she married a rat and gave birth to a rat baby. She made the best of it and loved her family though they didn't deserve it. One day a magical wind blew into their house and took her away to a better place where she was rewarded with fine clothes and as many books to read as she wanted and a warm fire and a comfortable chair to read in. From the better place she was allowed to watch her rat husband kill himself like a coward and be buried in the dirt, and her rat baby give birth to a dark and beautiful creature. All of this made the dressmaker very happy indeed. As a final reward, the dressmaker was allowed to forget all about the rat and the rat baby and even the beautiful creature, and only to remember her happiness for eternity. Amen.

What remained of my mother left the house then, and Father filled the empty space. I was sad, deeply sad. I stood up. I felt strong in spite of my sadness. I didn't go into the parlor, where I used to meet my women, or upstairs where my ancestors sat around in the dark. Those pasts were too near or too far to keep me here. I told Father I was going to the cellar for his tools, and he followed me down.

In the cellar Father watched me throwing his tools into a box I had found there — hammer, nails, crowbar, whatever seemed useful, and many things I didn't recognize but took anyway, partly because I might need them in the future, and partly because I could, just as I had taken and sold his furniture so long ago. I did it quickly, though it seemed to take hours, and when I finished, I realized I had been crying. The front of my coat was wet. I told Father he could settle on my heaving shoulders and in my lungs, he could course through my blood, but he could never return to flesh himself. This was what he wanted, I thought, to return to the overworld, because down where he was, even the worms in his eyes and in his heart complained about the quality of their food, and wouldn't forgive him. He would never make amends. He wanted revenge for the life that had cheated him. I wouldn't forgive him, either, I told him. He had cheated himself, he had surrendered, and what had been his now belonged to me.

The cellar doors slammed shut over me.

I climbed up the stairs and pounded on them. I could hear a

wind whistling, and with each punch of my fist I could see a little crack of sky opening and closing. The doors wouldn't open. I called for Maddie. I pounded some more. Exhausted, I gave up and crumbled on the steps. After awhile I tried the doors again, and screamed out for Maddie. The whole day passed like that. My fists were bleeding and my throat was sore. The silence closed in. The world outside began to fade away. I called out to my mother and my brothers and the silence swallowed my words. I tried to make a deal with Father, told I'd never come back, told him I'd move away, but he knew I was lying. He had had enough. When I couldn't talk anymore or raise my arms I sat and listened for Maddie. The last light faded and darkness came down, and cold. Little sounds rose up from the floor beneath the steps. Rats. In the crack of dim light through the doors, I saw their red eyes gathering. Then they were on the lower steps, sizing me up, then higher, higher, higher. I kicked them away and they huddled on the floor below. Maddie wasn't coming. The crack of light above dimmed to violet. I sat there with the creaks and pops of the unsettled house above me, and the scurry of rats beneath me, a seething little puddle of black fur and red eyes. Slowly, the cellar vanished into black, and then the steps, one by one, until there was only the pair of steps I sat on. The world was gone. The house was Father, and I was buried in him. Alone, afraid.

I will not surrender.

I will not surrender.

*****

Floating in the cold deep of Father's heart. Darkness stretches away. If I move from this step I will fall forever.

January 13

Dear Traveler:

Perhaps there is no one to be. Perhaps there are only things to do. Keep walking. Along Main Street, the air bites at you and the sun glares off hot metal surfaces. You have a headache, a throbbing pain that keeps time with your footsteps, as though your head and your feet were in cahoots against your purpose here. It doesn't matter, the pain doesn't matter. Only that you are here, that you have a purpose. Keep walking.

And along the way, torn pages fall from your hand and flutter away from you...

People frown at them and walk away, mouthing the words.

Across the way there is a card shop with an alley behind it. The card shop wasn't always there, but the alley was. Enter on the south end and ignore what you see. The pavement, the cars, the dumpsters, the lights and security systems — they are not real. Here is Delamond:

A narrow, rutted dirt track passing between a row of stores on the right and a line of sagging wood fence on the left. Empty crates and wooden barrels, bits of rotting food, puddles of water, a mangy dog hunting for food and a home. There are always angry voices shouting from over the fence, men and women and children squabbling over food, money, time, love. Through the open back doors of the stores you might hear businessmen courting customers, the sounds of sweeping, or whistling, or the ching of cash registers. It is a secret and powerful place here. You are in the midst of families and business, but you are invisible. Sometimes, when the businessmen are standing at the front of their stores, you can sneak in through the back and snitch an apple, a piece of taffy, a bolt of fabric.

Walk to the fifth building and stop. You'll be at my spot — the space between the fifth and sixth buildings, one and a half bodies wide. Here the sky seems dimmer above the leaning buildings, flatter. The air doesn't move. For twenty minutes on any summer afternoon the sun peers into this space, chases away the shade and must. Then the shade returns. How many long days spent here before I found that twenty minutes of light. You can see a sliver of Main Street between the fronts of the stores — men strolling, women bustling with packages and children, sometimes a car rolling by. From this secret space where no one sees you, Main Street looks like a movie. But it's real. It's all happening. It's always happening, over and over.

Stand in my spot. Count seven bricks in from the corner and twenty three bricks up from the ground. You'll have to look close now. From the left half of the brick onto the right half of the next. The rusty stain of my blood. Go in closer, touch it. You can almost feel the cold brick across your skin. Go in closer. See? The brick is not solid but riddled with valleys and caves and tunnels where dust that has traveled the world for eons and taken bits of history into its fabric settles and stays. This is how a place remembers you, by giving a home to your time. How does this wall remember me? It shelters my blood, which has forgotten my veins. My blood has traveled far, too, farther than I have. Familiar with ancestors, earth, sweetness, and pain, it knows more than I do. But it has settled here, in my spot, where I have only one question.

I press my lips to my blood and ask, *why.*

It returns me to a moment in school, an awkward boy mumbling at my shoes and I can't even remember now what he was talking about. A boy, perhaps in love with me. A boy who deserved better. Is this why? If I had been kinder Brice might have been gentler. He only gave me what I gave him, what I deserved. No one deserves this… Why did *this* happen to *me?* If only I had spoken a few kind words to him, or not even gone to school that day, things might have been better for Brice. Or if I had just been cruel to him all along, like the rest. If war hadn't broken out, if he hadn't run away, if anything different had happened — I might not have become me. We might even have raised a family. But I couldn't prevent the war. There is still a war in me.

I press my lips to my blood and ask, *why.*

I see schoolmates running from me. I see townspeople watching me from the corners of their eyes, storekeepers watching my hands, I hear a hundred times *Get out* shouted, whispered, hissed. I see the cold river swirling over my head, the loggers cursing the water, the dead congregating on the shores. The dead in my house, and the dying. I see Father frowning through job announcements in yesterdays' newspaper, boarding off another room in the house, pacing through the field of long grass, kneeling by my mother's death bed, building my cottage at the edge of our property. I see other forces guiding us — our ancestors, Delamond, fate, chance. Even me. Did this fate choose us, or did we somehow draw it to us? A cry in the Hayes' blood, passed through generations. An attraction for certain destinies. Maybe Father had no choice but to do what he did and be who he was. And maybe he surrendered, turned away. Maybe I pushed him out, and left an empty space for Brice to invade. Could I have avoided all this? Should I have fought harder, should I have accepted what became of me? Should I fight it now, or turn away? Would I be a better person if I were a different person? A better mother, daughter, lover, woman?

A better pariah?

No. Win or lose, war will always break you. All that has happened, happened.

I press my lips to my blood and ask, *why*.

Dear traveler, I have tried to understand. I have searched for justice and patterns. There is pain, and nothing. I can scream, I can write — my barbaric yawp, signifying nothing. I hate, and am hated back. I hate myself. I cancel me out. There is no why. There is war and the blind anger of men who will bring their wars to you and make them yours. They don't even remember what they're fighting for. Only the dead remember, and hope. There is also hope, because without hope, this would not be hell. Without hope, hell is just home. Hope keeps us all moving, keeps the dead pressing in around you. It's all you have now, the dead will never leave you. They will be a cold comfort. There is beauty here, and terror. They will be your hope in hell.

And understand me, traveler. Eventually, you came from this — born of their wars, molded by their anger. In the eyes of Delamond's people you are the crime, because you left, because you returned, but most of all because you are a Hayes. Their anger makes you a Hayes. And you'll have to carry their anger home, wherever home is. People will see it, they already have. You've seen it reflected in their faces. It reminds them of what they carry on their own shoulders. Even the sky stares back at you flatly, empty. How it disfigures you. You are in danger here. If you leave by the alley now someone will see you, and the memory will pass to others like a sick wind, and they will be upon you. They will take your home from you, take you from you: who you want to be from who you are. Limb from limb. Feel it?

Scatter my pages across the ground now, dear traveler. See how they lie? My blood is dead but dreaming. A crush of teeth, tightened fists, stifled screams. A thorny heart and a broken body. Blood and weeping. I am thirteen. I'm afraid, I'm afraid, I'm afraid. All of this my blood remembers.

I could remember more. Sun and wind chasing each other through long grass on a summer afternoon. Warm firelight and shadows making words dance in a book of stories. The footsteps of my children thudding over the field, dinner bubbling in a pot, birds calling out to each other as the sun sets. I could say I'm bigger than this wall, see that I am more than this moment. I can't see it. But I see you, dear traveler, dropping pages as you go. It's enough to move on, move out, move away. Hope for a better place.

I press my lips to my blood and ask, *why.*

January 14

Do I haunt my own children? Do they love me?

I still search for signs and patterns. They're all around us, if you look. You read a road sign to know which way to go, you follow a pattern to make a dress. They say there's even a mathematical formula, the Golden Ratio, behind the patterns in certain shells, and in flowers and stars. A pattern is a plan. It means there's order and purpose and a guiding hand. Some people find hope in this. I don't. If there's a God, I don't believe in him. I doubt he believes in me! When I find signs and patterns, I don't know how to read them, though I try. It isn't the message I'm interested in, though, it's the words themselves. There's comfort there, if not hope. *Solace.* When I was a girl sewing dresses, the pattern was the pleasure, not the sewing or the dress or even the money. I could sew dresses all day. Now my hands are cramped and my eyesight's bad, so I write. The pencil fits perfectly into the stiffened crooks of my fingers. When the patterns start to break down I get uncomfortable and panicky. When I can't think straight. It means the story's ending.

Are people a part of a cosmic alphabet?

Today I found my sometime sister Agnes in the garden. She

was writing a list for me, Martha, of things to take care of around the house while she was touring jazz clubs overseas with Buddy. Water the plants but not the cactus, and feed the cat, and watch for a letter in the post from a Mr. Pound, who she had sent a poem. She was whirling around the lawn, touching everything and moving on. She wore a floaty, pale yellow dress — an evening dress, really, wonderfully inappropriate — and a white woolen cape with a hood. It had turned warm for January, but not that warm. Agnes was a night breeze. Usually I play along when Agnes is like this, they say that's what you're supposed to do, but I wasn't in the mood. I was thinking about my children. I had seen Maddie one time after they took her away. By that time, I don't think she even knew she'd been taken away. In the psychiatric ward she sat in a rocking chair in the corner of the room with the other crazies and stared out the window. She didn't speak a word. The doctors said she never did. To see her — to see your child's eyes so empty, looking right through you. She was like a shard of broken glass, beautiful and dangerous and hardly there. Her hands were smooth and cold. The doctors told me not to come back. I tried to come back, I raised holy hell, but I never saw her again. She's still alive there, I believe. The doctors would at least give me the courtesy of telling me if she was dead. Wouldn't they? I write her letters now and again, send her cards on holidays and birthdays. I never hear back. She wouldn't come back to me, anyway. She was never really with me to begin with. Her whole short life with me she spent transforming into the strange angel she is now. And Morrow, too, is in too many places at once. I have hurt many, many people.

Now, watching Agnes in another world, and preparing to leave me twice removed for some make-believe Paris — I was too tired to play along.

"Everyone I love leaves me behind with the people I hate," I said. "I even hate your stupid cat."

"Please? Just do it," Agnes said, coming to rest on the edge of the stone bench to add another item to her list. "I'll bring you something from Paris. I'll get Mr. Pound to write you a poem."

"Agnes, Mr. Pound is dead by now," I said.

She stopped writing. The whole world stopped with her. She dropped the list on the ground between our feet. I stared at the paper. Agnes was crying silently. A few tears fell, tapped on the crinkled paper. Little star shapes appeared on the ink. I'll never forget that tiny sound, the quiet force of it. A distant hammering against a wall.

Agnes wandered away and began picking dead flowers from the garden. The sun shone but the air was close and chill, everything sounded nearer. You could hear the traffic like the ocean in a shell, and now and again a crow calling out across the empty field. In the winter, all the pretty birds leave the crows behind. It's a pattern in nature. Agnes picked through the beds near the fountain in the middle of the garden. She hummed a little tune that seemed to wrap itself around her. I didn't say anything more, I had done enough damage.

Old Ed wheeled himself into the doorway and looked out. He looked into the garden — in her white clothes among the dead things, Agnes was almost invisible. Old Ed pushed himself along the walk to the stone bench where I was still sitting and sat there. He acted like I wasn't there and stared into the garden, listening to Agnes singing to herself. He was wincing. He uses that same wince for a lot of different emotions. Love, for example. Agnes and Old Ed have grown madly in love, though they still won't admit it. You can see it in the pattern of their days. They argue about the war. Agnes saw cities destroyed, friends flee their homelands and die. Old Ed was there, too, but he saw victory. He waves his *Time* magazines in his fist. She hurls them across the room and slaps brand new ones in his lap. This is how she apologizes for past arguments. After she leaves him, Old Ed paws through the new *Time* slowly, drinking in each page. Later she returns to the day room where she finds him watching television. She sits beside him without a word and they begin a grumbly conversation. One wants the History Channel, the other wants cartoons. They end up watching infomercials. He calls her flighty and floozy. She calls him crank and curmudgeon. He winces, and they settle into silence.

"Are you in pain?" I asked him. He didn't move. "Look. I have something for you." The days had been slow and our gang had been growing impatient. I had been saving a green for just in case. I held the green out in my hand. He snatched the pill up before I changed my mind and closed it into a fist in his lap.

"It won't be enough," he said.

"I'm not trying to kill you."

Through the trees we saw a flash of Agnes' faded yellow dress. Once it had been the bright yellow of a canary. We stared but she had disappeared, we could only hear little wisps of song floating out. I thought of my mother. Once when she lay dying, I thought I heard someone singing outside her window, a song and voice I'd never heard before. Once I thought it was Agnes. I thought if I could have caught hold of the song it might have helped her. If I could have learned the words, but there aren't any words.

"Do you know that song?" I asked.

"I don't think it's a song," he said. "It's just Agnes."

"It's beautiful, isn't it?" As we stared into the garden, I watched Old Ed out of the corner of my eye, noticed how relaxed he'd suddenly become. His entire body was listening to Agnes' song.

"She's an odd bird," he said.

I made a point of not looking at him. If you looked at him he would flinch, wheel himself away. Old Ed had things to say if you agreed to look somewhere else and pretend not to listen. I wondered what lie buried in his past that he felt deserved such punishment. Even I wanted people to look at me once in a while.

I asked, "Do you love her?"

He froze, and he didn't speak for a long time. He said, "I don't love her so much as I hate her." Then I did look at him. There was that wince.

"Then why do you love her?"

"I don't love her. I hate her. I just told you. She's a pest."

"You're no dance around the maypole, either."

Old Ed caught his breath. Agnes appeared from the dappled shadows of a poplar. She looked at us, then slowly turned back into the garden.

"Why do you talk to me?" said Old Ed. "No one else does."

"It's you who talks to me."

"You're not one many people want to talk to."

"Neither are you, you old crust."

"I didn't ask for a conversation."

"You won't get one."

What children we were!

Agnes' song trailed in and out. I tried whistling back. For a moment it seemed my tune fit into hers, but it was only chance, and the song fell apart. Old Ed opened his hand and looked at the green I had given him.

"Do you love your children?" I asked.

"Why all the love questions?"

"I wonder if my children love me."

"Children? I thought you had just the one crazy daughter."

"You're an ass."

He sat for awhile looking at his hands in his lap. I hated him, I really hated him then. He made me sick, all of them did, everyone who thought they knew me and my family. Then, in a quiet voice I had never heard from him, Old Ed began to speak.

"My children don't love me," he said. And I don't know if I love them. I used to. Now when they come, they act like they're doing a favor. They lie to me, and they don't listen to me. I don't even know them. They don't understand what I went through in the war — that's where it all started."

"What was it like — the war?"

Old Ed was silent for a long time. I thought he had forgotten where he was. I couldn't see or hear Agnes anywhere. A car slipped by on Highway 8. A little later, another one passed. How easy it would be to hitch a ride out of here, but no one ever does. We're time travelers, not space travelers. Old Ed sat right next to me, but in his mind he was still storming across Europe with a muddy rifle in his hands.

"I saw a lot of dead bodies over there," he said. "Sometimes all together in one place. That wasn't a big deal. A pile of bodies is still just a pile. A field of bodies is just a field. It's the single bodies that get you. The ones you come across after they've been lying there for days, or weeks. A single body — that's still a person. Sometimes one that trusted you with their life. And after it starts to rot, a body looks like every other rotting body. It hits you that you'll look like that someday, too. In every dead face you see, you start to see your own face." I was watching Old Ed out of the corner of my eye. His hands were shaking. After he stopped talking, his mouth hung open like a word or a sound too big for his throat was pushing its way out. He swallowed it back down and wiped his lip with the back of his hand, cleared his throat. "We won the war. We did our job and the country was proud of us and I'd do it all again. But now I'm closer to Agnes than I am to my family. Hell, I'm closer to you. Doesn't make sense."

"Why do you keep all those magazines?"

Old Ed scowled and waved the question away. He was done revealing himself. "Why do we do anything?" he asked.

Agnes emerged from the garden again. She carried a small armload of shrively flowers in a bed of dry grass. She had stopped her song and was smiling a private smile as she stood before us.

Little smudges of dirt hemmed her gown where it brushed at the earth. That pale yellow gown, like a memory of sun. *Halcyon.*

"I'm very tired," she said.

"Who are the flowers for?" I asked.

Agnes glanced back toward the garden. "I've been out here awhile — I don't know." She looked back at the garden again, then at her flowers, frowning.

"Are you alright, Agnes?" I asked.

"All night?"

"We're not here to do anything," said Old Ed.

"What was that song you were humming?"

"Nothing. But here I am. Isn't it queer?"

I laughed suddenly, surprised all of us. Something was happening. I listened, but there was no sound. We stared around, it could have been hours, each of us trapped in our moments, moving like three hands of a clock toward a single, blind second. There was something we shared or we wouldn't be here, there was something we couldn't share.

We had already forgotten my laughter. Agnes was gazing out toward the treeline and Old Ed was staring at his knees. I couldn't remember what time it was. The day passed around us. It was the end of time. I didn't want to stay behind. I didn't want to go alone. I had seen this pattern time and again. Suddenly it seemed important to know what time it was. I shivered and looked up to see if a cloud had blocked the sun, but there wasn't a cloud anywhere. The sky was low and stretched away forever. Agnes was dying summer, fading into that paling sky. Had the second passed? A crow called out. Agnes carried the rich, bitter smell of freshly turned earth on her skin. There was something we needed to do, something urgent, but we just sat there, frozen. Why didn't we move? Move where? When?

"Does anyone remember what time it is?"

Agnes smiled down on Old Ed. "These are for you," she said,

dropping the flowers in Old Ed's lap. "They're dead."

"And for you," said Old Ed, reaching his hand up to hers and setting my green in her palm. "Take enough and you'll be dead."

"Please, does anyone remember the time?"

"Thank you, darling," said Agnes. "Why I could just kiss you." She leaned over, took Old Ed's head between her hands, puckered and gave him a loud smack on the cheek. He blushed and squirmed. "There," she said. "The kiss of death." She was blushing, too.

Later

Patterns. All the men in my life are one man. All the women are the same woman — faces on a fake diamond with a single, deep flaw. In the order of things here, I am the disorder of things.

Just a little while ago Agnes and I looked at the list she had been writing earlier, in the garden. She couldn't imagine what it was for. We held it up and watched how the light glowed through the star-shaped tear stains. I tried to count the points on each tearstain, to see if they revealed a pattern. I examined their arrangement on the page. The tears were too small to count their points — how they had pounded into that page! — but there was something else there: letters, stars, light, quiet. Messages for the dead stained with tears and glowing with hope, replies in silence. Father was silent. Whatever he was searching for out in long grass, he never found it. My mother found it in stories. Now that's all she is. I tell myself Brice loved me, and Maddie, and Morrow. Wouldn't it be grand to believe Delamond has had high thoughts of me, but I think it has not thought of me much at all for many years. Yet we are tied together — words in a sentence.

I am not thinking clearly.

I haven't seen the dead for a time, but I feel them moving around us, faster and faster, around my hand as I write this. *Expectant.* Is this my sentence, you dead? Am I dying correctly? Have I found the right words? *Fitting. Seemly. True.* Oh Mother, how I hate these stories! No one will ever know you. I have hurt many, many people. I hate who I am.

January 20

I fucked a priest.

It's true. That's exactly what it was. I thought it was loving. It felt like love. He might tell you the same, if he's alive. Agnes would be proud, But it wasn't love, it was — that other thing. I won't write that word again. This will have to do for the dead. *Appease. Atone.*

People gathered to Father Geoffrey Still like sleepwalkers, searching through one world for a thing that existed only in another. He led services at the Church of the Assumption. Church of Assumptions, more like — the joke escaped the Delamondians. That a man could find God, that He would hear them, that they deserved to be heard. That God was still hanging around. You don't see the wind, you only get the sad and beautiful signs of its passing. Father Still was deeply troubled, like a tree in the calm, waiting for a breeze that never comes, waiting so hard it trembles itself, and tells itself the trembling is a sign of God.

He had a habit of walking when he wasn't preaching. In town I would watch him wander along Main Street. Mostly he stared at the sidewalk, glancing up from time to time as if to see if someone was calling his name. A dark little shadow of a man, inward turned. I wondered if he was a Reverend Dimmesdale, driven by a dark secret. I didn't see him as an adulterer, though. No, his crime against God was simply doubting God. Father Still's white collar was a privilege and a yoke. I could see all this in the way he walked, and in his eyes. He had a searching look in his eyes, always. When he looked at you his gaze always said the same thing:

God is here — is God here?

Father Still did not seem aware that he had a body. He was his questing, and his questing dragged his little body after him like a load to market. He had the pale, unmarked face of a child, with a small red mouth that barely moved when he spoke, which lent an air of mystery to him. His arms hung at his sides when they should have been swinging, and his hands never tapped or fidgeted or brushed at his collar or brow. The only thing that did move, besides his mechanical legs, was his head, which swiveled and jerked at every sound that might be the approach of God. Children ignored him, mostly. Adults were a little afraid of him, though drawn to him. It was clear that Father Still was a comfort in his way, as a dark rock jutting up from a churning ocean is a comfort to the drowning. My women talked about him in words they couldn't find.

His words are so...

The service was so...

And their tongues froze, and they stared off at nothing. The words were out there somewhere. His legend had practically built itself in the short time he'd been in Delamond. Delamondians had to believe in something.

Father Still began a campaign through the doors of those too troubled or ignorant or sick to worship in his church, and he brought God to them. My women must have told him about me. The Hayeses were certainly troubled. I waited in my cottage for His solicitor with an ugly smugness, and finally, he came. Father

Still sat at the kitchen table where Father used to sit. He was nervous and serious in a boyish way. Handsome. I was pleasant with hate. I served coffee and biscuits. He started a number of conversations — lovely home, delicious coffee, do the two of you live out here alone? — that spilled into silence. He rose stiffly, walked to the window, sat down again at the table again for his coffee, rose. Outside, Maddie dug holes in the garden. Father Still watched her, glanced at me, and looked at his hands, which had come to rest on the window sill, as if they intended to hoist him through the pane. His hands had suddenly grown active. He picked up his coffee and spun the cup slowly around on its saucer, the handle like a clock hand, perhaps wishing he could speed the time.

He said, It must be difficult. He glanced at me again and licked his little lips. He stared into the dark center of his coffee. He said, Look. It's always an outside force that moves the inside. The coffee moves to catch up with the cup.

Does it ever catch up? I asked.

He frowned and said, There are forces beyond our understanding.

He looked outside at Maddie again. She was staring at something in her hand. She held her face close to it, tangles of hair like a ragged curtain falling to either side. I should have known about the power of names, how we become them. I should have named her God Help Us. Why don't you come to church, Father Still asked me, his voice sudden and loud.

It startled us both, this small volcanic burst. His face reddened as I stared at him, not knowing what to say. He didn't look away. People always looked away from me. It made me angry that he wouldn't look away, it made me want to laugh at him and his inconstant god. I wanted to ask, Where was God when the land was sick and my family was dying? Who was God that He needed a man to lead me to Him? I wanted to tell Father Still the joke about the Assumption and make him weep or turn redder or just go away. But he wouldn't look away from me. And as I stared at him the anger cooled into something else — a feeling I didn't recognize. When I didn't answer his question Father Still asked again in a steadier voice, Why don't you come to church?

And it struck me — he sounded like he was asking me on a date. Or how I imagined that would sound. My first date. I had heard boys speak like this to other girls, the girls who later in life became my women, and spoke the same way about Father Still. It might even have happened to me once, long ago when I was a schoolgirl. I realized quite suddenly that he wanted me, and that he didn't know it yet. His body was betraying him. I had only ever been with one man. I didn't feel I had a choice this time, either. And then I did laugh. If there was ever evidence of God, I thought, this was it. This cruel joke. This love affair begun without the permission of either of us and predestined for tragedy. It really was a bad novel, a *Scarlet Ripoff*. My laughter must have sounded harsh, though I didn't mean it to. As much as I hated the Prankster, I loved the joke. I remember an afternoon I spent with Helen watching television in her room. I was curious because she holed up there every afternoon to watch her "stories." That's what she called them. In her stories, everything looked fake, comical. Yet everyone was so sincere. That's how I felt in my kitchen with Father Still, getting caught up in some silly story we were a part of. It wasn't silly at all, though. My laughter was the sound of years alone on the edge of this dead field, waiting, just like Father Still, for something to carry me away. Never expecting this.

Father Still rose to leave. I apologized for laughing and asked him to stay. Maddie appeared in the doorway and held out her hands to us, a dead mouse cradled there. She looked at it thoughtfully, then at each of us. I smiled at her. She fascinated me and she frightened me a little, the way new and alien things can. My strange angel.

Take it outside, dear, I told her. Bury it by the violets. She returned to the garden, and Father Still sat down again with his coffee cup.

It's a difficult age, he said. Everything is new and wonderful, but so confusing and dangerous, too.

Are you talking about my daughter, or the times?

He glanced at me and spun his coffee. He commented on the transience of life, its unpredictability, the need to be certain of salvation for our children. I'm sure he gazed out the window with a troubled or poignant expression. It was dull, what he said, but how he said it, as though posing a problem to himself he wasn't sure he could solve. He'd been grappling with it for a very long time. Father Still assured me the church could provide guidance for Maddie and me. This he believed — I could see the certainty on his face, and the fear. He was afraid of me. He encouraged us to attend services, or to visit him in the rectory sometime for conversation. Then he left.

What a child I was.

What a fool you are.

Father Still encouraged his congregation to visit him for private conversations whenever they had questions or were troubled, and so many Delamondians took him up on the offer that he began scheduling appointments. I started going to the church during these sessions, but never went inside. I would sit with Maddie on a bench near the rectory door and watch others come in and out. There was a courtyard where people could gather, but no one did. Someone had scratched out a little flower garden. The courtyard was more peaceful than Bulb Park. I told myself I was there for the peace, but I was watching for Father Still. I wanted to laugh at something. I was so full of hatred! But I was lonely too, and not just for people. Maddie would bring a doll or a piece of paper to draw on, but she would always wander away into the garden and dig in the dirt. Like everyone else, she had another place to go to.

All the Delamondians who came out of Father Still's sessions were conspicuous. Some wanted to be seen, as though the sessions were proof of their commitment to spiritual progress and their powerful connection to the middleman between them and God. They scanned the whole town as they slowly paraded down his steps, trying to catch an eye wherever they could — any eye but mine. They glanced away from me and looked around the more fervently to wash my gaze from their eyes. These Delamondians weren't aware of their real problems. Others looked ashamed, and slid out the door and quickly down the sidewalk. They were too aware of their problems, and their shame was another problem. Problems on top of problems. Here is Delamond.

One day I saw Father Still there. This was not long after he had visited my cottage. The last of his appointments had scurried out the door. Maddie was burying flowers and watching the quiet little mounds of dirt. Father Still stood in the doorway. I don't know how long he had been there. The sun was high, and everywhere there was only brightness and black and nothing in between. Father Still blended right into the shadows. I could see the little white square at his neck, and his little red mouth framed by his pale cheeks and the dark of the church.

He said, Will you come in?

I won't, I said.

The church has room for all God's children, he said.

I hated talk like this. It sounded like he was reading from a script. I said, If you're going to talk, say something. Say something right now.

He opened his mouth, and nothing came out. It was exactly what I wanted to hear. I gathered Maddie up and said goodbye. I thought I was proving something to him. I felt his warm stare on my back the whole way home.

By dinner that evening I still felt him. Maddie sat at the table

sopping gravy with a crust of bread. I wasn't hungry. Father Still
was so flawed, a contradiction. A fatherless father whose children
were lost. His rituals would only bring them as far as the church
on Sunday. God wasn't in Delamond. Father Still was lost too,
searching for a better place he wasn't sure existed. I did not love
him, and I did not want to love him, but I was falling in love with
him. Or it felt like love. The light was fading outside, and Maddie
wanted to visit with her flowers. I let her slip out the door and
busied myself with the dishes. I kept a clean house, an ordered
house. I let the door open to let in warm night breeze. I could smell
the butterfly violets and the soil and Father decaying. He could
only come inside this way, now. I had patched the holes in the
cottage well enough to get us through the rains and the winter.
Then I heard a voice outside, a man's voice, and for a moment I
imagined Father had found his way back to flesh after all. I
glanced at the shovel behind the stove, the one that had buried
him. I would kill him this time. I rested my hand on the shovel.
Then Father Still was there, standing in my doorway just as he had
in the doorway of the rectory.

May I come in? he asked.

I was going to kill you, I said. Are you hungry?

While Maddie played outside Father Still sat at the table in
front of a plate of bread and gravy and asked about my life. He
asked just like that, direct, an arrow to its mark. He had finally
said something. I felt something break inside, and the unfamiliar
feeling I had had the last time he was here washed over me again.
Before I knew what it was I set the dishes down and sat in the
rocker by the stove, and I told him. I told him the whole story of
me. The land, the house, the books, the stories, the long grass and
the river, the wind and the dead, school, Brice, war, Maddie. It
came easy, like it wanted out. It took a long time. I hadn't talked
that long since my mother was dying. I felt giddy and a little sick.
When I finished, the story filled the room and hung there between

us. Father Still stood in front of me and touched my head. He was crying. He was crying for me. His warm thumb made a little cross between my eyes. I didn't want to laugh anymore. I could feel the cross tingling into my skin, into my brain and my blood. I wanted it to stay, that feeling. I was afraid it would go.

Stay with me, I said.

And for awhile, it did. We made love, then. No, not love. It was violent like love, and it was lovely, but we weren't making anything but trouble.

That should have been the end of it. If it had been, the feeling might have stayed with me longer, might be with me even now. But I was still afraid it would go away, like everything else I had loved went away, and like a selfish child, I wasn't happy having enough. I craved more of it, all the time. I began visiting Father Still at the rectory for conversation. Maddie came with me. That was the worst part. Father Still had a box full of toys and dolls and books for children to play with while their parents gutted themselves in his lap. Maddie played silently with the dolls, her back to us. Listening, I think. Father Still was a comfort — the Delamondians were right! This odd little man. He took your problems into his own private maelstrom of problems, they were all the same to him. I didn't really have any problems, though, it was just my life. I gave him that. Or maybe I was giving it to Maddie, trying to tell her, to confess to her, so she would know that I hurt for my sins. Maybe I would have given my hurt to anyone who would have taken it.

Father Still seemed to crave it. He sat in his chair with his hands propped and folded before his mouth, head titled down a little, staring intently at me. He rarely moved, though I imagined a steady trickle of whispers pouring into his praying hands. He was inhaling my whole life and exhaling it through his prayer and up to God. But the way he stared — if he was praying, it wasn't for forgiveness. It was a calling out: *I see her, God, but I don't see you. I see pain and misery and loneliness, but I don't see grace. You don't exist. You don't exist. You don't exist.* He was searching. He must have searched through all of Delamond, and then brought the search into his home. Sometimes he would offer up a gray ray of hope — *God works in mysterious ways. It is not ours to question, but to have faith. He will reward us in the end.* What drove him into the ministry to begin with, what event first cast a shadow over his delicate faith, I never found out. I didn't care, really. He was a liar. That's what I loved about him, and why I kept talking. Because I sure wasn't feeling any signs of grace, myself.

Sometimes I would stop to talk to Maddie or play with her. Father Still would remain motionless, still staring at the place I had been, and only after a long moment turn to us. Maddie and I played at dolls. She never made sounds, and I never knew what she was imagining when her doll bumped into mine. Hers shook a little, mine swayed a little in response, and they went their separate ways. Something passed between us, but I never knew what it was. I never knew if she was happy. I wanted her to be happy. I wanted her to be normal. After awhile I would realize that Maddie had stopped playing with me. I would shake a doll at her doll, but her doll couldn't see me. She had gone far away. Father Still would smile down at us. He had a gentle smile, a smile I could believe in. It was far away, too.

Only once did Father Still and I talk about God. I asked Father Still about Him. We were sitting in the rectory as usual, and a silence had fallen. Father Still was watching Maddie play, and I was watching Father Still. Even after all our talking and after I knew I was falling in love with him, I was still trying to hate him. Still trying to laugh at us falling in love. But in that silence, I suddenly felt something pressing — something physical. It was the church. I still hadn't been inside it. Something in the church had been bearing down on me, and I realized I had been feeling this pressure, like a hand on my shoulder, since the first day I came. Sitting in that silence, I suddenly remembered the cross I found hanging on the wall of Father's old house so long ago. My mother had been alive then, and the world, though barely. That cross was still there on the wall, and my hand, reaching up to it. I was still curious, still longing. Still a girl.

Father Still toured Maddie and me around the church. He showed us everything — the rooms, his clothes, all the silvery objects. As we touched and stroked each new object, Father Still gave everything in the church its proper name. *Sanctus bell. Icon. Chancel. High altar. Nave. Ciborium. Tabernacle. Eucharist. Chalice. Censer. Ave Maria. Gloria Patri. Host. Blood.*

Daily Missile? I asked.

Miss-*al,* he said.

I wasn't trying to be funny. From the beginning I had been trying to understand God and Father Still and what they had to do with me. I was thinking with what I already knew about God and men: stories and war. Father Still wasn't offended by my mistake, he was excited at the chance to say *missal* again. He spoke in whispers, like he was sharing secrets. He was in love with God, or at least with the mystery of God. For him, the world was alive with this mystery. I remembered when the world was like that, when I was a girl sitting in the long grass, or reading books with my mother. Maybe God could give that world back — I held out no hope for it myself, but maybe for Maddie. She held the candles and the chalice up to the light and studied her funhouse reflection. Maybe God could save Maddie. That was when I really started thinking about God.

Come to high mass, said Father Still. God will show you what you need to see.

And just as soon as hope had filled me, it poured out the bottoms of my feet. I knew what I would see. Father Still could let us wander through God's house now, and maybe God was there with us. But on Sunday, God still belonged to the Delamondians.

They wouldn't share. They would push us out, and God would let them. Why would God want a single fallen woman and her bastard child when He could have an entire town at his mercy? As soon as I started believing in God, I started hating Him for playing this cruel stupid joke on us. But I stopped trying to hate Father Still.

Father Still and I never talked about God again, but we were always talking about faith. Not directly — conversation always circled around Delamond, flowers, dressmaking, coffee, walking, sunlight, paper and paper mills, war, swimming, school, crayons. But in this way we were always talking about believing in something permanent. I don't think either of us had any faith in anything, but we wanted to. We started having faith in each other, though in different ways. What had happened in my bed hung between us like the cross on the wall in Father's old house, a half-forgotten secret waiting to be remembered. I had faith that we were doomed. My cottage had set the first chapter in a story with a predictable ending. How could a story like ours be different? If it had turned out happily, I never would have believed it. I would have been unhappy with my happiness and pushed Father Still out.

Session after session, we kept talking. Father Still kept asking about my life, not just about what happened, but what I thought about it. I told him everything I could. Getting carried away in the story, I may have made some things up. Times I couldn't stop talking, as though the story, true or false or something else, had been waiting my whole life for an audience. Then one day, suddenly, it was over. I stopped talking. Father Still was leaning forward in his chair, his mouth open a little. I was staring into the black space between his lips, and a silence — a different silence this time — wrapped around us. The silence and the dark in Father Still's mouth reminded me of the nights closing over the long grass outside Father's old house when I was a girl. I thought of that quiet, how it surrounded the house and suffocated us. How it felt almost pleasant, dying like that. Maddie played in the corner. She never made a sound or looked up. Between Father Still and I, all of our words lay at our feet like dust. I did not feel purged. I had only told a good story, and the pain of it lingered. The pain needed a better story. I looked at Father Still, who was watching my hands spinning my teacup in circles. We both needed something more. The clock ticked. Hands opened and slowly closed on the hour.

That was the first time it happened in the rectory. We left Maddie behind in the room — she didn't seem to notice. I felt terrible leaving Maddie behind like that, but that moment felt inevitable. It would have happened exactly like this no matter how I tried to make it different. *Predestined.* I was certain of it. I'm not so certain anymore, but it's too late now. I have hurt many, many people. Father Still and I went into his bedroom and closed the door. After that time, it happened every time. We wallowed in sin, we abandoned ourselves to it. Whatever *it* was. *Voracious.*

I was nervous at first, after Brice, but Father Still was easy to fall into, because he was so imperfect. He was not a leader, as I understood priests should be, he was led, by his doubt and his guilt, to commit crimes against God. He starved for God's love and forgiveness, but he craved God's punishment even more. I was everything he wanted from God. And he was everything I wanted: proof against God's perfection, proof against God Himself. And more: proof against Delamondians. Father Still was respectable, upstanding, well-liked. Being with him meant I was like him, that I was as good as all of them.

Being with him also meant that he was like me.

They were all like me.

*****

We were lovers for two months.

No, not lovers.

Father Still and Maddie and I were seen in public from time to time, picking out dolls or crayons for Maddie. Father Still was like a talisman that allowed me entrance anywhere I wished to go in town. We walked together under the guise of spiritual counsel, as shepherd and lost sheep. The necessity of the trick didn't spoil the treat. I walked slowly to savor the moment. I imagined we were a family. I imagined knowing the people I passed, stopping along the sidewalk to inquire after families, discuss politics, gossip, all the things they do on street corners and in the stores. The looks on their faces — pleasant surprise to see me, heads tilted and smiling as I explained Maddie's latest escapades, shaking my hands with both of theirs and wishing us all well, inviting us to dinner soon. I saw myself sitting in Bulb Park with other mothers and watching Maddie play with their children. And after, taking Maddie with me to the store for groceries, then back home to cook dinner for the three of us, fire in the fireplace, reading by its light before bed, sharing news of the day, sleeping in the warm nest of his arms through the night. But did I really want to belong to such a world after the way it had treated me?

Yes, I did. I believed we were up to something beautiful — seeking God through a web of stories we told ourselves was true. And the truth was in there somewhere, though God left us before we found Him.

As Father Still and I walked with Maddie between us, passersby took solemn note of Maddie and I and nodded approvingly at Father Still. They held Father Still in too high regard to suspect anything untoward. Storekeepers gave Maddie candy, which she immediately ground to sticky crumbles in her mouth. And they were polite to me. Kind, even. I was grateful to Father Still. Trips to town without him were usually much faster, with no talking to anyone, storekeepers watching my hands, glancing at the clock, wishing me along, no hellos, no thank yous, no come agains. If the townspeople looked at us at all it was out of the corners of their eyes, and when I caught them they sniffed and walked on. Not a word to Maddie, as though she were as guilty as I. I wanted to wrap my arm in Father Still's as we strolled down Main Street, as much for vengeance on Delamond as for my own comfort. The Delamondians could have used the shock. I resisted out of gratitude for Father Still, and out of respect for his office and the turmoil I knew he had been putting himself through. Not that he didn't have a secret pleasure in walking with me, too. For him there was the immoral pleasure of walking down the street as a normal man with a woman, as Geoffrey Still, a sinner who worried about his soul and his soul alone, and only on Sundays. The rest of the time he loved and quarreled with his woman, played with his daughter, worked a humble, menial job, drank too much once in a while, swore at the weather, slept in ignorance of meaning, grew old and died, satisfied that he had done what he could to raise himself and his family up from the muck and into the promise of an afterlife.

Once Maddie and I visited him before the church service. I don't remember why we were there, this wasn't our usual session time. Now it seems like we came to see what we saw. Father Still's rectory was a humble little cube compared to the stately girth of God's House. Inside, his house was full of straight lines and large empty spaces and sunlight. Clean, so clean you could smell the light. We walked quietly through the rooms, whispering after Father Still. Maddie held my hand, trying not to touch things. Against all the white space and light she looked like the smudge a dark moth wing leaves. Father Still wasn't there.

We walked outside and through the back entrance of the church. Our heels clicked on the wooden floor. We found Father inside the sacristy at the end of a narrow hallway, and we stood outside the doorway and watched. Father Still was kneeling in prayer. Through a heavy curtain on the other side of the room we could see the church sanctuary where he stood to deliver the service. We could hear the low, swelling voice of the congregation. In here, though, the warm, still air hugged us close. We had entered the heart of the church, Father Still's heart. He pressed his head into his folded hands, which he squeezed tightly together. Before him, on a little table, a Bible and a crucifix. He spoke in Latin to God, the walls absorbed his words and murmured them back. I had never heard Latin like this before. A tear dropped down his cheek and into the corner of his mouth. He was smiling.

Then he rose and crossed himself. I opened my mouth — I don't know what I would have said. I wanted him to know that I had seen him. Not that I had spied, but that I had shared. He walked through the curtain before words could come. Maddie and I entered the room after him, the air like held breath, and watched the service from there. Father Still chanted everything in Latin, except the sermon. At one point I think he saw Maddie and I hiding behind the curtain, though he made no sign. I wondered what the words meant to him, but then it didn't matter. He sang a hymn for us, the words before us and the meaning beyond. The song left our memories behind. We made our own meaning, and believed it.

*****

Father Still kept up a steady supply of crayons and paper for Maddie, and she developed an interest in things that could fly. She drew birds, bats, butterflies, moths, insects. When I told her some squirrels and fish could fly, she began drawing all animals with wings, flying. Rabbits, cats, bears, then even trees and rivers and, once, me.

Where am I flying to, Maddie, I asked her.

She said, You're flying apart.

You mean away, Maddie? You mean I'm flying away?

She shook her head and pointed at the picture. Apart, she said. When I looked closer I noticed my wings were separated from my back by a sliver of empty space. So too my head from my neck, and my hands from my arms. I began to notice this more and more in Maddie's pictures. There were always more and more spaces — not only hands separated from arms, but fingers separated from hands, and separated again by the joint. The spaces gradually grew larger, too, so that a rectangle of paper the size of her head was only big enough for a picture of her mouth — teeth, gums, lips, tongue, straining, it seemed, to fly from the force that held them together. She stopped visiting her flowers and drew for hours every day. Body parts lay all about our cottage, in cupboards and under chairs and stuck beneath the window. I found a few outside in the garden and in the field, as well, as though their own momentum had carried them out of the cottage. This was the death I feared would come for Maddie. I tried to hold on to her but she was slipping away. When I called her name she didn't hear, the rub of her crayon across the kitchen table answered for her. I held her while she slept, whispered songs into her ear. She didn't move, the songs passed right through her. I even prayed with Father Still, and wept over my folded fists, and tried to bargain with God.

Anything you ask, I told Him. Take me instead.

The invisible forces that patterned the universe for me weren't strong enough to hold it together for Maddie. Even this was beautiful, in its way, the birth of a new universe, though this did not comfort me. It was more bitter than sweet. I grew furious. For a short while Maddie had become my second chance at growing up right. I had thought that she could be me without all the mistakes I had made, that she was my salvation from myself. I shook her once, and she stared at me wide-eyed. I begged her to stay, but she was already gone. In those black eyes there was nothing, not even night sky.

As Father Still and I lay in each others' arms in his bedroom week after week, I worried about Maddie, who played in the sitting room while Father Still and I wrestled in the bedroom. I knew I should be with her during her last days, and Father Still worried about aggravating our sin by committing it so near an innocent child. I explained to him the danger of resisting natural — or supernatural — forces, the discomfort it causes. He explained to me that with the Lord we are never alone. As soon as we'd settled into our lies they unsettled me. I couldn't swallow them, they wouldn't go down, they sat on the edge of the bed and stared at me. With words you can say anything, be anything, believe anything. Nothing is real because anything is possible. For a moment I felt the stories that held me together dissolve. My past, my universe, was a fiction held together by thin strands of a faith in words I suddenly doubted. I watched it all fall away like leaves from a tree. Lying in Father Still's bed, on my back, listening to our breath, I detached from myself and began to float away in pieces. Nothing held. There was a pang of panic, and longing — was it mine? Our breath became the sound of parts moving through space, and then breath, too, dissolved. Once the pieces began to drift they would not be stopped. I did not want them to stop. They were not mine. Nothing was mine. Everything was paper-thin. Between the fragments there was nothing, not even space, not even silence. It spread around and through me. It was neither death nor rebirth, but a new consciousness entirely. Madness. I understood my daughter. I looked at Father Still, the loose collection of his features, bent pole of an arm, shifting, shapeless torso, arbitrary nose, eyes absurd as eggs, two dark lips like wet twigs haphazardly pressed into the open field of his weathered face. He was a shabbily constructed lie I chose to live with and love. We didn't matter, nothing did. Nothing held us together but stupid beautiful lies. That was Maddie's secret. The understanding brought Maddie and I together. We were connected,

I believed, she and I, we were drops of the same water spilling over the edge of the earth. Our bodies may split apart but our essence would not separate.

This, too, was a lie.

*****

The affair had already ended by the time I discovered I was pregnant. The mystery had removed itself from the man. It was the lies we had told ourselves that I loved, not Geoffrey, and it was the Latin and the ritual, the solemn, secret chant and the graceful bow, all words of a story opened up to me in a language I couldn't read and bound in the character of Father Still. I had lain with Geoffrey, bodies folded together like hands in prayer, yearning after Father Still. There is nothing in the world more tantalizing than the story you cannot read, the book you cannot touch. There is nothing you yearn for more than this. But I had lost faith in the fiction, and beside the story stood a man, just a man. He knew it too. Beside his troubled faith stood nothing more than a woman. We began seeing each other as we were, naked and plain, and we were ashamed. For the second time in my life a better place receded and another world reared itself up, as it had in the alley while Brice rubbed my face into the brick wall. There is no getting over this pain. You recreate the world you lost, but all you accomplish is the disinterment of the pain.

In the dead of winter Geoffrey sent me away to wait for the birth. I told him I didn't need to go away. I told him I wouldn't tell, which was true. Father Still was already a memory, and Geoffrey was just another Delamondian. But he insisted, said there was a seminary in Harrington where the nuns would take care of me. He would take care of Maddie while I was gone. That's why I agreed, because I thought Maddie might do better without me. It hurt to leave her. The seminary was the same one Tom had lived in. I don't know if Tom was there then, but he must know I had been there. He must have heard about Father Still, and he must have seen me as a real she-devil. Evil. The nuns didn't seem put off by me or my condition — I guessed this was something they did a lot. I wondered what other women had been here before me, what other Delamondians had buried their secrets here.

My room sat at the back of the seminary, away from the men in the quarter where the nuns lived. It was small and plain with a low white roof and a ground level view of what I was told was a meditation garden, buried under clean thick drifts of snow. I could see the cross and the bell tower of the church, both humble affairs, rise over the garden. In my time there I never attended a service. I pleaded illness, which wasn't a lie. The old familiar nausea of pregnancy had settled into me and would not leave. But the truth was I could not bear to enter another church, I had grown too familiar with its sad story. The nuns were patient with me. They came to my room and whispered prayers and tried to save my soul. They wanted to baptize me and give me communion but I couldn't let them. A part of me wanted to let them, but it was the part that still remembered Father Still and the Latin and the lies. The nuns looked too sad, I didn't believe their arguments. I was sad too. Their rituals were lost to me.

The nuns' patience wore thin over the winter months, melting away like the low white hills of snow in the garden. As the winter passed, the shrinking snow revealed benches of stoic stone. Skeletal shrubbery huddled nearby. In time the shrubs bloomed lush green with little red berries. Nuns swept the stone walkway that wound through them, and when the weather warmed I ventured out and followed the path around and around. Behind my view from the window there opened up a little flower garden and a pond with a marble statue of Mary in the center pouring clear healing waters out of a pitcher. The water in the pond was dark, as though tainted with the collective sin of all who passed by.

I sat here through long slow days. There was a stillness and a quiet I didn't feel elsewhere. It was not peaceful. The black gurgling fountain water warned against thoughts of contentment, but that was exactly why this spot attracted me. The restless murmuring of the fountain was my own heart. There was a beauty in the ugly black water, and a frightened tremor in Mary's graceful hands, that calmed and unsettled me. The nuns walked by in their black and white frockery without so much as turning their haughty heads. It enriched the garden.

I wondered how Maddie was getting on with Geoffrey. She was capable of tearing him apart. I kept expecting word that she had disappeared — run away or just broke apart one day into little pieces that dissolved into the air and drifted off on the wind. Geoffrey only sent little notes now and again that said nothing.

All is well here. I pray for you. Go with God. — G.

He had gone back to being the man I had wanted to hate all along. I wrote on the backs of his notes and returned them.

Dear Maddie: Wait for me.

From that cool bench in the garden I watched the last of winter pass into spring and the nuns shed coats and scarves for umbrellas. In time I knew the name of every nodding leaf. I watched the blue of the sky deepen through the branches of the maple tree behind and above me, the leaves glow with burnished sun. Against the page of the sky I read my life in the letters formed by the bare branches, and held myself and shivered. My belly swelled. I had grown afraid of what would come. I could not change the past or what I had done, but if I could have averted what I felt was coming I would have. If I could have prayed. I spoke to Mary but she didn't answer, or maybe I wasn't listening. My ears were clogged with sin. The nuns looked at me with flat, distant eyes and quietly shook their heads. It was too late for me. They had given up waiting and now satisfied themselves by caring for the unholy creature. They let me stay with them, and they were discreet with their opinions of me, but they all wanted to know more about me without having to ask me. I was a curiosity, a demon in a cage. It was my own fault I was here, but now that I was here I couldn't see the nuns as anything but displaced Delamondians in special robes. I wouldn't surrender to them. I wanted to be a girl again, running through the long grass, before all this happened. I could still feel it, if I closed my eyes, the slender blades swiping my shins and brushing my face as I sliced through it like wind. But that was a long time ago.

I meditated on my past and my future. My future was always a penance for my past. I had trouble with men. My misdeeds had been visited on Father, on me, on Maddie, and now — what twisted thing churned in my belly now? Surely lying with a holy man was a bigger sin than what I had done with Brice. It made sense that the price to pay would be larger, too. I held my hand to my stomach and watched the stony Mary. There was no forgiveness there. Mary's was a wasted effort. I could not divine my future in the pure steady stream coming from her hands. My future lurked in the murk of the pond below. At times I stood by the pond's edge and longed to fall forward, breathe in the blackness of all that accumulated sin, and die. I was an evil woman, I was wrong in every way. I felt the blackness of my own sins seeping out of my pores. I was a mistake, and the mistake was my fault. I wished one of the passing nuns, just one, would stop and speak to me. I felt so fragile I would have broken to pieces. Just touch my cheek the way my mother used to.

These were dark days for me. I could feel the sickness coming on that had once had me standing beside Father's grave and loosening my grip on baby Maddie. The sickness would pass again this time, I believed. I would see it through to the other side. Not because I believed the other side would be better. I knew it wouldn't be. There would still be Delamond and its people, my cottage, the ghosts of my family, my guilt. I wasn't blind enough to think that would change with the wave of a god's magic wand. And I wouldn't see myself through for my children, who would more than likely be better off dead than inherit the Hayes legacy of poverty and scorn. No, I would see myself through this dark period because I would fly in the face of all that, because not seeing myself through was exactly what was expected of me. From now on, I would write my own endings.

But the world had different plans for me. One night I felt the stabbing pains. It was too early — I wasn't due for months. I cried out. This time I was not alone. The nuns knew what to do. They gave me things to bite on, and they prayed. They were calm about it all, moving around me quick and sure. They didn't say anything to me or even look at me. They were here for the sake of the baby. I pushed. The thing inside me was stretching me wide and pulling me apart. I pushed all night, until the night began to fade into light. The nuns were tired and short-tempered and told me to push harder, I had to push harder. I wanted to die. I pushed through all the pain, I was trying to force my own life out of me. As the nuns stood over me I stared out the window. I remember seeing the cross on the church emerging from the blackness. Then something, finally, was coming out of me. The nuns grew frantic, yelling at me and grasping at their rosaries. In the final moments I was screaming for death, I was demanding it. Then suddenly everything came easy. In the morning light I felt the weight slip out of me, tired and heavy, and it was over. The nuns stopped yelling and praying, the rosaries swung from their dropped hands like pendulums, and the room fell silent. The baby must have been too tired to cry, I thought.

What is it? I asked.

Twins, they said. Boys.

The nuns faces were white.

The nuns wrapped my babies in white blankets and tried to hurry them out of the room. But I saw them, just for an instant. Of all the memories that *could* fade — I could tell a million new stories, but this would be the only one I would remember. Do I really want to forget? I saw their faces. Their mouths were open a little. I didn't know lips could be so white. I saw little white fists. I saw them. I see them. They are beautiful. Then the nuns covered them up and took them away. I thought they would bring my babies back in a moment, once they were revived. One of the nuns was crying, another started praying again. They brought me a special tea to help me sleep. The tea helped a little. One by one the nuns left the room, and it was all quiet again. I watched the sun push up from behind the church, slow and easy. Outside my room I could hear faraway voices, hurried footsteps. I waited for someone to come to me with my babies. After awhile I stopped waiting. Things grew clearer in the light. My babies weren't coming back. My babies were dead. I understood the fact, then, but not the reality of it. I had screamed for death, and they had obliged me. This could never be forgiven. I stared out the window at the brightening red shrubs, a flock of geese arrowing north, the bell tower signaling mass, the nuns hurrying through the garden to pray my babies and me away, the stony Mary and the distant church, and the cross up there on top staring down on me and saying, *Get out.*

*****

I called at Geoffrey's the day I arrived back in Delamond. I walked through the door without knocking. It was a Sunday, and Geoffrey was on his way to the sacristy before the service. Maddie sat in a wooden chair in the corner of the sitting room while he hustled about, gathering up sermon notes and crosses and whatnot. A book sat in her lap beneath her folded hands. She looked like a painting. She turned her head toward me as I entered and her expression didn't change, as if a wind had sneaked through the door, nothing more. I think Geoffrey believed he could straighten Maddie out. He had tremendous, useless faith. But Maddie was worse, if anything. When I entered Geoffrey stopped what he was doing and stood in the center of the room. Word had already been sent to him about the twins, that was clear. He wouldn't look me in the eye.

Come in, he said, holding out one hand to his side. Maddie rose and took it. He said, I was just —

I won't stay, I said.

We stared at each other for a moment. I read his open face, and we were both surprised at what was written there. He blamed me for his own guilt. For everything. He hated me. He knew he shouldn't, but he did nothing to check the anger, like a hammer, pounding at me. He was lost, more lost than I was. As an outcast I was allowed the freedom of losing my way. He let go of Maddie. She walked over to me without a sound, and stood there. The move seemed rehearsed, a dance step Geoffrey had trained her in. There was something grotesque about it, the silent grace of it. I looked down at my daughter. She looked straight ahead. She hadn't waited for me. She had finally flown apart. I was left with this little piece.

I didn't want to stay any longer in this room where I had once been so happy. Where had my happiness gone? I was not angry, or sad, or disgusted. I did not feel pity. I did not feel anything. When someone you love fails you, you are disappointed in a way different from any other kind of disappointment. Something is lost forever. I had not loved this man, but the feeling now was the same. For a short while, we had almost been a family. I felt it all fall away.

January 26

Dear Traveler:

I never did attend a church service. No baptism, communion, confession, no hope of heaven. Geoffrey Still is long gone. He never said goodbye. One day I saw a stranger at the door of the Church of the Assumption, a dried up old man with no humor or passion, and soon after, my women told me about it. Geoffrey had left rather suddenly, made an announcement at Mass one Sunday and a few days later was gone. He said he had been called to another parish. My women were divided — most believed what he had told them, but some wondered if there wasn't a personal reason for his leaving, since his behavior had grown odd, and his sermons dark in tone. He was a sort of Dimmesdale, after all. If he believed his own lies about me, there is no reason he should have said goodbye. But I don't think he believed his lies. I don't think he blamed me for everything. He saw himself too clearly, that's what attracted me to him in the first place. So now he's some other place, in a city or in a grave, still searching for proof against God and punishment for believing it. He never said where he was going. I don't wish Geoffrey anything, harm or goodwill.

I don't miss Father Still, either, though I miss missing him.

When I missed Father Still, I could still feel the ghost of the cross he drew between my eyes seeping through my skull and warming into my blood. Now it's just a memory of a memory, cold and thin and useless as an old bedsheet. Are you religious, dear traveler? Maybe if we had been religious the Delamondians would have let you stay. If I hadn't been so determined to be unlike them, to be unliked. It would be perfect now to break off a brittle corner of the journal and place it reverently on Father Still's tongue, watch him grimace gratefully as he works it down his throat. I remember thinking he had a beautiful throat, full of Latin. But I don't remember the throat now, and I don't speak Latin. Most times I'm already past goodbye, but in weaker moments I try to recapture that memory. It's like trying to hold an echo.

The Church of the Assumption is a massive white block and a tall square bell tower with a heavy rusted sanctum bell inside. The tower has a short, peaked roof that makes it look like a sort of spear. There is something beautiful in the strength and severity of this house. It wears its fear on its sleeve: *Maybe we're just singing to an empty sky.* It is brave and determined in spite of itself. Father's house must have looked the same, before Father came along. When you stand outside the Church of the Assumption, even on a weekday when there are no people inside, you can hear the echo of the pipe organ and the pop and creak of the wooden pews as the flock rises and falls in place. Old ladies clicking glass rosaries against the backs of the pews, low voices chanting in Latin. The quiet fervor of incense hanging in the holy air, smell of pain and faith. The church is a space in your mind where echoes fade, but never die.

Inside, the church is silent. The air is close and sweet with old incense. The air breathes out the silence. It makes you a part of it. The stations of the cross hang in little paintings on the side walls. The paintings and their story are poorly done — too melodramatic. But even a heart hardened against God trembles and cracks just a little, wanting to believe there's a real story behind this cheap one, a story of hope. Walk down the carpeted aisle between the pews to the sanctuary where the priest normally stands. Behind the altar, a Jesus hangs on a massive crucifix, staring up with tortured sadness at God, who isn't there. Jesus will go to a better place, though first, as the story explains, he has to go to a worse place. Not that it matters now — now he is gone. You can do what you want here and Jesus won't know. You could spit in the holy water. You could say my name. But you won't do these things, dear traveler, even though you are angry enough to. Where was God when the men were leading you away from Delamond? Where is He now — conjuring winds in the forest? Sipping absinthe in a Paris café? He's gone. Everybody leaves. Only words remain.

Sanctuary. Relic. Hymn. Missal. Pater Noster. Offertory. Passiontide. Communion. Sacrament. Vessel. Joyful Mysteries. Glorious Mysteries. Sorrowful Mysteries. The Fifteen Promises. Homily. Epiphany. Confession. Contrition.

Something here makes anger childish.

I didn't want him to go. I pushed him out, anyway. I shouldn't have laughed at him. I should have told a better story.

Rip pages from the journal and let them fall to the floor, dear traveler. Let it be the last sound you make here. There's an echo only God could hear. When a wind rushes in it sweeps the pages around like dirt. The pages settle in the aisle, among the pews, in the corners. Though you are leaving, this is not goodbye. The pages will wait. And if He ever returns to this place, He can find us easily. If He wants us.

January 30

"Smashing day," I said, taking my seat at the café table with Agnes.

Agnes didn't look at me. She was staring out glumly at the Paris throngs. Tom and Alice were playing checkers at the table next to us. Helen was plinking away at the piano. Old Ed crouched by the television, watching a war documentary. The usual handful of others were moping about the window or the nurse's station, waiting for medication. Marilyn was back in the kitchen, and Onion wasn't in yet, so nothing else was going on. For weeks Agnes and Old Ed had been snapping at each other like half-crazed dogs, and then just a few days ago they exchanged words they shouldn't have. Agnes said Old Ed's cocooning himself in pain and self-pity was a childish attempt to not grow up and face death. Old Ed said the same of Agnes' slowly creeping dementia. Truly hurtful words, and they hadn't spoken to each other since. Old Ed was too wrapped up in his own misery for any but the bitterest words for us, and our gang was tired of him. We hated that Agnes was in love with him, but I understand how you can hate the person you love the most. You don't choose to be in love, love chooses you. You have to just get on with it.

Agnes said, "'So this is where people come to live; I would have thought it's a city to die in.'"

"More Rilke?" I asked. Agnes nodded.

"'O lands! O all so dear to me — what you are, I become part of that, whatever it is.'"

I wanted to cheer her up. Our gang wanted to talk her into her love for Old Ed. Most of all, I wanted to keep her here with me. Agnes had been losing herself in time more often than usual — I kept finding her in the back of the garden by the fence, waiting for Buddy to come for her. I was afraid she would wander out of the home one night and never return. But I needed her here in order to continue as I had grown accustomed to continuing. We all did.

"'City people hang in the air, hover in all directions, and find no place where they can settle,'" she said.

"'Answer. You are here — life exists, and identity; the powerful play goes on, and you will contribute a verse.'"

Agnes sat up and frowned. "Wrong answer," she said. "'Henceforth I whimper no more, postpone no more, need nothing, done with indoor complaints, libraries, querulous criticisms, strong and content I travel the open road.' Now there's your Whitman."

"Are you going somewhere, Agnes?" asked Alice. She had just jumped Tom's last checker for the win. She always won, or he let her win. Tom always looked self-satisfied about losing. Alice joined us at the table and asked Agnes again where she was going, but Agnes didn't answer. Helen joined us, too. We had planned this. We were going to talk to Agnes about Old Ed. *Sabotage.* Alice was supposed to say something nice about love, and we would take it from there. Alice could make love sound inviting, even necessary. The rest of us would have botched it somehow.

"Ripping good music, yes?" said Helen. "Mozart and Paris are like chocolate on strawberries."

"Bollocks," I said. "More like a paper crown on a queen's head. Jazz is for Paris."

It struck me how violent our British was, with all its smashing and ripping — and I don't know what a bollock is, but I think it's a body part. We weren't a violent people, except in love. Peevish Tom sat at the next table behind yesterday's newspaper, snapping each new page open in protest. He wouldn't join us. He refused to be a part of our "meddling." Men are strange that way. They understand violence, but not love.

"Jazz is like…" said Alice, searching for a way to turn the conversation to love, "Jazz is like — is like having sex on fire." Tom's breath hitched and he nearly tore his paper in two. We could almost feel his face reddening in rage. What blasphemy! We were all a little shocked, even Agnes, who snapped out of her funk and stared at Alice. Alice blushed, deeper and deeper. She tried to appeal to Agnes' boldness. "You know," she stammered, "hot and screechy. And bouncy." Tom was coughing and retching. Soon he would raise his holy fist into the air, the heavens would crack open and smite these sinners. We ignored him. Agnes was beaming at Alice, who was shriveling back into herself. We had planned on being a little more subtle than this, but there was nothing for it now. Alice had ignited us.

"I know who could use some jazzing up," said Helen. "Old Ed."

"Look at him over there," I said. We did. Old Ed was a world away, lost in black and war footage. His body was so still it seemed a part of his chair. I looked around at the other residents, everyone in their own worlds, even the orderlies, joking and lazing behind the front desk, as far from us as possible. Even us at our café table, trying to get to Agnes' Paris by pretending we were already there. Where time is meaningless, here is nowhere. We are already gone, and our bodies are a traveler's log book. Old Ed was ravaged and barely visible, a faded signature nearly forgotten.

Agnes, even sulking, was like a fresh breeze through an open door. Coming or going? I wanted to say something more about Old Ed, something funny that Agnes would laugh at, but the moment had gone stale, and she was already far beyond me.

"I say," said Helen. "What a rip it would be if one of us sat in Old Ed's lap."

"Make him shite his knickers," said Alice.

Tom rose and marched out of the room. Alice stared nervously at her lap. Later, she would sit next to Tom at the dinner table and cut his meat for him, and after dinner she would fetch the checker board and they would settle into their familiar silences. She had nothing to be nervous about. Love's victor is the more skillful surrenderer. Alice let Tom let her win at checkers.

"I say, Agnes," said Helen. "You're the flamboyant one. Why don't you go round to him?"

"I dare you," said Alice. "Sit in his lap."

The way a landscape alters beneath swift storm clouds and a bright sun, Agnes' expression shifted from deep embarrassment to hot anger to dark suspicion, then to a calm nothingness. She stared at a point in the air between us all. A grin twitched over her face and disappeared. Her eyes watered a bit and she seemed suddenly old beyond her years, and suddenly very, very young, too, a girl who has been hiding in the dark for a long time from something that has just snuck up and tapped her on the shoulder. What were we doing, who did we think we were, meddling with others' hearts? I reached across the table to touch Agnes' shoulder.

"I'm not afraid," she said to me. She looked at us all. Paris was gone. Agnes was all here. "There's nothing to fear."

"But fear itself," I whispered. Something felt wrong. Wrong and unstoppable. I could only watch. Agnes rose and walked to the middle of the room and paused. Old Ed hadn't moved. Beside me, I heard Helen giggle. Alice looked at me and smiled like she was unsure if she should. I was holding my breath. I thought of things

I might do to stop the plan before something happened. I thought of yelling something, jumping on Agnes' back, faking a hip injury. I could have done anything. I silently sent Agnes my apologies. She turned back toward me, still grinning a little. Helen and Alice and I moved over to the couch and chairs, paged through magazines, peeking over the tops.

Agnes slowly made her way over to Old Ed and stood beside his wheelchair. She said something and he jumped, looked up at her with angry surprise, then softened. She talked while he looked at the television, and when she finished, he glanced up at her. He looked like a little boy afraid to ask for what he wanted. He started to say something and Agnes held her hands over her hears, said "Stop!" Old Ed shut his mouth tight and Agnes dropped her hands and they stood there like two shaking tea kettles about to boil. They were both staring down at the floor. They wouldn't look at each other. Finally Old Ed pointed at the television, and they watched the war for a minute before Old Ed started talking again. It sounded like he was defending the Allied's right to demolish whatever city they were demolishing. Agnes laughed a little. She had a beautiful light chuckle from her time as a young thing courting danger in Paris. She rested her hand on the back of Old Ed's chair. The way she stood, straight, easy, proud, I could see her as a young, silver-tongued femme fatale wooing and crushing the spirit of wanton European cities, and the men who would come back to her again and again. And her dress, old now, the rose sash faded to a pale orangey-pink, yet still the regal gown of a queenly socialite accustomed to power and its abuses. Old Ed was no match. They argued for a few minutes, then stopped. Agnes touched his shoulder with tips of her fingers.

The three of us glanced at each other over our magazines, six shifty eyes pacing across the top edges of unread pages. When I looked back, Agnes still had her hand on Old Ed's shoulder. He was staring down toward his feet. She was saying something only he could hear. She was deadly serious. When she finished neither of them moved. We watched. It took me awhile to see that Old Ed's lips were moving — he talked like that for a long time, mumbling at his feet. As he spoke, Agnes leaned further and further over him, her face turning a shade redder with each inch that closed between them. My gut churned. It wasn't exertion or love consuming Agnes, it was rage. Old Ed kept talking.

Agnes never looked over at us, or at me. We were invisible, watching a silent drama unfold. My stomach churned. Drama is different when the characters are real, when you've helped create the plot. There are consequences for this, and you can't walk away. Agnes set her hands on the wheelchair's armrest and leaned further over him. Old Ed grimaced and crouched into the other side of his seat. He stopped talking and closed his eyes against her. Agnes started whispering. A vein stood out in her neck. She had lost all her cool grace. I imagined he had rejected her because he wanted to be sick, not in love, though he was in love, and now she was telling him to die, though she loved him, too. She spat out a quiet, steady stream of hatred, shoving the wheelchair on the important points, and he leaned away, leaned over the edge of his chair, and then the whole thing toppled over. Old Ed tumbled out and lay in a twisted heap on the floor, moaning. Agnes backed away, her unfinished anger confounded by concern and fear. Marilyn burst out of the kitchen at the noise and hurried over. Old Ed was moaning about his hip, Agnes had broken his hip. Marilyn poked her head out of the kitchen, then ran over, made him lie on his back and wait while one of the orderlies called for an ambulance. I got myself over there and held Agnes. She curled into my arms and shook with a sudden cold. I saw Alice jump up with a little cry and run out of the room. Helen snuck out soon after without a backward glance. Old Ed was turning white and losing consciousness. He raised a finger at Agnes, said she would pay for this. He'd have her kicked out of the home, he would sue.

"Get her out of here," Marilyn barked at me.

I led Agnes away. We shuffled past the closed door of Helen's room, where Helen was playing her opera records too loudly. She was as shrewd as she was cowardly. If Marilyn asked, Helen would say she hadn't even been in the day room. She would suggest that Marilyn talk to me. Further on I saw Alice in the hall outside Tom's room. She was weeping into his shoulder and couldn't look at us. Tom's hard eyes bore into me.

"It's OK, Alice," I said. "Everything's going to be OK."

"I told you," Tom said to me, fuming. "The very idea — a whore meddling in love — why it's... "

"Like a priest peddling God?" I said. And there was more to say to Tom, much more, but this was not the time. He didn't know the first thing about me, or Geoffrey Still, though he acted like he knew everything.

I took Agnes into her room and lay her on the bed. She hadn't spoken a word since Old Ed fell. I sat in a chair next to her and held her hand. I wondered if she'd be so obliging if she knew our gang had been up to no good behind her back. I wondered if this would be the last time we would be friends. If Old Ed was hurt bad, everything could go wrong. I hoped that if Agnes and I weren't going to be friends anymore that I would be forced to leave the home, because I couldn't bear to be around her if we couldn't be close. But it wouldn't be me who would leave. I tried to remember the scene exactly as it had occurred — had Old Ed fallen out of his chair, or had he been pushed? I couldn't be sure. Old Ed was stupid enough to fall, and I believed he deserved to be pushed, so I saw it happen both ways. I couldn't trust my memory.

Our gang had felt so bold and self-righteous. We hadn't learned a thing in all our years. I was so tired now. Tired of running from my age. I looked at Agnes. She was staring up at the ceiling. Her eyes were half closed, and shallow, wispy breaths whistled in and out of her throat. She looked old, too. Mother of my dreams.

Agnes sighed — she was full of sighs, secreting through her lips in little warm breezes. I caught words on them — she was saying something. She was reciting Apollinaire:

"'Love elapses like the river
Love goes by
Poor life is indolent
And expectation always violent

The night is a clock chiming
The days go by not I'"

Her heart was breaking. Our gang had done this. I had done this, and I wasn't sure I could fix it. What would Whitman say to Apollinaire?

"'There is that in me—I do not know what it is—but I know it is in me ...
I do not know it—it is without name—it is a word unsaid,
It is not in any dictionary, utterance, symbol ...
Do you see O my brothers and sisters?
It is not chaos or death—it is form, union, plan—it is eternal life—it is Happiness.'"

Agnes chuckled under her breath. "You Americans," she said. "You're so..." Another sigh and she closed her eyes. A queer sort of light was falling through the window, a heavy yellow light I had never seen before. Something was fluttering in my gut, something was leaving. The light settled among the towers of books and photos across Agnes' floor and faded. We sat there quietly while shadows rose up around us. Agnes folded her hands across her chest. Except for a little stitch in her brow where she was thinking, a still, peaceful sadness settled over her like a blanket. That's how she would look in her casket, I thought. That's how Father had looked on his death bed; content, like he'd gotten away with something he deserved to get away with. In death, Agnes would have gotten away with herself, with the woman I would never have known. I realized then how slippery Agnes was about herself — I couldn't remember a single time when she had spoken her heart to me, plain and straight. She told everything to Martha. She only told me things through the poetry we shared.

"Agnes? Are you awake?" She made a little noise. "Tell me a story, Agnes. Tell me where you were born. And about your childhood. I don't know a thing about you. Tell me everything you remember."

"'My   youth   was   nothing   but   a   black   storm
Crossed now and then by brilliant suns.'"

"That's someone else's childhood," I said. "What happened to yours?"

"'Memories are hunting horns
Whose sound dies on the wind.' Apollinaire."

I wanted to cry. I started to. Agnes lay with her eyes closed. The room was getting too dark to see her face clearly. The shadowy towers of books and bric-a-brac began to take the form of a silent tribe of people gathering around us, a different breed of dead than my own — Agnes' dead. How they must have congregated here, night after night, in thrall to their high priestess. Friends and lovers, writers she'd never known, scenes invented from abstract paintings she collected and turned to memory. I wanted to believe Agnes had been places, seen things. It was all I knew of her. If she had never known a Buddy Baker, if there had never been a Buddy Baker, if she had never been to Paris, sipped absinthe, reveled with surrealists — if it all vanished in the light of truth, then what would remain? Who was lying on this bed? There was a time when I hadn't cared. Back then our gang hadn't seemed so breakable. Leave-taking was a lark, then. Now Agnes was barely ever here, and whatever stories our gang had tried to believe about better places had suddenly grown brittle. If Old Ed died, our gang would die, too. Outside, I could hear residents shuffling past. Soon it would be time for medication, supper, bed, the rest of our lives. No more leave-taking, no more hijinks. Beside me, Agnes was falling asleep, or dying, or slipping away. I wanted her to stay. I wanted a glimpse of what was real in her before she left for good. No one else made me feel so lonely. I loved no one else so completely.

"'Whoever you are, I fear you are walking the walks of dreams,

I fear these supposed realities are to melt from under your feet and

hands.'"

"'Common sense tells us that the things of the earth exist only a little, and that true reality is only in the dreams,'" said Agnes.

"'I accept reality and do not question it.'"

"'I believe that I am in hell, therefore I am there.'"

A rap on the door startled us both. The door opened and white light cut across Agnes' hands. They looked like marble, a warm white sculpture. *Artifice.* Marilyn stood in the doorway.

"Are you OK, Agnes?" she asked.

"I'm fine, dear. Resting."

"How is Old Ed?" I asked.

"He's staying in the hospital tonight," said Marilyn. "I'll need to talk to you — both of you." She watched us both for a moment, searching for early signs of guilt. She always looked at our gang like this, but now it was serious. We didn't give up anything. "Medication time soon," she said. "I'll see you in the day room." She closed the door. I listened to her footsteps fade down the hall — I could always tell her footsteps, they were the only ones in the whole home that were no-nonsense.

Agnes was staring at the ceiling. I looked up. I turned on the nightstand lamp and looked up again. There was a hairline crack that snaked from the doorframe over the bed and petered out near the middle of the ceiling. I tried to see what Agnes might be seeing there, but all I saw was the crack. The light spread in a cone around us. Whatever tribes of the dead had climbed out of the dark walls had returned to their own worlds. The piles of books and photos were just piles of books and photos again.

"I never did sit on Old Ed's lap," said Agnes.

"No. You lost the dare."

"Next time our gang needn't interfere," she said. "Old Ed and I can manage ourselves." I felt myself blush. Had our gang been that obvious about our plan? Of course we had. We were children acting like children. Agnes squeezed my hand. "The plan worked, anyway," she said. "I think I really bowled him over."

"Be careful what you say, Agnes. You'll confess to assault." I watched her face for a confession, but she only gave up a grin. That little grin of hers. "Why were you saying to him, anyway?" I asked. "He was terrified."

"He tried to recite poetry to me," said Agnes. She was serious. I could feel her frowning. "It was something awful. It rhymed 'true' with 'blue.' I wouldn't abide it — not after we had just agreed to be in love."

"You told him you loved him?"

Agnes nodded. I thought I saw a little blush. "That's when he started with the poetry, and I told him to stop. We started talking about the war instead. Then we agreed we shouldn't talk about the war. Then we didn't have anything to argue about, so we moved right on to love."

We laughed and squeezed each other's hands close and hard and didn't let go, even after we stopped laughing, even after the laughter seemed a faraway thing. Agnes watched the crack in the ceiling, and I watched our hands folded together. This was how prayer was supposed to be, I thought, hands held tightly, voices sending laughter up to heaven. We pushed God out when we started being too earnest. This at last was the real Agnes, this was what we had had together, and what Agnes was leaving behind. I squeezed her hand again. She pulled on me until I climbed onto the bed with her. We lay side by each, staring up at the ceiling, holding hands as though waiting to see what would open up through the crack. From outside, the silver ting of a bell rang out and vibrated around us. I wanted to show Agnes my journal, then. I didn't care to know what was on the other side of that crack. I wanted Agnes to forgive me and I wanted us to live forever in this sanctuary and pray with laughter. I would never be alone. My dead would never enter here. I would never have to write again, so the story would never end. I switched off the lamp and we lay in the dark, listening to our breath. There was our breath, our voices, a globe of heat around our hands. Everything else had been a fiction.

Agnes' breath hitched. It was so quiet I thought I heard a tear drop into her pillow. "Do you think Old Ed'll be OK?" she asked. Her voice was small and raw, a sad little girl's voice.

"With the extra pain, he'll be better than ever."

"Do you think we'll ever get to Paris?"

The question seemed to hover all around us. Agnes curled into my arms, and I held her close while she cried. I didn't know if 'we' meant Agnes and Old Ed, Agnes and Martha, or Agnes and me. It didn't much matter. I wasn't any of those people, and neither was she. We were just our hands and our prayer, waiting for an answer. I didn't want to say yes or no. I wanted to tell the truth. I said,

"'Imagine, ma petite,
Dear sister mine, how sweet
Were we to go and take our pleasure
Leisurely, you and I —

To lie, to love, to die
Off in that land made to your measure!' — Now there's your
Baudelaire."

Agnes didn't respond. She had drifted off to sleep with her
head on my chest. The darkness wrapped around us and I listened
to the sound of our breathing, felt the weight of her head rising and
falling against my heart. My heart was calm and strong. For a
short while, all the questions disappeared.

February 7

One day in spring I found a deer, dead, out in the long grass between my cottage and Father's old house. It was the first thing I knew of that had died out there since Father's cows dropped off. I thought it was sad that the deer had made it through winter only to die when the earth was coming to life again. But nature didn't care if I was sad, or if the deer was dead. I could have buried the deer, but it was no bother to anyone. No scavengers came sneaking around that weren't already there, and the days when Maddie played in the field had long passed. Maddie had grown into a woman, and the dark thing that Brice had passed on to her had grown deeper into her. It looked like it hurt. As a woman, Maddie was more feral. She reminded me of Thora, Brice's mother. Maddie had moved out of my cottage and into Father's old house, where she paced the halls or rocked in a chair by the kitchen window, staring out. When the weather was fine I would stand or sit in the doorway of my cottage and stare out at the field and the old house, too, watching the weather, listening for life in the old house. I was still young, but I wondered how we would die. I wondered what Maddie thought of the dead deer. She didn't have much to say to me.

I half suspected Geoffrey poisoned Maddie's mind against me. It wouldn't surprise me. As he waited for me to give birth to his sons at the convent and watched Maddie be Maddie, as he thought on all that we had done, the sin piled on sin, seeds might have been planted in her mind. He saw me in a different light when I returned, and Maddie wasn't Maddie anymore. Over time she stopped playing in the long grass, and the butterfly violets she had so carefully tended grew wild with weeds. By fourteen she had started going into town. She wouldn't tell me what she did there. Sometimes my women would say they saw her downtown, wandering Main Street, hanging around the schoolhouse, or sitting in Bulb Park, drawing pictures — she still loved to draw, then. My women would wait for me to say something about her. They were fishing for rumors. I said nothing. They didn't need me to say anything. I could imagine how *Hayes* was gaining new definitions. I didn't care about that, I cared about Maddie. I couldn't control her — she wouldn't stay at home, and I didn't want to imprison her here, anyway. I wanted her to find a way to escape this diseased patch of earth, this family, this city. I wanted her to be safe and happy somewhere. I didn't know what to do, any more than I did when I sat with my dying mother, worrying over my swollen belly. I still don't know what to do. I should have done something. I sat in my cottage and worked for my women and watched time bury us. The field of long grass never looked so empty.

Maddie grew into a young woman increasingly at odds with her father's inheritance. I used to love how courageously she was transforming into something strange and beautiful, even as it saddened me. But after Geoffrey, she fought harder against it. She began looking at me differently. She looked at me like Geoffrey had after I returned from the convent. As she was flying apart she tried to hold to something. When she was fifteen years old she said she wanted to marry and have a family, and she wanted her family to live in the old house. We fought, then. We fought for weeks. I told her all about men. I told her I didn't want her in that house. The more I talked the more resolved she was to contradict me. I felt like I was fighting against Geoffrey and Father. Geoffrey would somehow absolve himself of me if he could turn her into a right woman — a married Delamondian with a proper Delamondian family. Father would want Maddie in his house to watch over her, to keep her away from me, to punish me.

That house is a death trap full of hateful ghosts, I said to her.

They only hate you, said Maddie.

A man will take what he wants of you and leave you in that house to rot, I said.

I'm already rotten.

You can go anywhere. Go somewhere new. You can do things. Anything's possible.

You're wrong.

A part of me believed Maddie was right, and that Geoffrey and Father, who were looking at me through her eyes, were right. The Hayeses would only ever find new ways to be Hayeses. The hulking old house, our land, Father — all living dead — they proved it every day. I could change my name a dozen times and I'd still be That Hayes Girl. Just ask any Inchbald. Yet I wasn't willing to give up. Maddie wouldn't escape this place the way I had hoped, but maybe she could find another way. I hoped that if I let her go to the old house that Father would be satisfied and lie quietly in his earth. Maddie would be my penance for all the hurt I had brought to my family. I deserved that. And I would still be able to watch over her, and make sure she didn't grow into the woman Geoffrey wanted her to be.

So I surrendered. I gave her most of my things and she moved into the old house, and the house moved into her. As the days passed, whatever passions had pushed her out of my cottage left her, and the fire in her eyes grew cold, and died down. She grew as cold and hollow as the rooms of the house. All that was left was a shell of the dark thing she had inherited from Brice, hard and sharp and pointed at the world. She still wandered downtown most days, but I never stopped seeing her. Whenever I looked at Father's house looking back at me, there was Maddie.

Not long after she settled in, she found a man. The man's name was Vincent, a wiry, unwashed young man who had a way of sauntering around the old house like it was the spoils of the war, though his eyes were shifty because he knew he didn't deserve a thing he'd got in life, which wasn't much, and because he knew another man could take it all away if he wasn't careful. He was a rodent. I could read his whole story just watching him. He had no family to speak of. He worked at the mill sometimes but more often spent his days at The Lumberyard — the millworkers' tavern — getting drunk. He had no friends, only fellow schemers who were allies and enemies alike. His body was stronger than it looked, but inside he was selfish and overconfident, which made him weak as a baby.

I knew it was only a matter of time — a short time — before he would leave, and in that time, I knew he would do something hurtful, and he did. I let him. Maybe I shouldn't have. Maddie wouldn't have allowed me to intervene, though, and maybe it was for the best, somehow. I stayed away from the old house, except to leave dinners and things on the doorstep. Once I was leaving some flour and coffee there when Vincent walked around the corner of the house. Without a pause he snatched up the goods and said, We'll take some more of those biscuits, too, when you got 'em. The back door opened and Maddie stood there, in a white dress I had made her long ago, framed by the dark of the house's insides. In the shadows I could see the corner of the kitchen and part of the old stove where my mother and I used to read books, and the doorway leading into the back room where she died. The house breathed out the same stale air I had breathed as a girl.

Maddie was staring right through me, staring so hard I had to convince myself that whatever she saw wasn't there, and that I was. Then she quietly closed the door.

It went like this for a few months, until Vincent disappeared. That's how I knew he had gotten her pregnant. I didn't need to search for a cosmic pattern this time — it hit me over the head like a shovel. Even after she began to show awhile later, Maddie didn't say anything to me. I watched her coming and going, leading with her belly. I waited, and when she was near due Maddie finally let me into the house. Even then I didn't want to go in. I remember the first trip over. Somewhere between my cottage and the old house I stepped back in time. My steps grew small and I watched the path at my feet, the gentle razors of long grass grazing my shins. A breeze picked up, bruised clouds rushed over, the light changed to another time. I could hear the river again, carrying the voices of loggermen downstream. I could see patterns in the long grass, and almost read them. And as I stood on the back steps of the old house looking at the kitchen door, Father rested his hand on my shoulder. In his hand I could feel the Indian arrowhead, its tip sharpened on his teeth and pointing now through the window at Maddie. I understood then that Father would never lie still in the ground as long as I was alive. His rough hands formed the dome of the sky.

Through the window I saw Maddie in the rocking chair, staring out at the gray horizon. She was waiting for Vincent. I stepped inside, pretending to close the door behind on Father, knowing that I was only walking further into him. Inside, the house was cold — Father's cold. The only sound was the rocking chair marking time against the floorboards. The past closed in around me, filling my ears and nose and mouth — warm fires and cold fires, stories by firelight, light of another world lighting my mother's face, the weight of the world on Father's shoulders, waiting and watching for something to happen, watching it watching us. I stood next to Maddie and looked out the window with her. Her belly was small and round like an unripe melon. Too small for being so far along, I thought. She stopped rocking and I rested my hand on her head, smoothed back her hair. We didn't need to speak. We watched the day fade toward that gray line in the distance. I wanted to hold her like I did when she was a girl, I wanted to tell her a story that would clear the foul air out of this house for good.

All the men came and went, and never came back again, I said.

Maddie started rocking again. I set about getting the kitchen in order, and made up a little supper for her. I did this every day. Vincent had done a little work to make the place livable — the stove worked, and there was a rickety table and chairs in the kitchen. The bedroom had a bed. I couldn't go in there but once, to gather the sheets and blankets for washing. The other rooms were still closed off, along with the parlor at the front, where I had once sat with my women, hiding my own belly and wondering where Brice was, what the future held, and where all the magic in the world had gone. Maddie sewed clothes for the baby and stared out the window and spoke even less than she had when she was a girl. She had stopped grinding her teeth long ago, but there was a churning inside her that was not the baby. My strange angel was traveling farther beyond than she ever had before. As a girl, her flying apart seemed to have a purpose, the way a caterpillar's transformation into a butterfly follows some unseen logic. But now it was different, less a transformation than a migration. Maddie wasn't waiting anymore, or searching for something. She was simply moving along with the days as they rushed toward their permanent exit.

She gave birth to a boy early one morning. He came out quickly, with a purpose. We were barely prepared before he was there, in Maddie's arms. She held him close to her dry breast while he mewled and shivered. I asked Maddie for a name. She whispered something in the baby's ear and he stopped crying and fell asleep. Maddie fell asleep, too, and I sat with them through the morning, watching. The boy would live, but with trouble. He was small and blue, and his skin was so thin I thought I could see his bones. The blue came out from deep in his bones. His bones were troubled. There was a sadness in them. He wrapped himself into a little ball, and Maddie too curled herself into a ball around him as they slept. A world within a world. I stayed with them all day. Maddie lay in bed while I tended to the boy, sleeping or staring up at the ceiling or out the window. When she held him there was no expression on her face, she just stared deep into his dark eyes. Deep in the night Maddie turned her head toward me and mumbled something in her sleep. It sounded like *marrow,* or *sorrow,* or *tomorrow*. In the morning she told me it was the boy she had been dreaming of. He had told her his name. Her forehead was damp with sweat, and she stared into the baby's eyes the way she stared into the field of long grass, hopeful and fearful of what she felt was coming.

*****

Morrow grew into his bones. A pale thing with a splash of dark hair spilling over his frail brow, he looked more like Brice than Maddie or Vincent or me. That's where his sadness came from, I thought, he had felt the dark thing in him that Brice had passed on. By the time it was passed down to Morrow, though, it had been watered down. It wasn't hard or sharp. Morrow would never hurt anyone with it, though it might hurt him. He seemed to sense this, and seemed stronger for it. He wrapped the knowledge around himself like a blanket, secure and comfortable in spite of it. He was a warrior.

Maddie was gone away for good, it seemed. She was barely able to keep house, to keep her family fed and clothed and warm enough inside Father's cold heart, and she was never really there. She spent her days in the rocking chair by the window, sometimes humming little songs from the past. She let me have Morrow. In the evenings I sent him back to the old house with foodstuffs and other supplies, but during the day he was all mine. He made me think of my other sons, and another life where he had uncles to escort him through the world of men, to teach him how to avoid becoming That Hayes Boy. My women didn't take to his company any more than they had Maddie's, and my business suffered more. I didn't mind. I didn't need the looks they passed over us — when I thought about this, it seemed like in the past I did crave those looks some, like I wanted some judgment passed down on me. I needed it less after Maddie was born, and now I didn't need it at all. It wasn't that I didn't feel guilty anymore for all my crimes. I was reminded of the evil creature I was every day when I looked at Maddie, or as I watched Morrow sleeping, his eyes shivering beneath the gossamer veils of his eyelids. I had hurt many, many people. I had brought pain to the ones I loved. But while I had a family near me, it was easier to surrender to all the things I had done than to struggle against it. They were a part of me, and without them, I would not be Tru. Much as I hated myself, I didn't want to be someone else. Not then. I made enough money to live, and that's all I wanted now, to live for Morrow, to keep him alive.

I tried to fatten Morrow so I wouldn't have to see his bones, but he rarely ate. He was like a little bird. I watched him sleep, and learn to crawl, and I saw his first footsteps, with his arms stretched out and panicky like he was trying to fly. Later I watched him play — he took a liking to drawing, as we all had. I still had some crayons Geoffrey had bought for Maddie, and some paper. And in the old house, I found more paper Father had brought home from the mill, brittle as dead leaves. I showed Morrow the books my mother showed me, and he held them like I had as a girl, not like Maddie had. I read to him as much as I could, and he listened.

Morrow could be still as air. He didn't play in the long grass, even in the summer when it beckoned softly to us in the breeze, unless I led him out there myself. I showed him the family gravesite, and pointed to where the noise of the rushing river came from, and told him never to go there. I taught him all the things I tried to teach to Maddie about the soil on our land and the things that grew out of it and the things that grew into it. Father did not approve. I showed Morrow Maddie's butterfly violets by the side of the cottage. They still grew strong, but weeds had been choking them out of the garden for years. We spent some time pulling the weeds out and turning the soil and giving the flowers some water. Morrow sat and looked and what we'd done.

What's wrong with Mommy? he asked. He kept looking at the flowers, as though he were asking them.

Nothing's wrong with your mommy, I said.

Doesn't she love the violets?

She loves them very much. She's just not much of a gardener.

I wondered if I should teach Morrow how to fight. He had the kind of quiet about him that people mistrusted. I remembered how good fighting felt, but also how bad it was. The world already knew enough of war. I kept him on the books instead. I gave him as many books as he wanted and he kept them in his room in the old house. He liked the math books most of all — algebra, geometry, trigonometry, physics. He read them before he knew how to read. One day when he was old enough I took Morrow to the school. He was happy there, and did well. After that I didn't see him as much.

I spent my suddenly empty days like Maddie, watching the old house and the open field. That was when I spotted the deer, dead, in the long grass. From my kitchen window I couldn't see the deer, I could only see a space in the field where there was no grass. I walked out and looked at it. I would like to remember that the deer looked peaceful, like it was only sleeping, but it didn't look peaceful, or meaningful. It only looked dead. I stood there wondering what I should do about it. I wanted to do something, but there was nothing I could do. I walked back to my cottage and busied myself with work from my women and making a dinner for Morrow and Maddie. When there was no more I work I looked out the window again. Nothing had changed, the grassless spot was still there, and the field, the graves of my family at the far end, the old house and the crumbling remains of the barn, and the silence that had grown over our land since the logging camps moved away, and Delamond spread further south. I watched it all, and kept coming back to the grassless spot and the dead deer, and the rest of the long grass waving in the waning light, and how time seemed like one short day, how just this morning I was a little girl running through the field, and now it was afternoon, the sun turning its back on our land and heading toward the horizon, and the long grass growing still, and very quiet.

Over time the deer rotted and crumbled into the ground. I was tempted to read it as a sign, and wonder if nature was trying to say something, but it wasn't. In nature, there are no mysteries but what we create. If a person lay dead in the long grass, nature would conspire to do away with the body, same as it did the deer. Vermin would pick at the flesh, and birds would take the hair for nests. Wind would dry and polish the bones. Rain would push them into the ground, worms would eat what's left. Nature wouldn't know the person's history, the person's name or dreams or victories or defeats. And if it could know, it wouldn't care. A person's history is a story we believe is true. Nature puts no stock in tales of that sort. In nature, everything is what it is, and what you see is what you get: wind, rain, birds, vermin, living, dying. But seeing a dead person, we ask unanswerable whats and hows and whys, and we invent funerals and stories of afterlives as answers. Sometimes the stories we tell live longer than we do, because we need them to. Sometimes they should die with us. Sometimes we kill them off when we shouldn't. The Hayeses could have learned a lot from nature, if we had been natural.

Though I didn't want to make things worse for Morrow by being seen with him, sometimes I couldn't resist walking him home from school. The other children were a little afraid of him, and even his teacher, Miss Kranz, watched him from a distance. Where the other children left the building in twos and threes, running and laughing, Morrow would emerge alone, and the others would part a way for him, nervous even to brush against him. He would walk out to me with the same blank face his mother wore as a girl, touching, but always moving away from you. *Tangent.* Morrow had a gentle and curious light in his eye, though, not Maddie's coldness. I should have taught him how to fight. It was only a matter of time before the others brought their wars to him.

By the time he was eight years old, it was clear that Morrow had special abilities. He understood the language of numbers, and could read the world through mathematics. And he was a chatty little boy, eager to talk about the things he read in his books and in the world, which was for him a magical landscape of equations he only understood a small part of. Baseball was all about the shape of the playing field, the speed of the ball and its arc as it flew through the air. Plants were interesting for the patterns of veins in their leaves and the repeating numbers of petals in their flowers. Morrow would lead me by the hand all the way home, and the world became a place I had never seen before. He would lead me back into the old house, too, ignoring me when I said I couldn't go in. Father let me in. He wanted me to see what I had done to the family, and he followed just behind me as I followed Morrow through the long dark halls. The house smelled of time passing slowly, indifferently, the air clogged with silent crowds of dust motes we had to push out of the way as we walked. I called after Maddie but she never answered. When she wasn't sitting in the kitchen she wandered the empty house as though looking for a way out. Sometimes we could hear her footsteps on another floor, or just the creak and pop of floorboards, or her hand brushing against the wall as she walked past Morrow's room, humming her little songs.

Morrow had moved himself into a bedroom on the second floor. The room was as dark and empty as the rest of the house — there was a bed and an old dresser, a curtain drawn against the view of the field, and the books I had given him arranged in a low wall along the floorboards, white candles standing at attention along the top. There were candles in the fireplace, too, and when he lit them they looked like a little glowing choir. My favorite of his books were the geometry texts. I liked the shapes cut by lines and arcs and letters and numbers. Beneath each design was a list of explanations — Morrow called them *axioms, postulates,* and *definitions.* They were full of symbols and Greek letters that made each design true. Morrow called the whole thing a *proof,* and I called each of these texts a book of proofs. The patterns were everywhere in the world, Morrow explained. We sat on the floor by the fireplace and he read the proofs out loud as I traced over the designs with my finger. Sometimes we invented new definitions, and called new patterns into being, still too young to see yet. Together, we were making a new world, a true world. When the world was finished, we played number games.

Twenty three times seventeen, I said. Go!

I began writing the numbers on a piece of paper while Morrow's eyelids half closed and began to flutter, and his hands, raised up beside his face, fingers crisscrossing and touching each other in a blur of motion, finished their calculations before I had the problem written out.

Three hundred and ninety one, he said.

I took his word for it. We laughed and clapped to drown out the echo of Maddie's footsteps. He couldn't explain how his counting worked. I liked it better that way. I liked the way he let me hold him. There was a trust between us. Except for my mother, my relationships with people had always been based on mistrust, or stories we wanted to believe. I asked Morrow to read from the book of proofs, and he did. He spoke in whispers, with reverence. I thought of Father Still, leading his service in Latin. Something had opened up to me then, and it revealed itself again now. It hovered in the candlelit air on the coded breath of Morrow's proofs. For a moment, there were no endings. There was only this quiet, floating Now. If there was a God he lived in the words passing between Morrow's lips, thin as a whisper and breathing out beyond the walls and the field. After a time Morrow stopped whispering, and I pulled him to me. We sat there in the glow of his math. Beneath his shirt I could feel his shoulder blades, like little wings.

I regretted the life I'd led most during the time I spent with Morrow, and when I had to leave him. He followed me out of his room and down the hall a ways, then stopped, let me kiss him on the forehead, then turned away. We were supposed to be a family. The house was supposed to be full of light and warmth. I wasn't supposed to go. I will always remember the way Morrow walked down the long dark hallway away from me in Father's old house. It was the same way he walked away from me in the courthouse a short time later — awake to the shadows, a little soldier, brave victim, stoic survivor.

I deserved my lot. I had to live with what I'd done. Still, I tried to tell myself our family could be an ordinary family. I had to try. And I had reason to hope it could come true, especially after Brice returned.

When I reached my cottage door, I noticed it was open a few inches. I never left it open like that, because animals would sneak in looking for food or a place to nest. Someone had been there, or was still there. Maddie never came over, and my women were like vampires — they never came inside unless I invited them. Everyone else I knew was dead, and didn't bother with doors. Once inside, I knew immediately that Brice had been there. His smell settled over every pot and table, book and bed. His musk and sweat, the smell of his sex and his war. It didn't look like he had touched anything, but something was missing, and I couldn't place it. I stood at the kitchen window and looked past the old house toward Delamond. Across the field, I imagined Maddie sitting by her own kitchen window. Above, I saw a pale glow of candles from Morrow's room, where he sat reading from his book of proofs. In another room across town, maybe Brice sat staring out another window. Hatred nettled my gut, and a warmth spread through my breast — it was hope. If I could have floated up above Delamond and pinpointed the location of each of my children and Brice, I was sure a pattern would have revealed itself — a new geometrical expression wanting a proof.

*****

Brice did not come back that night, or for several days after. My women didn't say anything about seeing him, but they all had something to say about the day Thora had gone to Filbert's for groceries, her dress freshly pressed, her hair combed, her head up. She had skipped past the canned goods and bought trimmings for a grand meal, and a steak from the butcher's. Everyone thought she had fallen in love, and speculated on who it was. Men's histories were examined and read in new ways. Everyone was a suspect. Several women even retold Geoffrey's leaving in light of an affair with Thora, and wondered if he might be hiding there now. There were things about Thora that Geoffrey could have loved, but there were too many things about he and I that he hated for him to return to these parts. Too many things to retreat from. Geoffrey wasn't a fighter. I wish I could have explained all this to my women. Thora's change had changed them, too, and much as

I hated them for their gossiping and bad stories, I loved watching how excited they were about it, like children at Christmas.

Something was happening. It was looking at me. This time, I didn't want it to pass us by. While I waited for Brice, I set about turning my family back into a family. Thora knew how to do this, too. I started with a proper dinner. I had money stored away that I was going to give to Maddie when she was ready to leave Delamond. Instead, there would be roast beef and Yorkshire pudding, fresh bread, cold milk, apple pie. There would be a warm fire, and we would sit down at the table and eat and talk, and gather around the fire afterwards and rub our bloated bellies and read stories from the books, and grow drowsy and nod off, dreaming all together.

I asked Morrow to sit in the kitchen and read from the book of proofs while I cleaned and made the dinner and cleaned again, then went upstairs to find Maddie. I never grew accustomed to the hallways. They were unusually narrow and high-ceilinged. I felt like I was walking lengthwise through the walls themselves. I imagined my ancestors must have been raised in close quarters, and when they bought this land they sought to expand beyond the confines of their past with a large house and wide open pastures, but in the end they couldn't build past their childhoods. They had been comfortable here, I remembered their calm as they moved about the rooms and the halls when I was a child. They weren't here anymore — they had vanished when I emptied the rooms of their furniture and their paintings. And though they had bored me as a girl, I missed them a little now. Maybe they had followed their belongings. Maybe they wandered the halls of strange new homes, getting lost in searches for the old drawing room, or for each other, and all over Delamond families frowned at the bewildering chills that chased through the house, and set another log on the fire, and wondered at the faintly creaking walls.

Only Father still lingered behind in the walls and the thick, chill air. He reminded me this was his house, his body and soul. He would not allow me a family here. This is what he said, shadowing me step for step. You disgraced our family. You killed your mother. Get out, get out. And I wanted to run but the walls seemed to close in like a fist. I thought I would be trapped if I tried to turn. Father was right, this was not my home. But neither was anywhere else. Tonight I would make a home with my children, we would settle in the kitchen downstairs and make it our kitchen, against the time before this evening, and the time to come, which waited for us in the night just outside the door.

I found Maddie in the room on the third floor I had stood in once as a girl, looking out the bay window onto Delamond. She was standing by the window looking down on Delamond, through the thin mist that descended every evening over the town, little lights shown up. Delamond was settling in for the night, families were gathering around tables.

Time for dinner, Maddie, I said.

Maddie turned to me, surprised I was there. Her pale face absorbed the moonlight and glowed. There was still a little life in it. Something glowed in her eyes, too — hatred and hope. She shivered and let me take her hand, and I led her downstairs.

I sat my children at the table and they ate like they were just discovering food after a lifetime of hunger. The fire snapped over the lush sounds of gulping and sighing. While we ate I kept waiting for Brice to walk through the door, hang his coat on the wall, and sit down to eat. I thought this dinner might somehow conjure him to the house, but it didn't. I knew he was out there somewhere, though, and for now, that was enough. My family didn't talk. We didn't need to. It was the best food we had ever eaten, and we didn't stop eating until everything was nearly gone. I saved a plate for Brice, and while I cleared the table I let Maddie and Morrow sit and stare. Even their staring was full and satisfied. After, I tried to pull Maddie's rocking chair near the fire, but she wouldn't let me. She said it was fine right it where it was, and sat in it, and didn't move. I laid blankets on the floor and Morrow and I kneeled beside the fire. He had picked out his favorite stories and he read them to us. Maddie watched the fire. She sat still. Some part of her was listening. I could see in her face a hint of my mother I had never noticed before, something in the gentle curve of her lips. The flicker of the firelight made her mouth look like it was trembling toward a smile. And in the crackle of the flames I could almost hear Father turning the pages of yesterday's newspaper, looking for odd jobs for odd folks, still full of hope. The whole room was full of hope, full of proof.

*****

When the stories were finished I carried Morrow upstairs and tucked him into bed. Maddie stayed in her chair. Without Morrow and his proofs, the kitchen had lost something. The fire in the stove had already begun to die, and the red embers had changed Maddie back from the glowing ghost of my mother into the smoldering creature Maddie had become in the present. Maybe it wasn't Morrow's leaving that caused the change, but my staying. This wasn't my home, there was nowhere for me to lie in this space we had created. I wasn't sad. Something of the good remained, there was still a little warmth in the stove. Maybe it would return again if I left it now. I wrapped a blanket around Maddie's lap and made my way along the dark path through the dark grass to my cottage. It was late spring, and warm. The moon cast a silvery light over the field of long grass, which was full and strong and wide as an ocean. Had we conjured this weather, too? As I neared my cottage I walked slower. I could already hear summer in the long grass as it brushed dewy kisses across my shins, my woman's shins — I wasn't a little girl anymore, yet a certain magic hung in the air as it had back then. I stopped at my door and looked back over the field, the old house. It was a new time. A pregnant time. Whatever was happening hadn't passed us by yet, after all.

And so, when I saw the door of my cottage was open again, and a little candlelight shone from the kitchen, I didn't hesitate, but walked right into the future. Brice sat at the table, where Geoffrey had sat, and before him, Father. I could almost see lines of white light connecting them all, growing brighter as they reached Brice here at my table, the warm candlelight in a wavering sphere around his head. The spell we had cast in the old house had worked after all. I had only been waiting in the wrong home. Brice's head shot up as the door creaked open, and he flinched backward.

It's you, he said.

It sounded like a proclamation. Suddenly I was me, a new me. I was Trudy, I was Tru, I was Gertrude, all together for the first time. *Convergence.* I gathered myself around myself for a moment while I looked at Brice. Brice was also new — the same thorny boy I had known, shot through with age and experience that made him appear more solid and permanent even than the brick wall downtown that still held fast to our last moment together. Brice had seen many things and learned many things. I saw them all written on his face. His dark hair had receded a little from the lines newly carved into his brow, but it still curled up and forward in a troubled wave, and his face was still a stone, all hard-weathered into rougher planes and edges. His glassy little eyes shone out from under his upturned eyebrows, and the long bridge of his nose, more rugged than I remembered, the wet, puffy little mouth, open a little, the jagged teeth inside, quiet now. His shoulders had broadened into strong, tired mountains. And his hands, curled around the candle, the long fingers I remembered, rougher now at the knuckles, and dirty nails bit down to the nub. While I looked at him I stood by the stove. The room began to disappear, until there was only the cool weight of the stove at my back. Formalities and pleasantries, too — how are you, you look wonderful, it's been so long, let me take your coat, can I get you something to eat? — all vanished as soon as I thought of them. Only the story of the past lingered in the shadows, and the question of the future spreading out in the steady candlelight between us. And suddenly, up through the soft hope that had been swelling in my breast, there rose another feeling, colder and hotter and thornier. It thrust itself up my throat and I spat it out.

Why'd you leave me? I said.

Brice looked at me for a long time. He wouldn't look away. He was afraid, but brave, and when he finally spoke, his voice was not the boy's voice I remembered, but a man's. He said, I was scared.

Then why'd you come back?

I waited for the explanation Brice didn't want to give me. I held his face in my stare. I thought about killing him, not for the last time. He saw what I was thinking. He wasn't afraid to die, but he wasn't ready to just yet. He opened his hands up to me. They were calloused and scarred. Then, for the first time since I'd walked through the door, Brice looked away, into the shadows.

I found my way to the war, he said. I didn't tell anyone where I was going. Not even my ma. I just up and left one night. I found a place where they didn't care that I was too young to be a soldier, and then I was in Italy, fighting. I was scared, real scared. I didn't make no friends in my platoon. I killed a lot of people — soldiers. It felt good for awhile. For awhile I wasn't scared no more. But then I killed one of our own. I think it was an accident, but I don't know. That guy had it in for me. We hated each other worse than the enemy. My gun went off while I was cleaning it. It shouldn't have been loaded, but it was. I don't know. There was going to be a lot of trouble for me, but the Army knew I wasn't old enough to be there, so they just sent me home, and made up a story about the accident. I traveled around awhile. I wasn't happy about anything.

I had nightmares about the accident every night. Everywhere I went, every new town, every new job, the nightmares followed me. After awhile, I started thinking about Delamond. Coming home. I had written my ma once, from Germany, but never heard back. I thought she was probably glad that I was gone, and'd be even gladder if I never came back. But then I started thinking about you. That was as bad as the nightmares. I couldn't get you out of my head, and then you were in the nightmares, too. Instead of the soldier, I was killing you. Night after night. That made me more scared than ever.

And? I said, still hating, still hoping. Brice looked at me again — afraid, curious, a little sad.

And so I came home.

You worried your mother sick, I said. Does she know you're here?

Brice shook his head. But she found out I was here the last time, he said. I came once before, you know. I went to the other house over there looking for you, but no one answered the door, so I came over here. I knew this was your place as soon as I walked in. I could smell you, and it looked like your kind of place. Clean, nice. I was just sitting at the table waiting when a woman ran in and started screaming Get out, Get out. She looked just like my ma, only younger, and crazier. I never seen the like. If I'd've had my gun I would've shot her, but I just ran away. When I got home my ma saw something had happened, and she got it out of me. She told me not to come back.

That was your daughter, I said. You would've shot your own daughter.

Brice looked like he had just been shot. Oh Jesus, he said. Oh Jesus.

He covered his face with his hands and sat like that for a few minutes, muttering to himself. I thought back to that afternoon I found my cottage door open. I had been inside the old house with

Morrow. Maddie must have seen Brice, but what had made her come running? Did she somehow recognize the father she had never seen? The father who had planted his dark thorn in our family and then run scared from us, only to embrace war and the slaughtering of strangers? The father who sat here now, head in his hands and crying like a scolded child? When he looked up again his hands were pulling his face down into a grotesque mask of pain. Oh Jesus, he said. His hands let his face go and his mouth popped up into a wide, awkward grin — a grin I remembered from our last afternoon together, just before he took me into the alley. I imagined he smiled like that every time he fired his gun at the enemy.

We have a daughter? he said.

If you smile like that again I'll kill you myself, I said. I was serious. But he couldn't stop smiling, not even through the shock of what I'd just said or the hard thinking he was doing now.

He said, But — but we could have a family!

We did have a family! You ass! Did you think about that at all while you were off killing people and touring the country? Did you think about me? Did you think about how you raped me and just left us here all alone? Do you know what this town did to your daughter and me?

I wasn't thinking, Trudy, he said. And I'm real sorry for it — for everything. I was just a scared boy.

My name is Tru.

Brice opened his mouth to speak, then stopped. He stared at me and thought. His face went soft and he looked like a boy again, the boy I had ignored in school, and had hurt, and who had given me what I deserved in a dark back alley. The pregnancy, the birth, Father's *get out* and my mother's death and Father's death, the endless stares and whispers, the stupid gossip of my women, the thousand disservices of all Delamondians, all clambered out of the shadows, and the loneliness, losing Maddie piece by piece, losing my sons, losing Father Still, the lost days staring out at an empty field. I wanted to kill Brice. He had started this. I wanted to finish it. I wanted to choke him to death and drag him out into the field where I could watch him rot like an animal. I believed he would let me — he was that sorry. I would have let him kill me, too, if he had wanted to. I believed we deserved to kill each other. Love is, after all, violent. I was only mad because I loved him, and didn't want to. I had stopped being angry with him long ago, that's why I couldn't say all the things I had thought about him over the years. But the thought of being angry, the habit of it, had stayed with me. I wanted to be angry, but I was in love, and that made me mad. But the dark thing that had raged inside him as a boy had turned into something else, maybe hope, maybe resignation. All the killing had helped him, I think. Such a price to pay for something that wasn't his fault. You don't choose love. You have to just get on with it.

What's my daughter's name? he asked.

Her name is Madeleine. She has a son. His name is Morrow.

Oh Jesus.

I realized then that I was still holding the plate of food I had saved for him. It had gone cold. I could have started a fire and heated it up, but I didn't. It was an accident. I set the plate front of him, got him a fork and knife and butter and milk. He stared at the food dumbly for a moment, then grabbed the fork and set to. He ate like the rest of my family had, but without the crackle of a fire, the sound of his chewing and slurping filled the kitchen. It was disgusting, and lovely. I would start a fire after all — just a small one — enough to warm us, but not enough to welcome Brice to stay.

I knew I was being ridiculous, telling myself that he might not stay, that I might control his coming and going. That anything had ever been uncertain. For a moment I even pictured us all leaving Delamond together, forever. That was ridiculous, too. I belonged to Delamond and the pattern of its history. What was I without Delamond? I imagined myself in another town, in the bustle of a big city, with a good paying job and clothes and food and a home — a home, a place that would be me and mine. Details quickly filled themselves in: ceramic dishes above the kitchen sink — running water! electricity! — and a table with flowers in the center, a small yard, a small dog, a widow living in the house to the left who needed help getting around, a young married couple to the right with cute nasty children who walked through my garden on the way to school. I would not be me in such a place, I would be someone else entirely. Such a normal, happy life was too believable. The place where I belong has always been more impossible, a place mine and not mine, on the edge of somewhere and nowhere.

I stood by the stove and blew on the flames and watched them struggle to spread, listening to the click and scrape of silverware on Brice's plate. I had raised Maddie by myself while Brice went off to fight his mad war. Yet, I reminded myself, Brice's madness had been there for her as much I had, protecting her and guiding her and tearing her apart. We had always been a family that way. But we could never be a real family. We could never be real. We would always only be someone else's gossip. Brice's being here was proof enough of the pattern that had emerged so many years ago in this family, when the wind first blew through the window of the old house. I wasn't undivided, as I had felt when I walked through the door. I could never be whole. What I had felt when I opened my cottage door to Brice had passed me by already. The pattern of our future was already set. I wasn't bigger than the pattern, I was only a fraction of it. There was no use fighting it. There was a certain comfort in belonging to something, no matter how ugly it might be.

While I warmed my hands over the fire, the door swung open. Maddie stood there, dark against the darker outside. She stared at me quietly, hardly breathing. Her white gown floated around her and her black hair hung down over her shoulders. Her beauty always struck me, so absurd and useless in this place, in this family.

Madeleine!, Brice yelped. He stood and backpedaled and smiled around a mouthful of pie. Maddie looked at him and his smile. She didn't move. Maybe I was wrong, I thought. Maybe it could work, maybe we could be a family. My breast was on fire with it.

Sit down, Brice, I said. Maddie, come in. I have something to tell you.

I turned to set another log on the fire, and that's when I noticed what had been missing after Brice's first visit: the shovel, the one I had used to bury Father. A few crumbs of dirt had dried against its empty space against the wall. Maddie must have taken the shovel when she chased Brice out. That's why she's here, I thought. To return the shovel. What had she wanted it for? And when I heard the sounds, the grunt from deep in Maddie's chest, the whoosh of the shovel flying through the air, the dull wet skullcrack and the heavy drop of Brice's body to the floor, the space behind the stove where the shovel had been all those years seemed to widen to a vast open field. It was all over, just like that. Without turning around I dropped the piece of wood I was holding and squeezed calmly into the open space. I could hear Maddie breathing. Then she dropped the shovel, and walked out the door. I stayed there behind the stove a long time, curled against the warm iron back of it, until the space shrunk again around me, and the warmth died and grew cold. When I opened my eyes I saw a few dry clumps of dirt from Father's grave just inches from my nose. Dirt as hard as a fist. Father had called out to Maddie that first evening Brice was here, made the shovel fill her vision of the future. I got up on my knees and looked out at Brice, laid out flat on the floor on one side of the table, his face a bloody pool, and the shovel by the door, a cake of red paste glistening on the back. Brice's fork waited on his empty plate, a normal thing, only missing the body and the hunger to attend to it. Maddie had left the door open. The night air trickled in along the floor, curled around my feet. Outside, a breeze wished by in the long grass. Then everything went quiet.

*****

By the time the first light crept over the horizon, I had buried Brice in the family plot, next to Father. Brice deserved a better place, but I believed he could hold his own against Father, and Father would come to regret what he had done. After Brice was in the ground I drove the shovel deep into the earth at the top of Father's grave, where it would stand as his headstone. I sat to catch my breath, and closed my eyes, and saw Brice in his final moment. I still see it now. Maddie heaves the shovel up over her shoulder and out. Brice sees it coming. The shovel is heavy — he has time to duck or fall out of the way. Instead he sets his fork down. A calm falls over him. He had not expected the end to come this way. He had hoped to die fighting his war, but the war has come to him. He is disappointed, and sad. The shovel swings further out, gaining momentum. He can see chalky white lines in the blade where it has scraped against rocks. Brice rests his hands on the table. He glances at me to say goodbye, and back at Maddie to apologize for everything. And as the shadow of the blade falls across his face a sudden dawning lights up his eyes — the pattern of our lives has come clear in the arc of the shovel finishing its round. There is no leave-taking without returning to something else. He and Maddie would both return to a better place. He would wait for me there.

And when I opened my eyes and watched the dim light of morning spread across our land, the rest of the pattern revealed itself to me. Within a day Thora would come looking for her son. She would bring the authorities, and everything would be found out. They would take Maddie away to prison or a mental hospital. The Delamondians would not let a whore raise a child, so they would take Morrow away, too. But they would make me stay here, a prisoner on my own land, where I would live out the rest of my useless days, alone with Father, waiting for an ending. Everything around me was always ending.

I was the ending. This suddenly came clear to me. I had opened the window that let in the wind that ended my family. I stood there and let it happen, as I had let Brice run away, and Father Still, and let Maddie fly apart, and my sons die in my womb rather than force them into the longer, slower ending that would be their life as Hayeses. That was my place in the pattern, the role I'd been assigned. I couldn't change it. The proof was already in place, the pattern was already true. But Morrow and I had invented new proofs, too, ones we hadn't seen right away. One of them was forming before me now.

I would gather up my children from the old house and bring them out to the family plot. I would wrap them in blankets and surround them in a perfect circle of books — a bunker. I would light fires in the stoves, and spread kerosene around the old house and my cottage. I would burn down the old house. I would burn down my cottage. From the gravesite, my family would sit and watch the fire spread through the long grass. We would listen for a fire engine while Morrow repeated the necessary proofs, adding strength to them, and we would watch our endings unfold in the flames licking at the sky.

February 11

Dear Traveler:

On the outskirts of a city far south of Delamond, your mother sits in a cold pale room gazing out a window onto a little patch of grass where people sit or stand or walk in circles. This is the Pinecrest Mental Health Facility. Don't let the romantic name fool you. It's a blocky beige building with hard angles, dark windows, and a high fence all around. People are brought here and drugged senseless and never allowed to leave. Beside the building is a vacant lot of hard packed dirt, and across the street sits a lifeless warehouse with a parking lot of tired old farm equipment. In front of the warehouse is a bus stop where you can sit and watch the sparse freeway traffic whoosh by, or read the graffiti markered and carved into the green plastic bench. The bench is a log book for travelers. Peace symbols and swastikas, names of passers-through, free advice — *Shit, Fuck, Get on that bus, Don't get on that bus, UR Krazy 2*. The bus comes every two hours, stops and hisses at you, and goes. On the sidewalk to the right of the bench there are ancient black wads of gum that form the pattern of the big dipper, and to the left, through a crack in the pavement, a dandelion grows and dies every year. You could sit here and watch the building for hours, days, months, years, hoping for a glimpse of your mother, but you'll never see her. You'll have to take my word for it. They won't let you in, they say it upsets her too much. They say she went berserk when she saw me and started clawing and pulling her skin off. They're liars, and when they see your grandfather's face in yours, they'll know you for a Hayes, and lie to you, too.

Your mother sits in a rocking chair inside, wearing a simple white dress with butterfly violets circling round the hem, neck, and wrists that I made her one year for Christmas. Her unwashed hair is long and black, her hands are dry and hard as the wood of her chair, and her eyes are black mirrors. She never speaks and only moves on her own to rock her chair. She smells like disinfectant, as though someone tried to scrub her craziness away.

What does she see out there through the window?

Your mother is not crazy, she is only misunderstood. It's my fault she's here in this awful place. To the orderlies, she is a mouth to feed, a body to clothe. They don't know her. They can't know her, but they don't even try. She inherited something from Brice, but it wasn't insanity. Brice was braver and more sensitive than most Delamondians, but he couldn't understand or control the dark thing inside him, which someone else put there — Thora, maybe, or Delamond itself, or God or the wind, who knows. Brice passed the dark thing on to Maddie, and she couldn't control it either. And neither could I. It took her apart and transformed her into something else. I'm not sorry for the strange angel she has become. To watch her change into this — it was as beautiful as it was heartbreaking. Now the pattern is clear to me, but back then I didn't see it unfolding as it did. She did what she had to do to become what she had to be. Is she at peace? She is what she is. She is home. That's all she sees through the window. How many people can claim they have never struggled against what they know they are? I wish I could embrace my role in the story as courageously as she has. I wish I was home.

Your mother always loved you, dear traveler. Can you conjure this — sitting in your room in the middle of the old house, reading your math books by candlelight. Could you hear your mother singing to you, then? She would sit in her rocker by the kitchen window, the creak of the wood like a metronome, and she would sing songs to you that I sang to her as a girl, that my mother sang to me. She had a sweet voice, like a small bird at dawn. The same songs over and over, while she rocked by the kitchen window, singing even after you went to sleep, and those sweet notes were coursing through your brain while you dreamed. Do you remember your boyhood dreams, dear traveler? You dreamed you were a prime number. You told me so. *Indivisible.* That was your word. And you dreamed of flying. But a prime number can be divided by itself — you taught me that, and Delamond showed us how, when the men sent you away and part of you stayed here with me. You never lost your knack for flight, though. It's what keeps you moving forward, and away from Delamond.

Your home is in the moving. Rest a page of the journal on the green bench, another queer message for another traveler. And at the fence of the asylum, push more pages through the bars and watch them scurry across the grass, searching for shelter under trees and bushes or at the front door. Your mother is watching you, dear traveler. She has been watching over you your whole life, and waiting for you to stop here. She will be at peace when you find a better place. She will meet you there. You will know her by a slight fluttering in the air around your ears and hands that vanishes when you stop, and returns when you start to move again.

February 12

Old Ed died yesterday.

Our gang was not to blame. Old Ed had not broken his hip. If anything, our mislaid plan landed him in the best possible position to be saved from the heart attack that killed him. The doctors said they were amazed he had lived this long considering how clogged his arteries were. He died before they could operate. It was as though his body had been waiting to be brought there before seizing up on him, in case it changed its mind in the course of events and wanted to live. The body is no friend.

Agnes was much worse. For this, we were to blame. She wore a beautiful black lace shawl of mourning, and since the news she had not spoken a word to the living. She lived in a constant state of departure. She was preparing to fly for Paris, always only one wing beat ahead of the death she had forgotten we were all rushing into. We watched her racing to and from the day room to her bedroom, attending to last minute details, piling her luggage up by the door, the corners of her shawl rising up at the corners when she ran. We let her go. She didn't understand how we could all sit around so calmly when there was so much left to do before the trip. She stopped at my rocker for a second, gripped my knees.

"Martha," she cried. "Do find my red velvet gown for me, will you? I believe I've packed it by mistake. You know Buddy loves me in that gown. We're going to a party as soon as I arrive. Buddy says some French poets will be there — Surrealists! Imagine!"

I wondered how much of this past was pure fabrication. Not that it mattered. Agnes believed it, she was there. But she was nowhere. I wondered why I didn't envy her more. It was because I have been nowhere too, and what drove Agnes' smile now was not happy excitement. When the boundaries of time and vision slip to reveal new worlds, or old worlds anew, it's not the thrill of opportunity that fills you, but the panic of finally understanding all that is already lost and only vaguely remembered. The impression of a dream. This was where Agnes was now, frantically packing her bags for desperate voyages across a globe as fragile as a bubble, yet still more stabile than this world, because it had not shattered yet. It takes a certain courage to travel this way. This world may be broken, but it is always here. That world may disappear completely at any moment.

It may be foolhardy to voyage there, but is it braver to live among the permanent debris and build cities from the shards of broken realities?

Our gang was broken up, too. Alice was mortified by what we had done and couldn't sit still for long. She had no other worlds to travel to, nothing to escape to. Stoic Tom soothed her in his way. They walked through the cold garden when checker games became too motionless. Alice hardly looked at him. She was lost to him. He hadn't spoken a word to me except with his eyes, remembering what I had done to Father Still, and now this. Helen carried on normally, as though everything were normal. She stuck to the facts: the hip was not broken, the heart attack unrelated to anything we did. She built a piecemeal armor from the broken reality and avoided the rest of us. When Marilyn asked about Old Ed and Agnes, I told her nothing. She had a long, private conversation with Agnes and came away with nothing. I know this because of the way Marilyn looked at me afterward, grudgingly conceding the battle. The other residents watched Agnes more closely, wondered when she would leave for good, but nothing else had changed. Old Ed was dead, that was to be expected. That's what we're here for, that's what we're waiting for. The fact of his death made its circumstances easier to forget. It was better that he was dead. It gave the others something to rebuild on.

Rebuild what?

With what shall I busy myself?

There was something important to discover here. I followed my feet through the home, kicking through the rubble to find it. I had been walking in the garden, too, pulling up dead plants, clearing the land. I would have liked to set a fire, a controlled burn I would lose control of, a purifying fire. In the garden I unburied a little stone I believed at first was an Indian arrowhead. I rubbed it clean. There were tiny flecks of something shiny in its rough grayness, little squares of a reflective mineral. They looked like hardened pages of a lost book scattered across the cold plain of a blasted planet. *Calcified.* When I found the stone it had been pointing east. I carried it to the eastern fence behind the pine trees and looked beyond the flat land to the wavering cars passing like insects along the distant road. That road eventually wound its way around to the front of the home and into the heart of Delamond. The stone in my palm seemed to point beyond the road, though.

I have spent my whole life looking beyond, seeing nothing. Have I grown up yet?

Onion was his usual self. He held to the facts, too. He doesn't understand death. He distracted us from our sense of loss with noisy games of Boggle and Yahtzee. "Life goes on," he said, "we must keep busy." He asked Helen to play the piano, and she did. She played nicely and her warbling, off-key voice seemed appropriate to this newly broken world. My heart lay in the middle of the day room floor, stinging and raw in the sudden air. It wasn't Old Ed's death that affected me, it was the death of something else. I mourned the same way after Brice took me in the alley, mourned for the same lost thing — the magic that had died and left the world a cold, hard thing. My eyes couldn't shut, and each minute of every day was a little stone added to a string around my neck. Last time, this feeling had passed. It took more time than I had left, now. When Onion asked Helen to stop playing she didn't, which also seemed appropriate. He tried to lead us in song but we could not sing, we had given our voices over to silence and rubble. We were listening to the sound of us, Helen's keening over what remained of what we called home.

Fed up, Onion looked to me and cried, "Hayes! A song for the audience!"

That word, that name. It pierced me this time. I was surprised at the sudden stab, the instant bloodlust rising up in my breast. That name had always hurt, but not like this. Time caved in on me. My past rushed up from behind and my future closed in before me. Everything was here, everything was now. I wanted to throw my pain back at Onion. It was time to teach him a lesson. I told him we needed to go, and his eyes wavered back and forth, unsure of me. This wasn't a game. He couldn't pass. He told the orderlies a story about errands and we were off in the jade chariot.

We didn't talk at first. I rode in the front seat for the first time, propped on one end of the seat like a rag doll at the edge of the Great Divide, dangling my little legs into that cavernous space beneath the glove compartment. I didn't know what to do with myself in all that space, and I didn't know what to do with my pain. The space and the pain seemed somehow related. The air and the light touched me in too many places. If I could have drawn the car closer around me I might have felt better. I had to say something, surround myself with my own air. As we cruised slowly through town I gave Onion a history.

"Here is Delamond:

"This is where I used to buy sewing supplies from a Mr. Inchbald, who only looked at me once, to call me Hayes. This is where a girl running by me took my hat off and threw it under the wheel of a passing carriage that wouldn't stop for That Hayes Girl. This is where I fought with the kids who called me Hayes. This is where they stood and watched me walk home from school and said things to my back. This is the church that wouldn't let me in. This is where they called me whore, and Hayes. And here, and here, and here, and here. This is where I used to imagine living with a husband and children. And here, and here, and here, and here. This is where my sons would might have worked if I hadn't let them die. This is where they would have gotten drunk and fought and beat everyone who called them Hayes, and where they would still be called Hayes. This is the alley where a boy taught me about love and war. This is the street where my world fell apart and never returned. This is the world I was left with. This is what it means to be a Hayes.

"Do we understand each other, Onion?" I said.

Onion's eyes shot at me, his mouth pursed. "Yeah, I get it," he said. "You call me Onion."

What a fool you are, Tru! A sniveling whiny brat!

We drove on in silence. I listened to Onion breathing. His breath was heavy, and his knuckles were white on the steering wheel. I turned the radio on. He turned it off. I watched his knuckles like barometers. Slowly the blood returned to them, and his breathing grew quiet. I put my hand on his shoulder and stared at him. I had never touched him before. He didn't seem to mind my touching him. His shoulder felt more muscular than it looked. Beneath the skin and fat and muscle, I sensed the bones and the blood. It was real, his body was real. He inhabited it, this wondrous, flawed machine, he took it for granted. My hand, too, felt prickly with heat. He let me touch him this way because he believed we were friends. He had always felt a part of our gang, and we accepted him into it too, in our way. Onion didn't do what our gang asked because we were experts of manipulation. He did it because that's what friends do. And all this time, the way we had treated him. He already knew what it meant to be a Hayes.

"Onion's a term of affection," I mumbled, trying for humor.

"The same way Hayes is?"

I could never tell before if Onion was joking or not. Now, for the first time, I could tell. He was, and he was apologizing, too. He was more complicated than I thought, or I was dumber. "Yes," I said. "The same way Hayes is."

"My name is Gilbert."

"My name is Tru."

I wanted to cry. I wanted to cry for the way I had treated Gilbert, but also for this strange world where people stand next to each other and don't see each other, speak but never listen, and for these little magical moments when we do.

"You want to know something funny, Tru?" asked Gilbert. "I'm allergic to onions."

We laughed out apologies and forgiveness. Gilbert had a beautiful laugh. His face scrunched up and a sort of hiccup erupted from deep in his gut, where the good laughs always come from. I had heard him laugh like this before, and now I remembered each time.

Gilbert turned the radio back on and we drove around awhile longer, and he showed me his Delamond. There were restaurants, a park to sit in, a theater, a church. This was where he bought groceries, this was where he rented videos, this was his favorite song on the radio, this was where he had jammed a parking meter and parked for free and walked around for hours one day when he was sick of being fat. This was where a girl had told him he was cute. This was where he wrote poetry for the girl, and after he found out she had said it on a dare, this was where he had written poetry at the girl. This was where he took classes to prepare for the college entrance exam, and this was the highway that would take him to the college he was working to save up for. Some of the people waved at him as we drove by. Most didn't recognize him. It wasn't a bad place to live. It was alive with hopeful stories.

We arrived back at the home in the last light of day. All the curtains were open. The residents in the day room were stiller than normal, and alert, as though afraid to move. They kept looking out the window. Across the street, dull golden dusk spread over the farmer's barren field. Marilyn stood behind the front desk. When we walked in she snapped her head up, then her face dropped.

"Where have you been?" she barked.

I let Gilbert do the explaining. I was tired and a little dizzy, and I wanted to lay down. Alice scampered over to me, led me into the hallway and pulled me to a stop.

"Agnes is gone," she said.

"What do you mean Agnes is gone?"

"She's run away, Gertrude. She had quite a bit of money. I saw it. I don't know where she got it."

Tom had gone out with one of the orderlies looking. Helen had shut herself in her room and wouldn't answer when Alice knocked. The orderlies on duty would probably be fired. At first everyone had thought Agnes and I took off together, then they remembered I took Gilbert somewhere. Marilyn was in a state. Even Gilbert might be fired. As Alice jabbered on I thought I should panic, too. Agnes might be in danger. This home would not be a home without Agnes. I would have to leave, too. I was angry with her for leaving again, but mostly I was calm, even a little relieved. It was a peaceful hangover from my drive with Gilbert, and I was in no hurry to get rid of it, especially now when things were taking a sudden turn for the worse. Agnes was gone, this time probably for good, but things were finally ending. Better to have endings than not. I couldn't be mad at Agnes, and I didn't need to be afraid for her. She was not in danger. She was like Maddie, who couldn't be touched by the world, or confined in it. Agnes had been in more danger here with us, with all our waiting around. Now she was moving again. Now she was happy. She would be happy no matter what happened to her body, even if it died. And though her body might die, she never would. She was always already in a better place.

"I'm afraid she'll land herself in Paris," said Alice. "Then what?"

"Then she'll finally be happy."

"But what will we do?"

"Nothing. Wait. What we always do."

Alice's face twisted up like a tornado. "Why, you're no help at all!"

"No, I'm not," I said. I didn't intend to be cruel. I was thinking of Agnes in Paris. Not the Paris overseas, but Agnes' Paris. I was thinking of Agnes making it there. I was sad to see her go. I was waving goodbye.

"She was our friend, Gertrude, or have you forgotten? She could be hurt. She could by lying in a ditch somewhere. She could be — oh — "

I held Alice as she cried. How long had it been since I held a child this way? Had I ever? I could write a story. It only depends on where you are. In this broken world the stories are more difficult to come by. There are only a few to go around, and they are gray things, worn thin. Difficult to leave them behind, though. Agnes had. But she had never really been anywhere else. Her stay here was temporary, a detour. I wanted to follow her. The nursing home was a sham. The hallway seemed somehow smaller, the walls thinner, as though I could punch a hand through them. Outside would be Paris. We could already be there. We just had to see it.

"She's right out there," I said.

Alice pulled away from me and ran over to a window looking out on a corner of the garden. "Where?" she said. "I don't see her."

"Not there," I said. "In Paris."

Alice looked at me. "When you first came here I didn't listen to the stories I heard about you," she said. "People warned me. Tom told me to stay away. He told me all about you. You and that priest and the convent and everything. I was nice to you, anyway."

"You were very nice."

"I shouldn't have been," she said. Her mouth was working, struggling to find the last word. "Hayes," she spat.

Alice stalked off to her room. I heard the door slam. I walked over to the window she had been looking out of. Just a few feet away I could see the edge of the garden, a few tree branches and shrubs, growing out past the limits of the yard. A branch hanging low under a thin blanket of snow waved limpidly in the twilight. It could have been Paris. It could have been anywhere. I could go there, too. When I walked over to the doors leading out to the back yard, the doors were locked. I could see out into the rest of the garden, where the rising moon was beginning to glow over the snow. This would be as close as I would get to it. I stood there looking out for a long time. From the day room I heard the spill of game pieces onto a playing board. As the moon climbed higher, the garden would darken. The longer I stood there, the heavier each minute grew. I could feel each one around my neck.

What good does it do to see something beautiful if you can't get to it?

The relief I had felt just a moment ago faded away. With Agnes gone, all the illusions we had lived by began crumbling around me again. I tried to hang on, but it was useless. I felt sick. I was in Delamond. If I didn't end it I would be here forever, watching everything always ending around me. I walked down the hall past the resident rooms. I walked slowly. I couldn't hear my own footsteps. I stayed in the middle of the hall as I went, to feel the space all around me. The air was stale and hard. There were sounds, but they were distant. Most of the residents kept their doors open just slightly, glowy lights seeped out and the small noise of television audiences laughing and clapping. I peeked in as I passed these rooms, saw the corner of a footstool with a bath towel draped over it, an empty pair of shoes half-tucked beneath the foot of a bed, a paperback novel split open and resting on the arm of a chair. Other doors were closed, thin bars of light at the bottom, and others opened onto nothing but darkness. Each room was its own little world, and I was outside them all, seeing, unseen. I stopped at Alice's door and knocked. Knocked again. There was no light on. "Go away," she said. Across the hall I glanced at Helen's door. It was open a crack, and for a second, a dark sliver of her face appeared there. When she saw me she closed the door and played an opera record. I banged on the door. She turned the volume up.

"It's all over, Helen," I said. I pounded a fist on every word. "Over, over, over."

A door down the hall opened and an old woman's head poked out, scowling. "Keep it down!" it hissed.

"Oh, piss off."

I came to the end of the hall, which branched in two directions. My own room waited at the end of the hall to the left. One of the lamps in the wall had gone out. To the right, through a thick silence, I could see the door to Agnes' room. I chose the right. I stood in her doorway and flicked on the light. Her room was the same, crowded with little photos and paintings and letters and books. Someone had piled the suitcases she had set by the front door on her bed. A bit of red velvet poked out of one, like a tongue sticking out at me. Her perfume lingered in the air, smell of faraway places, better places. She would never tell anyone what that perfume was. The room felt like she had left a minute earlier and been gone for years. I took a step in to unpack her things, then stopped. She may send for them, I thought. Then another thought came immediately on its heels, a sentence floating up from some book I had read long ago: *And they never saw her again.*

I turned to the sound of footsteps behind me. It was Helen and Alice. They were in their nightclothes. Helen had a bluish paste smeared all over her face. They looked into Agnes' room. We all stood there looking into the room. It made us forget who we were, and the things that had just passed between us.

"It's so full of her," said Alice.

"She didn't take much along," said Helen.

"She doesn't need much, where she's going," I said.

"Do you think she'll be OK?"

"Nothing can touch her," I said.

"Do you think she'll miss us?" asked Alice.

"I hope not," I said.

Alice started crying again. Helen pulled her close and got a little dab of paste on Alice's forehead. Tom came around the corner quickly. He walked like he was made of wood. He stopped behind Alice, who rested her hand on his shoulder. Tom looked into Agnes' room shrewdly, as though calculating some practical matter we never would have thought of. They hadn't found Agnes. The police had been notified. When a runner makes it to nightfall, she either makes it all the way or she has an accident.

"We could make Onion take us out looking tomorrow," said Helen. "We can search all day."

"His name is Gilbert, and we don't have to make him do anything," I said. "He'll go if we ask."

Helen raised her eyebrows at me. They were all looking at me, all the eyes of Delamond. The difference between them and me came clear once again. They had been able to escape themselves more easily than me, leave their real selves behind and play at being what they once were, or being something else entirely. It was easy for them because they never really wanted to leave themselves behind forever. Why would they? Delamond was theirs, and they were comfortable. I belonged to Delamond. Our play wasn't play for me. I had always been Tru and That Hayes Girl at once, and not always certain which was one was real. Only Agnes managed a total escape, or had she? What you run from fuels your flight, even if you manage to forget it. She was faster than the rest of us, had more fuel to burn. I felt myself burning out, the exhilaration of speed had worn off. I had had my fun, but I wasn't a child anymore. All we are is a silence slowly filling with words. And when there are no words — what is older than silence? I saw our gang drifting away, cold stars growing smaller in the night sky. I could fill myself with words again, I could make every breath into a song, but now all I heard was the silence between the words and the stories, the silence of the grave and the black night sky. I wrapped it around me.

"I'm tired," I said. "Aren't you all tired?" They must have been exhausted. I was exhausted. "Agnes was tired, too," I said.

I watched the distance grow between us, until whatever might still have connected us stretched to a single strand of light, and broke. Alice and I would never make amends, Helen would never know me. Tom would go on believing what he believed about Geoffrey and me. It was too late for regret. My friends were a distant constellation now. I whispered goodnight to our gang and walked away. The hallway narrowed to a distant point, a doorway. I crossed over and stood just inside my room, examining it. I had always ordered things, there was no mess. The bed made, chairs pushed in, clothes put away. On the dresser, a few empty perfume bottles Agnes had given me — to spice the suite, she had said, but I had never seen the sweet in my room. The walls were bare, the curtains always closed. My view looked over a fence at Highway 8 curving into Delamond, but I couldn't see the city itself. I only ever saw people traveling from here to there, or there to somewhere. There is no smell to my room, just a stale warmth that carries a hint of dry age, like an abandoned hayloft. The light is dim.

I told Agnes once that I didn't need things, didn't want things. Even then I had tried to strip myself of the little belongings that told my story, even as I wrote new stories. Even as I write this sentence. Maybe I didn't need her, either. She didn't need me, anymore. Maybe she would write me from Paris, long letters on the backs of paper café menus composed as her gaze drifted along the Seine. Or maybe not. I let her go. I let all my things go. Nothing here was mine anymore except the journal in my hand and my pencil, hanging around my neck on a piece of twine with all the minutes that had passed. I sat on the bed and opened my journal. I liked to write in bed. After years of sitting at a kitchen table to do everything but sleep, I quickly accustomed myself to this unexpected luxury. I shifted into the mattress, finding my spot. Something dug into my hip. In my pocket I found my needle and thread, and set it on the nightstand. There was something else, too, the rock I had discovered in the garden. I turned it round, catching the dull light in the silvery flecks embedded in the rough gray surface. My little world-book. Tomorrow I would throw it into the field beyond the eastern fence. It would belong to the field. Nothing would come of it.

For now I set it on the nightstand beside the sewing things and found the first blank page in my journal, licked the tip of my pencil. And as I looked at the blank page in my lap I saw myself in the future — now, sitting here writing this line. As I sit here now writing this I see myself then, staring at the blank page. I cross over and cross over again, never stopping, never finishing anything. I haven't seen the dead hovering around for some time, they're busy settling into my journal. Agnes knew it would happen like that. She wanted me to leave them behind that way. And it hasn't been as difficult as I thought to tell the stories, to testify against myself to the dead. But all this time, it hasn't been the hordes of the dead that have scared me so, or leaving them behind in stories with endings. Even the writing itself has been a sort of cold comfort. All this time, there's only been one place I haven't left behind, and one person I've been afraid of. I have always been nothing more than my back and forth traveling — running away from Father and the old house — touching my hand to worlds as I pass, setting them in circular motion. And Father still lurks about the old house, and the old house has become my mind. Some endings are as easy as setting a fire and watching it burn, but others — I'm afraid, I'm afraid, I'm afraid.

February 27

Dear Traveler:

I remember a birthday party, revelers riding on cheated medication to faraway destinations, a silver bell ringing through time, a night sky full of stars shining in my forehead, beginning and ending points, a journal waiting in my lap. Waiting for me to make a choice. I made my choice, and it's led you and I here. If I stop now, I will never die, but I will not be living, either. You will be stuck here too, and I can't let you stay, welcome as you are. You have your own purpose to prove. If you start again, you know you are living. To start again, you must find an ending. I have tried before to write my own endings, and failed. This time, at least, may I fail right.

You pack your things in the dark. The warm, late winter air is heavy with the smell of rain, and a moist breeze has washed away the bitter reek of the paper mill. For the moment, Delamond is clean. You are the first to sense it — the rest of the town is asleep. Your joints ache dully, but you are ready to go. The night is a time of leaving. You cannot stay here any more than you could stay in your former life. Stand in the center of the dark room and listen. The breeze passes through the window and rouses the dust in the corners of the room, the dust carried in on the shoes and shoulders of countless travelers from countless distant cities, the travelers who once pressed you along a dream sidewalk as you watched your body fall to pieces. The world is a small place, contained in this room. Time folds easily as paper, and death is so much nearer to us than we know. You have only the endless time of the stories in the journal in your hand. This is where we have waited for you. Drop a few pages behind, on the floor. This is where you must leave us, scattered in travelers' dust. Outside, the night is passing. Pick up your suitcase and close the door behind you now. Follow the night.

You leave the room key on the front desk. The door behind the counter is closed, and beyond it sleeps the manager and his wife. They will be relieved to find you gone, and they will be suspicious. They will search your room and wonder at the torn pages scattered across the floor. They will read a few and try to piece them together and fail, though they will feel vaguely disturbed by what the fragments hint at. They will make up a story to tell the townspeople about you, and at night they will lie in bed together silently, staring at the walls, wondering what the pages mean and why the person lying next to them seems suddenly like a stranger. They will converse in their sleep and wake with forgotten knowing. You will not feel avenged by this. You will feel nothing at all. You are the knowing.

You walk, follow Main Street all the way up the lip of the kettle. You pass through the millworkers' neighborhood quickly, the squat houses with front doors yawning open, windows boarded shut. Further on, the road straightens and narrows, becomes a dirt trail, and the land opens to farmland and falls away into pale morning mist. A cloud of hazy dust rises up behind you and obscures where you've been. Smell of pine and manure and cool earth under snow that stays until April. No trace of the mill, which is downwind. I haven't felt this air in years and years and years. It smells lighter here, as though it has traveled from a great distance on its way to another faraway place. You can taste the distant cities on your tongue. The trail curls toward our plot of land. Father is standing in the field watching us approach. He tries to convince himself this is nothing to be afraid of, and he sets his jaw against our coming and fingers the arrowhead in his pocket. When you arrive, the silence of our land immediately rushes to you on the wind, squeezes you like a giant hand. Father's hand. You breathe it out and it and loosens its hold. This silence is a part of you.

The trail stops at my cottage door, or where the door used to be. There is little for you to look at here, dear traveler. My cottage is a burnt black rectangle in the ground. Brave and hungry weeds shoot up and around it. They do not care what had happened here. Nature knows a different justice than that of mankind. Step through the char into the open square, barely larger than your old room at The Manor House. There used to be a table in that corner where I made my family dinner and where my children used to draw pictures and do their homework. There used to be a rocking chair here where I used to sit and watch them. The nights were cold, our lives were blind. I see myself, stirring potatoes at the stove, glancing out the window, listening for my children. Or the quiet sound of crayons rubbing on paper, sunlight reaching for shelves of pickled vegetables, the click of a coffee cup on a saucer, the needle and thread and the chattering voices, then the wind brushing by, the days flying into still, watchful nights. Father is in the night. Father is in the land, the long grass, the sky, the water, in all the wood of my cottage. His hand is in the red paint on the front door. This was not my home, this was Father's home for me. I gave birth here, I raised children, made a living. I had a life and was happy sometimes. But always there was Father, Father on all sides, looking in on me looking out. And everywhere I went, I carried this land with me. The sun always exposed the disease in my heart, and when it stormed, the thunder was the sound of Father gnashing on the arrowhead in his mouth. I never knew how to leave it behind, because I was nowhere.

Nowhere = Now + here.

Now I draw my old self to me — all her rage and desperation, I hold it to me. It has been waiting for me here all these years, and it comes to me now like an infant to its mother's breast, and cries out. It tells me again the story of my children, Maddie, slowly ripped from my side by the same invisible forces I once hoped would unite us all again, Hayeses and Delamond, and my sons, born dead and still knocking at their casket walls in a convent cemetery, and Morrow, thrown mercifully and cruelly out of our orbit but sent for now with these little words. It tells me what a fool I have been, what a child, what a sinner, what a monster, to hurt the ones I loved and to seek an explanation in an unknowable fate. It tells me everything, the pain and the injustice, the helplessness and fury, until I think I will split, but I hold it to me, afraid to let it go, afraid to lose this part of me though it hurts me, because it is mine. So little in this world has been mine.

You look out toward the old house. From here it looks like a giant, black beast laying low in the grass. You stare into the air above it, try to picture yourself as a boy peeking out of one of the windows. You cannot see it. Now you are old. It has taken you your entire life to reach the place where your life began. You can still see the faint remains of the footpath that lead away from my front door to Father's back porch, little more than a scar in the grass. The land has not waited for you, it is eager to forget. The long grass lies in a tangled carpet of brown leaves and mud. The old house seems another lifetime away. You look down at your pants and his shoes, soaked in dew and mud-stained. You used to hate getting wet this way, and the damp that clung to you the rest of the day. It seems a small thing now, a thing of the past. You follow the hardened rut to the old house, and your hands push aside the ghosts of long grass, still feeling its sharp slip across your wrists. You watch the ground, the present parting at your hands, the green grass parting just ahead of each footstep. In the shadows before your feet I think I catch glimpses of the dark heeled boots of Father. Is he leading me on or walking away? Don't look up. He won't be there.

By the time you reach the back porch of the old house your hands and feet are soaked and freezing. You stand beside the foundation and follow the black line of it around with your eyes. Here too, the burnt remains of the house have nourished the soil, and dormant shoots of grass and vine lay over the silent wood, holding it fast even in sleep. On the other side of the house, the hill dips down to the town below, where lights and the tops of the downtown buildings show through the fading mist. To your left, what used to be a proud pine forest has been cleared away for the development of new homes, whose tall peaked roofs jut out of the thinned pine like spear tips and dully reflect the pinkish sunrise.

Miraculously, the four wide porch steps leading up to the old back door still stand — burnt and rotten, leading up to airy nothing. It took a long time for the firemen to get here. They didn't care, the fire was a blessing, the old house another ugly reminder of something everyone wanted to forget. I have not forgotten. I see it all now, measure imaginary steps through demolished hallways past my bedroom to my parents' bedroom. There's the corner where my mother lay dying, where Father found the coward's way out. There's the kitchen, where the table had stood and where I had colored so many pictures, invented stories to tell my mother. The burned out husk of the stove is still there. Father had paced back and forth before it, I can still hear his heavy tread. I can still smell the tea he brewed for my mother, and the cinders the house has become. I wonder if, as a little girl, some of the presence I had felt in the house wasn't my future self, my now self, looking in. I can see her now as she stands in the kitchen staring out the window.

Her father is wandering the field in the twilight, looking for something lost. He is harder to ignore when he's not inside the house. Inside, his quiet makes him feel empty. When he is outside, the emptiness he leaves behind is unquiet. The little girl's mother is laying in the next room speaking to the air. I see the mother twisting in her sheets. She knows she is dying. She calls out. I sit beside her. I remember so little of her, only the invisible world she saw, which became my world, too. She wants me to see it again. I lay a hand over her brow and say goodbye. She opens her eyes and looks at me, staring into the remains of a life, and says, Are you sad? *Breathe.*

Back in the kitchen, the little girl that was me presses her hand against the kitchen window and follows the light of her father's lantern through the dark toward the barn. When she draws her hand away she stares at the steamed imprint of her fingers on the glass. I try to say hello to her, I try to tell her that she will survive. I tell her she is a part of something larger. I tell her she is loved, then I tell her I have to go. She turns round into the kitchen and stands there, listening. I think she catches an inkling of me, she glances around the kitchen with a little smile. Then the smile fades, and everything else.

Walk into the house, dear traveler. You can see it, too, in the burned and rotten wood beneath your feet. You never knew your great grandfather, but he haunted you, too. He was the coldness slumbering restlessly in the walls, dead but dreaming. He wanted to keep you here, he wanted you to lift the family name up out of the disease in the land. He still doesn't understand that he is the disease, and though you left long ago and his daughter has finally passed on, he still haunts the land and his old house. He has forgotten why he stays here. His anger has become a routine. You still feel his coldness in the dark empty hallways, in a room full of white candlelight, a boy kneeling on the floor, a book of proofs spread open before him. His classmates have been teasing him about his a crazy mother. He told them it wasn't true. Prove it, his classmates taunted, and here the boy was, before the book of proofs, looking for the axiom to prove his wish true. The formulas and the drawings make visible the secret form of things, yet they cannot change the pattern that has been set for us. Down below, he hears his mother singing, but he can't hear the words. The words are important. The words are the proof. He follows the sound down the hall and the stairs through the darkness he has grown up in and into the flickering kitchen. His mother sits in the chair by the window, singing and staring out. The boy touches her hands and her bare feet. She is cold and hard as winter wood. He climbs into her lap and she stops singing. He looks through the window. Across the field of long grass he can see his grandmother's cottage, a candle in the window and the pale form of a face watching him.

Keep singing, Mama, he says. But the words have frozen and shattered in the cold of the house.

You turn your back on the old house and balance on the highest step of the porch, looking into the flattened clumps of frozen grass, the darker mud beneath, and the dark within the dark rising up to you. If you fall from this step you might fall forever. At the far end of the field, the familiar copse of trees still stands at the property line like an exit. In the summer, when the long grass was green, the long grass surrounded you like a sea of water and stretched away forever. Now in the winter, the dead grass lying frozen in the mud, the land seems a small, hard thing closing in on you. You are an old man now. You could turn around right now, find the road and walk away, but you would never be able to leave. You would trap the boy in the journal's pages and track Delamond's mud all over the world, and the world would imprison you in your memory. You didn't live out your life here. If you take it with you now, it will suffocate you. You are not the Morrow of the journal, but something else besides. After today you will only be something else. Step into the dead grass. Long ago I tried to show you the joy of running through the long grass in summer, and you played along. Now I could not persuade my legs to run, even if the grass rose up fresh and green to greet me. When I was a girl in this field I hadn't thought about my body. I was my body, it needed no prodding, it followed my thoughts immediately. Now it is stubborn, at best, a cantankerous mule. My body is not my home. Now my mind is a separate thing from my body. Growing up means growing apart.

You watch your feet as you walk, looking out for gopher holes and dead deer. Pale yellow sunlight burns away the low mist. You are surprised at how separate the world of the ground seems from the world above, how vivid and real, yet secreted away and unknown. It seems larger, too, and fills your vision. For a second you feel dizzy and stop, glance behind. You have come farther than you thought. The porch you stepped off is a small dark shape on the horizon, and your footprints are a faint, broken line through the mud, easily lost. Above, the bustling clouds muscle out the sun and the field dims, yet the rising daylight seems to open the sky to the land. At the edge of the field you see pieces of a fence. An old oak off to the left droops down into the ground. In the far distance beyond our land, you can see a low ridge of blue hills beneath a ragged rash of storm clouds, and in between, a vague white line, like the torn edge of a page.

When you make the fence line you stop. The fence is little more than an occasional wooden post tilting out of the ground sprouting broken strands of wire disappearing in the grass. There's a little clearing to your right, and you make your way over. Your stomach tingles. You curl one hand into your pant pocket and the other around the journal and squeeze them, trying to pump warm blood back into them. In the clearing, there sits a row of graves — five low mounds pushing up through the bramble. The two mounds on the end are barely recognizable for what they are —

your great uncles' graves. Two worn gray plates of stone lean back from them into the grass, unreadable. The next closest headstone is a rough stone slab chiseled into a rectangle and painted white. Nearly all the paint has chipped and worn away, along with your great grandmother's name. Beside her lays your great grandfather, marked by the rusted blade of the shovel used to bury him. The fourth mound is lower than the rest because it is empty — Thora took Brice's body away, but his marker still stands, the wooden stake with the dog tags hung over it.

You stand and look at your family, wanting to say something. You wanted to belong to something, a family you knew was yours, and a home you felt comfortable in. In spite of the purpose that brought you to Delamond, you were hoping to find these things, but all you've found is the remnants of a collection of strangers struggling to fly from one another, and failing that, to kill one another. Dreamers and killers, dumb and deranged, they are no better than the town they lived in. They became everything Delamond said they were. There is no home here to belong to. You want to be angry with us, you try to close your hands into fists, but your body will not obey you. Your body is a channel opened wide for the ocean of longing you have been drowning in — how long? The ponderous weight of a lifetime of searching for something that dissolved if you looked at it too closely. It was never there. The unlived life and the sham life, they were never real. You have been driven by fictions, we all have. You could try to be angry at Delamond — its hand buried us long before we died — but what would be the use? I tried hating Delamond, too. The problem was bigger than Delamond. We would have been Hayeses anywhere we lived.

If you need something to hate — the last is grave is mine. It has no marker because it's empty for now, but you can say whatever words you like over my burial. The dead have been calling me home from the start. From the first day of this journal they have been leading me here, to these graves and this page. And I think I understand now what the dead wanted from me. My journal has become a mirror, and a mirror can be a doorway — to a better place? Tired of their endless traveling, they had a destination in mind for all of us. I'm so close to it now I can feel Father from the grave, black waves of silence pouring off him.

When I was a child, Father, you demanded something I couldn't give you. You wanted me to be something else, go somewhere else. You told me so with your wordless hurt. You clothed me in your silence and your hatred and your loneliness, and the very thing that bound us together also drove us apart. We all wanted to be something else, somewhere else. Mama made it. You left yourself behind, too, but you never found anything new. One by one your family died off around you, your land grew barren, and I shamed you into death, where you waited for me.

Now you lie before me, still silent. When I was a girl I hated how you never spoke, I hated what your silence said. Your diseased land spoke for you, and your cold, dark, empty house, they told us you were eaten from the inside, and hollow. And you're still waiting for me to give you what you think you want. I told Mama stories and she spoke to invisible worlds, but you never heard a word to show you the way back to yourself. The only words you spoke yourself were, Get out. And I did. I searched for something else, somewhere else. I was afraid, singing against the dark in my cottage, watching your house watching me. I was just a girl, and then you died. Even in death I was afraid you were disappointed in me. I was full of hate, making clothes for women who scorned me, doing business with men who called me whore and Hayes. And I was full of hope, falling in love and giving birth and watching the long grass return each year, growing up over your grave and around your house. I became a woman, and strong. But you never went away, and I could never forget you, or stop fearing and hating you. Because you felt the same for me. I hurt many, many people. People I loved. I found many wonderful and terrible things, but I never found anything new, and in the end I wound up right back here, with you. And I feel like a little girl again, trembling and full of hurt and hate. But not without hope, now.

We are not so different.

You were an avid reader, too. Pacing through the days, searching through the long grass — you were reading for a sign to point us to a better place. You didn't find it there, you bought me books, and the books spoke for you, too. But I wasn't listening to you then. I hear you now. I remember all the stories. They were full of magic and hope. For a time, we all were. You gave us that. But they weren't our stories, and they couldn't take us where we needed to go, and everything began to die. When I was a girl I used to watch your hands, strong and calloused and paper cut. I wanted to read those thin red lines and feel them wrapped around my own hands. There was a story in your hands that you never shared, and there was strength, and protection from the world. You never held my hand. I had to read other things. I wrote new lines — here, in these pages. Are you listening? This is our story. Now, here. I have been writing, and I have become something else. I am Tru. I am the words you never uttered, I am the story you were afraid to tell. Are you proud of me, or ashamed? Would you open your arms to me or throw me out? The time for choosing is already gone, Father. It looked at us as it passed. I am the word now, the word that will bury you. Hold it close. Climb into your earth and don't be afraid. There is no better place for us.

*****

Severance. Dear traveler, what you bury in time, grows. My time has already sprouted and ripened into dully glowing words hanging like ambered fruit in a midnight garden. I lose myself there, on narrow paths lined with ripened days dangling from knotted vines. I touch them as I go, and they fall into the earth behind me — Father's hands, the dark, remote landscape of the twisted sheets over my mother's dying body, the perfect blue of a summer sky and the warm breeze around my knees, the rough rub of a cold brick wall against my cheek and the sound of Brice's gnashing teeth, the depthless gaze of my newborn daughter, the averted faces of townsfolk and the unabashed stares, the sweetly curled incense in the Church of the Assumption and Father Still's Latin chanting, Geoffrey's warm hand on my bare shoulder, the click and scrape of hopeful dinners with my hopeless family, the wet sound of a crushed skull, dull thud of earth over loved ones who never knew me.

I loved you, how I loved you all. I will bury no more family. They do not stay where they belong, but turn like jeweled fruit before my frozen eyes. How long have I been sitting here? I am sorry for my sins. I loved you all. When did it become so hard to move my limbs? I can feel their breath on me now, chilled whispers, I can make out their words. I'm afraid, I'm afraid, I'm afraid. Their hands, let them bury me instead. I have done my work. I will miss you, my family. I will miss you, Agnes. I will miss you Tom and Alice, Helen, Gilbert. Even you, Old Ed. I will miss you, Morrow, and I will miss you, Tru. I have written my stories. Look at me, dear traveler, watch me turn, my hardened eyes, my amber heart.

Now tear me apart and bury me. Give the memories back to the journal's pages, and tear them out and let them go. The pages scatter on the breeze. A few get up in the branches of the old oaks, strange fruit for curious passersby. Some tremble and cling to the wet, weeded headstones. Push them into the earth. They dampen in places, soaking through, and the penciled lines smudge and run. Other pages lift into the air, flutter over the field like white butterflies and settle in the long grass, or find their way to the burned out foundations of the old house and the cottage, waiting for Nature run its course. The storm clouds are approaching, heavy gray beasts in a slow march across the sky with nowhere to go.

You walk back through the field toward the road, dropping the last pages as you go. When you reach the beginning of the road at the doorstep of the cottage, something by the wall catches your eye. Reaching up through a bramble of weeds is a bunch of withered butterfly violets. You pull one out of the ground. It comes eagerly, as though it had grown only for this moment. It is a sad little thing, begging to die. You knew some happiness here, dear traveler. Much sadness, too. You knew you would have to leave someday, didn't you? That was the blueness showing through in your bones. You didn't want to leave, but the pattern was set. You were trying to understand the why of it in your math books, but we couldn't conjure a proof against it. You still can't stay. You are the pattern's motion. It hurts, but it's only memory. You pull the flower petals away gently and bury the stem where you found it. The petals scatter with the journal pages. Everything falls quietly into place. You pick up a blackened length of wood. What had it been? Now it is only a blackened board. Throw it, watch it fly end over end and land somewhere. No one will ever touch it again.

You feel the comedy and the horror of all your real and unreal lives dissolve together and tingle uncomfortably deep in your gut. It skitters around the walls and rises up into your chest. For a moment you think you might throw up. You hold your hands to your belly and feel the painful tickle rise up to your throat, stick near your Adam's Apple, then skitter out of your mouth as a little laugh, a brittle, shimmering thing beating a way through the air. It is sad and hateful and comical, beautifully absurd. It is all that you ever were crystallized into bittersweet, breathy hardness and delivered onto a random passing wind. Watch it go. Eventually its atoms will disperse into the air. It will spread across the entire planet, affecting weather patterns in Chicago, Paris... It will span the distance of time and reach down to me as I sit by the window with the gift of a journal in my lap, starlight mapping the lines on my face.

You don't get away with anything in this family. You just get away. Get out, now. Step onto the road. The longer you stay the harder it is.

What now is the word for home?

As you walk, your feet kick up a dust cloud around you. For a moment you lose yourself in the haze, then a sudden wind pushes it away. The new houses are still there where the forest once stood, and the land behind where you lived for a time, and Delamond below, and beyond, a highway leading back to another house you once lived in. You rest your hand on the journal. There aren't any pages left in it. The spine is stiff and the covers don't touch together. They still remember the pages that once lay between them. I am the empty space, and you are the future — my future. My hope is in your hands, your legs. *Axiom, postulate, definition.* You are my proof. Keep walking. As time and distance fill the space where the pages once were, memory will fade, and your traveling will form a new pattern. Count on this. Count on the empty pain in your chest filling with something new, somewhere else. You are not too old. You are on your way out now, going away home. The storm clouds gather behind you and drop a volley of cold rain down. The landscape grows more anonymous. You may travel north and find a friendly city. You may or may not buy a house, fall in love, start a war or finish one. You may or may not change your name. It is all so long ago. You're afraid, you're afraid, you're afraid.

Acknowledgements

Tru would like to acknowledge the authors whose work has inspired her own, and which appears occasionally throughout her journal: Walt Whitman, Charles Baudelaire, Arthur Rimbaud, Rainer Maria Rilke, Guillaume Apollinaire, Pierre Reverdy, and Marina Tsvetaeva.

Excerpts of *Tru* have been previously published in various guises in the following publications:

Divide: creative responses to contemporary social questions, 4.1 (Fall 2006).

The Paumanok Review, 6.1 (Winter 2005), www.paumanokreview.com.

Samsara Quarterly, (April 2002).

Identity Theory, (July 2002), www.identitytheory.com.

Also available from Flame Books:

Flame Books is proud to announce publication of the award winning 'How We Were Lost' by new author **Megan Taylor**.
ISBN: 0 9545945 8 4

Marking a superb debut novel, this contemporary story is fired with suspense and emotion as Taylor's compelling writing paints the trauma and longing of a gifted teenage girl who is desperate to make sense of herself and her life.

'How We Were Lost' *synopsis*

It's the start of the summer holidays, and two young girls have gone missing from a small seaside town. Escaping the lonely reality of her dysfunctional, motherless family and her hostile peers, 14 year old Janie begins her own search for the girls, unaware that it will lead her into a disturbing adult world. Precocious, unguided, and overwhelmed, Janie eventually penetrates her family's silence to unearth a heartbreaking secret of loss and abuse that lies far closer to home.

"Taylor writes beautiful, intense prose, richly evocative and with a strong appeal to the senses that's as vivid as it is tactile...Recommended." **Nicholas Royle, *Time Out***

**FLAME
BOOKS**

Flame Books is an innovative new publisher established upon ethical foundations. We aim to publish the most exciting contemporary English-language fiction by excellent new authors, and wish to offer fair contracts and royalties to authors whilst also supporting numerous worthwhile charitable projects. We seek to be closely involved in the writing community and to use the internet to establish new relationships between ourselves, authors, readers, and all involved in producing and distributing quality publications.

All titles published by Flame Books can be purchased directly from our website at a reduced price. International delivery is available on all orders. Our titles can also be bought at selected bookstores and via other online retailers.

www.flamebooks.com